Terra Mortem
Aliens. Idolatry. Wrath.

Ethan Proud

Terra Mortem

Copyright © 2018 Ethan Proud

All rights reserved. No part of this publication may be reproduced, stored in a retrieval system, or transmitted in any form or by any means, electronic, mechanical, recording or otherwise, without the prior written permission of the author.

Published by Proud Brothers Publishing, Pagosa Springs CO, U.S.A.

Illustration © Tom Edwards
TomEdwardsDesign.com

Printed on acid-free paper.

The characters and events in this book are fictitious. Any similarity to real persons, living or dead, is coincidental and not intended by the author.

Proud Brothers Publishing.
2018

First Edition

Ethan Proud

Other Books by Ethan Proud

Rebellion: Book One

Co-authored by Lincoln Proud

Vengeance: Book Two

Co-authored by Lincoln Proud

Onslaught: Book Three

Co-authored by Lincoln Proud

Terra Mortem

Prologue

The claxon rang out urgently as the red lights flashed in each of the corridors aboard the *Shrike*. The other ships in the squadron still bore ahead to the Second Earth, their new home, yet the passengers aboard the damaged ship could only stare helplessly. Their captain struggled to keep order as engineers and mechanics rushed from airlock to airlock, each carrying a kit of repair equipment.

"Captain Smith, this is Eric Taylor aboard the flagship *Gaia*. Do you read me?" A voice crackled over the intercom, interrupting the alarms.

Captain Smith sighed as he lifted the radio off the receiver. "I read you. There is nothing to be done for the engine. We are going to crash land on the nearest habitable planet."

Despite his outward calm, his stomach was in knots.

"We've already run a systems check for the safest planet within your reach. It's called AE625." Eric's voice came through again.

Captain Smith swore. AE625 had been hailed as an alternate to Earth nearly half a century before, but their hopes had been dashed when the first satellites reported nothing but sand.

"I said habitable," he said through gritted teeth.

"It's the only planet you and your crew have any chance of surviving on, I'm afraid." The voice coming from the flagship did not sound reassuring. "We will come back for you as soon as we can."

The radio sparked and crackled a moment later and the *Shrike* was offline. The Captain punched in the command for a crash landing on AE625. The ship jostled as it breached the atmosphere and its second engine almost gave out due to the strain.

The ship picked up momentum as it neared the planet's surface. In mere seconds the only thing visible from the starboard window was sand. The crew braced for impact.

Ethan Proud

Chapter One

The wind whipped the sand on the lonely exoplanet AE625 into a frenzy that pelted the two creatures slogging across its surface in search of water and sustenance. They were part of a larger colony formed when their ship, *Shrike,* was separated from the squadron due to engine failure and spiraled to the surface of AE625 three hundred years ago. The rest of the fleet of would-be-colonizers continued on course to Earth 2.0, which on clear days could be seen by those stranded on AE625. The planets were so close that they orbited each other while making a trek along the orbit of a sun.

The human of the duo, Yuto, was male and eighteen years old, but he resembled an Earthling thirty-year-old. On AE625 the average lifespan was fifty years. He had black hair that hung messily in his face when he wasn't wearing his goggles. Of course, with the wind picking up he had his goggles strapped on tightly. His slant eyes peered from behind the polarized lenses and tried to make out the lay of the land, but to no avail. The only part of his skin visible to the outside world was the bridge of his brown nose, which was scabbed and bleeding from the miniature sand-missiles that bombarded him constantly. His ancestors, at least from the time of the wreck, were Japanese and Columbian, and allegedly some of the smartest minds in the universe.

Back in the day, Earthlings considered their planet constituted the entire universe, and despite that glorious notion they still destroyed the one planet they had. Since the *Shrike* and its accompanying ships began their sojourn, all mankind had died out on Earth except for a few pockets of people living in areas such as the Midwest and Mongolia. These isolated cultures managed to thrive when the rest of the population died off after the power grid failed. They had yet to turn the power grid back on, and their populations were reduced to living in conditions similar to the 1800s, but with much more knowledge.

Next to Yuto, his companion floated lazily on the air, unperturbed by the wind. She was only as wide as Yuto's chest and the bulk of her was comprised of membranous wings. She had two pairs of wings, a larger pair up front and a smaller pair in the back. The rest of her body was long and serpentine, her head flat with a wide mouth and large black eyes. The underside of her body was covered in little suction cups which allowed her to move around when not in the air. Her body was turquoise, and she lacked any hard bones except the casing which protected her brain, spinal cord and internal organs, and the tiny fibers which spanned the length of her wings. She was a goni, or at least that's what the first humans had called them. They were a hermaphroditic species, and despite this Yuto had given her the name Aileen. She was pelted with sand as well, but her body was adapted to this particular set of living conditions. Her gelatinous cells absorbed the sand particulates through phagocytoses and expelled them through vacuoles on the other side of her body. She produced no waste, other than cellular byproducts. Once a month the gonis would excrete this from their pores. The gonis would then sit in the sun and allow it to harden into a film and then wriggle out of it, leaving an exoskeleton of waste behind.

Yuto and Aileen were on their daily mission, to find water. Their small colony sent out hunters every day to find new water sources. They would map these underground springs and once they had used up a spring, they would search for a new one. The maps they synthesized could later be used to return to a spring after the passage of enough years that it might have accumulated enough water to restore itself. Scientists in the colony would observe the spring's source and determine how many years before a spring might be habitable again. Gonis like Aileen were used to find water sources. The gonis did not need water, gaining enough from their diet. But the gonis did feed on the molla, which were fungal growths that proliferated on the rocks by the springs. It never took Aileen long to locate the delicious mollas.

She let out a burbling cry and Yuto followed the sound until he saw her perched on a rock face. Just to her left was a crack in the rock big enough for two humans to walk. She scuttled inside. If Yuto had been closer and the wind not so infernally loud, he would have been able to hear her many suction cups squelching as she moved. Yuto slid into the cave, relieved to find it sheltered from the wind. He pulled the scarf from around his neck and took a breath of the fresh, clean air. As he followed Aileen deeper, she began to glow. The hard parts of her body, as well as the mouths of her suction cups (which were made from the same cartilaginous polymers, albeit they had a different structure) were bioluminescent. All that Yuto could see of her was her glowing skeleton. As she traveled deeper she continued to warble her excitement, until she stopped suddenly. She had found the mollas.

Yuto flicked on the headlamp above his goggles and found Aileen perched above her find of mushrooms. The mushrooms had a thick dark exudate, which contrasted to their pale skin. Yuto drew a hand out of his glove and delicately cut one of the mushrooms at the base, careful not to disturb its hyphae. He ran his pinky finger across the cap of the fungi, picking up the dark gel that formed. He rubbed it on his gums vigorously and his mouth went numb. Next, he dug his pinky finger into the gills and retracted it, a clump of spores sitting on top. He proffered it to Aileen who made a screeing sound before her eyes lit up and she slurped it off Yuto's finger.

Yuto repeated the process but this time held his pinky up under his left nostril and snorted. The spores traveled up into his sinuses fairly smoothly, with a taste akin to Earthling coffee. The majority of the spores were absorbed into the mucous membranes of his nose, where they were broken down into narcotics within his body. Yuto's snot was always black and stained by the spores. Not all the colonists used the spores like Yuto did, most cooked the mushrooms whole. The heat caused the polymers within the fungus to break down far enough that the narcotic effect could not be felt, although the evaporating water was said to have healing effects due to the dispersed and weakened drugs.

Yuto closed the empty nostril with one hand and with the other he stretched the skin across his cheekbone to open up his sinus more. He snorted and gagged simultaneously, and the spores that had remained lodged in his sinuses hit the back of his throat, a steady flow of coffee-tasting fungi beginning to drip from his nasal cavity into his throat. His body instantly felt cool, which was a relief in this arid climate. After the initial cool sensation his body began to buzz slightly and his mind was scattered and focused at once. His heart beat faster and faster in his chest before it settled into a galloping rhythm that excited Yuto for the sake of excitement. He dug out more spores and chased them up the opposite nostril. The feeling was amplified and Yuto began harvesting mushrooms and putting them in his backpack.

The backpack was a myriad of patchwork, a relic from the first stranded Exos. Exos was the phrase used by Earthlings to describe the humans who would be inhabiting Earth 2.0, or in this case AE625. Each of the two thousand five hundred Exos on board had a backpack similar, and only three hundred and two survived the crash and many of those survivors met their ends on AE625. This meant that Yuto's backpack was three hundred years old, patched together with pieces of other backpacks, canvas from the ship, and fabric that was made from the molla (both the molla and the canvas were repurposed to make clothing as well). The pack was ugly and grey and sandblasted, but it had never failed Yuto. The backpack had been jury-rigged from its original multi-compartment form to have only three storage compartments. The first compartment on the bottom was waterproofed and the largest. It was used to bring water back to the camp. The second was slightly smaller and used to carry mollas. The third was a small zip up pouch on the front of the backpack in which Yuto carried a knife, a compass, and other necessities. The compass had been a gift from his father, who in turn had received it from his father. It was useless, however, as the poles of the planet were constantly moving due to the molten layer of steel beneath the planet's crust.

Aileen continued to lap up the exudate happily, which made Yuto's job easier. It had a vile, bitter taste and most of the colonists refused to eat it and washed it off before cooking the mollas. They also frowned on it being used as a narcotic, but short of stealing and murder everything on AE625 was legal. The black fungal sweat did have one drawback. It stained the user's gums and nostrils a deep purple or black color. In his youth, between the ages of seven to nine, Yuto had experimented with the molla along with his other friends, but unlike the rest he developed an addiction to it. Most of the hunters were addicted to the mollas or enjoyed using them recreationally, which made them the perfect candidates to go exploring unknown and dangerous regions for the little mushrooms.

When he had finished harvesting the bulk of the mushrooms, he began to explore the cave deeper, looking for water. The mollas only grew in dark caves that had water, so some of the life giving fluid had to be nearby. The water on AE625, however, was full of heavy metals and nearly killed the first settlers. Their gut bacteria couldn't handle breaking down the harsh chemicals and died in droves, leaving the settlers susceptible to dysentery, before chemical poisoning killed them. The gonis, perhaps looking at them as a new and exciting food source, investigated. They crawled all over the settlers for several days, attempting to eat the humans with their toothless, soft mouths. When the surviving settlers awoke, they found that the gonis had accidentally transferred their commensal bacteria flocs to the humans and the humans could now live on the planet. Since then, the two species had entered into a mutualistic relationship. The only anatomical differences Earthlings and the Exos on planet AE625 had, after three hundred years, was that the Exos had more robust livers and kidneys.

Yuto's headlamp illuminated the grotto and he finally saw the source of the water, a single drop that fell from the ceiling of the cave and into a tiny pool— no, puddle—only two inches deep, save for the tiny abrasion in the rock surface that allowed the water to seep back into the sediment. Yuto swore viciously and kicked his foot against the wall of the cave. His headlamp showed that it was a single hollow, with no side-branches or tunnels.

Aileen cocked her head and stared at him with her large, black eyes. She gently floated over to him, flapping her wings only once and landed on his shoulder, her tail wrapped around his throat for stability. The suction cups tickled his neck slightly, but he had grown used to it over the years. He glanced at the entrance to the cave and noted that the wind had abated, the sun beginning its descent towards the horizon. Yuto could see Earth 2.0 like a distant moon. As far away as it was, it was close enough that he could make out the swirling blue of its waters and the vivid green of the land masses. He often dreamt of rescue, though he knew it would never come.

Yuto and Aileen began their trek back towards their camp, following the cairns of stones Yuto had stacked to mark his path. Some of the cairns had been knocked over by the wind, while others still stood erect.

Chapter Two

Yuto returned to the camp, his pack full of mollas but devoid of any water. The camp was comprised of canvas tents around two holding tanks for water. One of the tanks was filled with fresh water, although rarely ever brimming. The other tank was for the Exos to relieve their bladders in. Each of the tanks was collapsible and could be brought along with the Exos. When times were bad, which they were now, the Exos would cook their mollas using their urine, and drink the broth afterwards to hydrate themselves. Currently, the water tank was empty, the urine tank beginning to go the same way. On Earth, drinking one's own urine was only done in times of dire need, or by a few strange individuals. On AE625 it was a way of life, and until the urine tank was a dark brownish gold color, it wasn't considered disgusting.

Yuto relieved himself in the second tank and took his day's treasures to the central tent where the other hunters were gathered. Yuto's childhood friend, Rio, had just exited the central tent, his own goni perched on his shoulder, snacking on a molla clasped between its forewings. His goni's name was Herma, shortened from the word hermaphrodite, since Rio wanted to name the creature something gender neutral. If Herma ever knew that its name was a slight to its sexuality, it never showed any indication. Rio was the youngest in the colony, only fifteen years old, but by that age he should have been married. Yuto himself had married when he was only eleven years old, which as a member of a dying species had not been viewed as irresponsible of him. However, with the water shortages, it had been impossible for any other children to be born. Pregnancies were commonplace enough, but the child never received the nutrients needed to survive to full term. Half term or shorter pregnancies were common but all ended with spontaneous abortions of desiccated fetuses. With food in such short supply, the fetuses were often cooked with the mollas and fed to the gonis.

Many of the women in the colony wondered why Rio had not married them or one of their friends. He was tall, broad-shouldered and extremely handsome. He could have any woman in the colony, even some who were already married. Yuto, however, knew why Rio shunned the advances of women. When Rio was six years old he fell ill to a serious bacterial infection that killed his parents and rendered him impotent. He found his encounters with women frustrating and embarrassing. The one female he allowed to be close to him was Dierde, a pretty girl with smooth alabaster skin, blonde hair and perfectly straight teeth, a rarity on AE625. She often tried to coax Rio into trying anything sexual, and when he relented nothing ever happened. Yuto often thought that Rio and Dierde would marry one day, if Rio ever warmed up to the idea. On AE625, marriage wasn't like it was on earth, with no ceremonies, no vows, and monogamy not the main goal. Marriage on AE625 had the sole purpose of picking a lifelong mate in order to raise children and make life on the planet a little more bearable. Infidelity was not taboo and was often encouraged. Shacking up was simply a way to make life easier.

"Find anything good today?" Rio called to Yuto. His gums and nostrils were as black as Yuto's. Snorting molla was one of the only pleasures Rio found in life.

"No water, if that's what you're asking," Yuto said glumly. He hated to admit when he had found nothing.

"Damn, well after you check in today let's smoke some molla," he suggested and Yuto shrugged in acquiescence. There wasn't much better to do, other than return for the night and have sex with his wife, which was always better after smoking molla.

Yuto entered the central tent, seeing several crates full of mollas and those backpacks with any water stacked in a corner. Three old men and two ancient women were counting and distributing the day's finds into crates, each crate marked for a family or individual. The Council of Elders always counted the day's find and were often up late into the evening and up again early in the morning. The Elders were aged thirty-eight to forty-six but looked like Earthling ninety year olds. They were wizened and hunched over, their joints swollen with rheumatoid arthritis, which made their task of counting and weighing the mollas even more painstaking. Yet somehow they managed. The oldest woman, Treya, tsked her disproval at Yuto for not returning with water. She took his day's find, turned her back and waved him off. Aileen, sensing her derisiveness, spat a gob of black molla cud at the woman's frizzy expanse of grey hair. She didn't feel it, and Yuto quickly took his leave.

He headed for Rio's tent first. For the most part he smoked molla before going home to his wife and it didn't bother her. She was at home all day tending to chores within the village, and free to spend her free time cavorting with whichever man or woman she pleased while Yuto was away. That didn't mean that Yuto was the unaware husband in the relationship, he had had his fair share of trysts, it was simply the way of life on the desert planet.

Rio's tent was an exact replica of every other tent in the colony. Each was a relic from the *Shrike*, a canvas exterior held up by a spherical contraption made of many rods, which could be collapsed, folded and fit neatly into a telescoping cylindrical tube. The tube was also collapsible and when opened completely made up the bottom of the tent. Everything else in the tent had to be carried in a backpack during nomadic phases. The only seating in any of the tents were cushions woven out of molla stems that could be filled with air. Every hour these cushions had to be refilled, the air slowly pushed out by the weight of an Exo being. Rio was already sitting on a cushion with Dierde next to him. He was busy loading dried molla caps into a pipe crafted out of metal. Dierde twiddled with a book of matches between her fingers. Her lips were dyed black with molla spores and she would often apply a paste of the spores around her eyes, a fashion statement that Yuto wished his wife, or any other woman in the colony would pick up on.

They greeted Yuto as he sat and Dierde struck a match and lit the pipe as Rio held it to his lips. He held the hit in his lungs for several beats before breathing out a blue cloud of smoke. He passed it to Dierde who did the same, before passing it to Yuto. Yuto took a hit and reveled in the strange taste that filled his mouth before exhaling a string of blue O's. As he exhaled his vision was augmented with bright colors and mild tracers that made the boring and drab tent look like something out of his dreams. His focus was enhanced, similarly to when he snorted the molla spores, but without the scatterbrained effect. The effect it had on his heart-rate was inverse and he felt calm. He and his friends fell into a bout of cackling laughter until the initial high subsided.

In the meantime, Aileen and Herma floated around each other coyly before sinuously rising in the air, each of their suction cups matched up. They flew upward, slowly and steadily in an S-shaped pattern before dropping to the ground in a spasm of coitus. The creatures' bodies became one and it was impossible to tell the difference between where one creature started and the other ended, even though Herma was a milky white color. Dierde's goni left her shoulder and joined the frolicking mass. This was a common occurrence but despite it, no goni had reproduced since the last Exos had been born. If a goni wasn't born when an Exo was, the human would die as it wouldn't have a bacterial donor. Gonis formed lifelong bonds with their owners and would not affiliate themselves with another human, and as such, newborn Exos needed a goni infant to inoculate them with the bacteria needed to survive on AE625. Dierde's goni was an electric blue color with threads of yellow running the length of its body. Dierde named it Dierde. The eccentric woman believed that she and her familiar were one being, a belief that was only slightly radical.

"I think we should leave," Dierde said, breaking the drug-induced chill.

Yuto and Rio looked incredulously at her.

"And go where?" Rio asked with an eyebrow raised to his hairline.

"Anywhere we want. We are hunters and we can survive without the rest of the clan," Dierde said, which was exactly what every hunter had thought on at least one of their travels.

"I think we should go to the original settlement," Yuto said, and Dierde howled with excitement.

"That's what I'm talking about!" Her eyes lit up, the molla making them look even crazier.

"But we have a responsibility to the colony," Yuto said, viewing both sides of the issue.

This time Rio disagreed. "There are other hunters, we won't be missed. And we won't have to drink our own piss half the time." Rio's eyes began to take on the same crazy gleam as Dierde's. "You're the only one with a wife, you can bring her with us or leave her."

Yuto thought about bringing his wife, Taiga, and feel a lump in his stomach. He'd rather leave her, and Dierde saw this.

"You don't love her, and you know it. She won't miss you and you won't miss her. You are only together out of convenience. How many other lovers have you had since you publicly announced your marriage?" Dierde asked. It sounded harsh, but it was just honest. The closest thing to love between two Exos Yuto had ever seen was Dierde and Rio.

"Probably every woman in this colony other than the crones and you," Yuto said and a laugh bubbled up from his stomach before erupting from his lips. "I wouldn't think twice about Taiga and she wouldn't spare me a second thought."

"So when do we leave?" Rio asked in a hushed, conspiratorial whisper.

"Next time one of us finds enough water to fill all of our packs. Instead of bringing it back to the camp we will mark it ourselves and the three of us will fill our packs the next day." Dierde grinned wolfishly and put her hand in the middle of the circle, the other two placing theirs on top of hers. "No one but us can know."

Terra Mortem

Chapter Three

Hours later, Yuto stumbled back to his tent, his mind still buzzing from the molla. The stars shone brighter than before, each wearing an aura of some fantastic color that was usually lacking. Yuto stopped and stared at them, enjoying the last remnants of his high. He entered his own tent and found his wife, Taiga, drying out their molla portions to make soup the next day. She had short dark hair that framed her flat, plain face. She wasn't unattractive, but she was plain nonetheless. She was short and stocky, with toned arms and legs. Despite her plainness she attracted many men and a few women with her gravitational personality.

"You are later than usual," she commented offhandedly. It wasn't an accusation. She and Yuto simply had no connection other than sex. They talked about their days, attempted at procreation, and then went to bed. They didn't discuss ideas, cook, or do anything together other than sex and small talk.

"After today's fruitless search, I smoked more molla than usual." Yuto shrugged. "How was your day?"

She shrugged in answer. For the past weeks, if not months, there had been little to talk about.

Then they threw themselves at each other. Their relationship had gone from having little meaning to it, to purely physical.

Terra Mortem

Yuto tore out of his clothes and began to remove Taiga's, his lips locked with hers. The faint taste of dirt lingered in both of their mouths. It didn't bother him, such was life.

X

Yuto and Taiga were lying in bed, naked and sweating. But for the most part, they were silent. The two fell asleep without saying another word to each other. In only a few more hours Yuto would rise and begin searching for molla and water the next day. It wasn't a terrible routine, but it was a routine. Its appeal had already waned on Yuto, and he wanted more now. It had been weeks since he indulged in an extramarital affair, but those too were losing their luster. Yuto sighed and rolled over and let sleep take him. Moments later it seemed, he was woken up by the warbling cry of Aileen. He dressed in the dark quietly, as to not wake Taiga. Hunters had to wake before the sun in order to make as much ground as possible before the scorching heat came over the horizon.

He exited the tent and Aileen floated over to his shoulder, her suction cups wet and sticky on his skin. He scratched her head and whispered, "Sometimes I think that only you understand me."

Chapter Four

In the opposite direction, Rio set off from camp, Herma perched on his shoulder much like Aileen was on Yuto's. His boots scuffed the dirt as he mulled over the previous night. He was fully committed to abandoning the colony, and the prospects of finding the first settlement thrilled him. According to legend, the original colony could be returned to in five hundred years. By then the water in the underground spring would refill enough to support the colony for another hundred years. It was a promised land of sort, but Rio would never see it and neither would the children that he couldn't have. He would never reproduce, he had no reason to live for a next generation—he only had himself to care for. Rio saw no reason to remain in the colony and even if he died in the wild, it would have little effect. In the grand scheme of biology, he was a one chapter book. After Yuto left, Dierde had begged him to try sleeping with her. He gave in like he always did, but nothing came of it for him, although she did—several times.

As a result, Rio was frustrated and a day spent wandering in the desert would be good for him. His goggles were equipped with night vision and allowed him to traverse the rock scattered terrain effortlessly. AE625 was almost pretty at night in the absence of heat, but in a devastated way. The wind blew the dry sand, weathering rocks in odd patterns as they reached for the sky in huge, twisting chunks. Canyons created by water a millennia ago dug out the landscape in deep troughs. When hunting, Rio usually explored the canyons and the caves that riddled them, hoping there would be something along the ancient waterways. It had been four days since he found water of any kind. Canyoneering was difficult for Rio because of his large frame. Some of the handholds wouldn't support his weight, and many caverns tapered down until he couldn't fit deeper in them. He was fit, of course, being a hunter, but he lacked the lithe figures of Yuto and Dierde.

The landscape changed little over the hours, especially from Rio's vantage point at the nadir of a canyon. The sun's slow creeping advance went unnoted by Rio, except for the subtle lightening of the sky. The canyon wound slowly and sinuously, and Rio imagined what it might have looked like with water in it. He had never seen a river before and he imagined a magnificent torrent of azure liquid barreling along its length, not the gentle meandering stream that was the likely culprit of the erosion. None of the colonists knew what any large body of water would look like. The only water that had ever amounted to anything was the stagnant water sitting in the tank at camp. Rio explored the caves in the region, scaling the walls to find them, often disappointed by their shallow ends, lacking both mollas and water. His hands were calloused and often bleeding from the jagged rocks he scaled all day.

Herma flew beside him, gently flapping its wings on the air currents. When Rio began to struggle it would land and wait patiently on the rocks for its master to continue climbing. Rio's hands were slick with sweat and felt soft against the hard rocks. Each point of the hard granite dug into his palms and another abrasion formed. His chest and stomach were similarly scraped, but he had a goal in sight, an opening in the cave wall another hundred feet up, large enough that he could stand in it. Panting, he steeled his reserve not to look down and reached for the next handhold. It stuck out bare centimeters from the rock wall and he wrapped his fingers around it, tugging to test whether he had enough leverage.

Not satisfied, he looked for a foothold, found a slight indent in the rock and pushed his body higher, using his tentative handhold while snaking close to the wall to avoid being caught in the wind that whistled down the canyon, moaning eerily like the ghosts of the planet. The ghosts of a long-dead, dry, planet. His muscles strained to hold his weight until his eyes alighted on another handhold and he ascended another foot. It was slow going, but he wanted to be cautious instead of getting himself into a predicament he couldn't get out of. He had to climb back down once he had explored the cave, after all. Despite his careful planning his route still wound across the canyon wall.

By the time he was halfway to the cave, the sun was creeping over the edge of the canyon, a sliver of light beating down on Rio. He began sweating more profusely and often he doubted his grip.

Regardless of the treacherous climb, he made it after another forty minutes and heaved himself over the ledge. His breath caught in his chest when he saw the cavern end before it had gone five feet into the rock. He screamed and heard his voice echo back to him six times over. Each time the sound faded, along with his hopes of finding water. Herma repeated his call forlornly, its voice, neither male nor female, containing a slight metallic quality. This was because gonis, like birds, had a syrinx, not a larynx, and could operate either side of their voice box independently, making each song a duet. Herma looked as defeated as Rio and the two sat in dejected silence, not looking up from the sandy dirt that clung to their bodies.

Rio blew out a long sigh in capitulation and swung his legs over the cliff, eying the canyon that wound before him. The muted tones of the canyon fit his newfound mood. He found a foothold and eased his bodyweight on to it before pivoting to face the cliff-wall and began his descent. If it was possible to trudge whilst rock-climbing, he managed it. Each of his movements bore more weight than his actual mass and were slow and dejected. It took him thrice as long to scale down the canyon as it did for him to climb up it. Though he was focused on each handhold, he did so mechanically. His mind was numb from his failure and no thoughts were spinning through his cranium as they usually did.

When his feet finally touched solid ground he stood there for a moment before Herma's bugling call brought him back to reality. He turned his gaze to the goni and saw what it was making a fuss about. At the base was a tiny pool of water; it barely trickled an inch onto the sand before it evaporated due to its glacial pace. Nonetheless, it was water. Rio examined the water and saw that it had eroded its way down the canyon, invisible until it crept out along the canyon bottom. Its source had to be at the top of the cliff. With Rio's luck it was probably at the very top of the cliff. He would have to scale the canyon wall again.

His muscles ached, and he knew he wasn't capable of climbing it again. His entire body felt drained and judging by the sun he knew he had no other option than to return to camp and try to find the water again tomorrow. He pulled a map out from his pack and did a few mental calculations on the poorly drawn canvas and lightly marked the spot with a cylinder of graphite. The makeshift pen left his fingers and hand blackened and shiny. He didn't mark the spot in an obvious way, though, and he definitely did not mark it as a potential water source. Instead, he smudged it with his fingers, making it look like a mistake. This way the Elders wouldn't know that he had found water. Hopefully it was enough for him, Dierde, and Yuto to make their escape.

Ethan Proud

Chapter Five

With her goggles pressed tightly against her face and a scarf wrapped around her neck and face, the pelting sand bothered Dierde very little. But what bothered her greatly were the sixteen figures she saw moving on the horizon. The last three of the caravan of wanderers pulled carts behind them and switched every half hour to not lose speed. Dierde had watched them for several hours now. She could tell they were at least humanoid and that they weren't part of her colony, and decided to move in closer to get a better look. Traveling in the shadows of the rock monoliths that burst from the planet's surface, she positioned herself so that she would intercept the troop's path yet still be behind them. As she grew closer, her goni became agitated and lightly cooed a warning. Dierde ignored Dierde, but the creature was persistent and gently wrapped its tail over Dierde's shoulder and drifted backward, flapping its wings slowly.

"What?" Dierde hissed softly and gently. She purred at Dierde in reassurance. "We will be fine."

The goni eyed her flatly before settling back on her master's shoulder. Dierde smiled and turned to resume her espionage and snaked around the base of the spiraling tower she was hiding behind. Much to her dismay, she rounded the corner right into the leader of the troop. He was as tall as Rio, but slender, and he

Terra Mortem

wore all black clothing. He wore a duster jacket that bore an insignia Dierde had only seen drawn in the sand and on maps. The Exos had called the symbol 'tree' and no one alive knew what it meant, other than the rumors that it was the symbol of the Original Settlement.

The man's face was concealed by a mask with wide orbs for the eyes, the mouth covered with two cylinders that filtered the air for sand particles and other airborne molecules. The rest of his party wore the same strange masks. This only took Dierde a mere second to take in before noticing the creature on the leash right in front of her. It stood nearly three feet tall and was a quadruped, but at the moment it was balanced on its hind legs sniffing the air. Its eyes were a milky white, and its skin appeared to be the same gelatinous texture as the goni's, except this creature had long spines that covered its back and were hollow like a needle. The blind creature's nostrils were nearly as wide as an Earthling horse's, and they constricted with each breath as if trying to capture a smell. The animal's snout was long and tapered despite its sizeable nostrils. Underneath the freakish nose, a fat purple tongue tasted the air. The beast's paws were shovel-shaped claws designed for digging. The creature took one final sniff before settling onto all four limbs and turning its blind face towards the man holding its leash. Its sinuous scaled tail swung behind it expectantly. The animal's body was exceptionally pale and that, along with its digging claws, led Dierde to believe that it was a subterranean creature. What the humans were doing with it, she had no idea.

The man in front pulled off his mask and squinted as the sand whipped across his face. His skin was dark brown, though not naturally, it had been burnt by the sun one too many times and had a permanent ruddy-brown hue. His hair was cropped close to his skull and Dierde could see a vein bulging above his left ear. The rest of his face was a myriad of piercings, three along his right eyebrow and two more at the corners of his lower lip. He eyed Dierde up and down blatantly and she felt both uncomfortable and excited. Dierde took a faltering step, unsure of what to do, but at the same time she felt her blood pumping with excitement. She hadn't ever met another Exo being who wasn't a part of the colony.

She found her words and spoke first. "Who are you?" Dierde's words came out clearly and she was glad she didn't stutter.

"My name is Jarrod. I didn't believe there were any other outcast colonies alive," he stated in a blunt monotone.

"Outcast colonies?" Dierde asked. She believed that the only survivors lived in her colony.

"We were banished several months ago from the *Shrike* wreckage," Jarrod stated plainly as if it was common knowledge.

"Exos still live at the wreck site?" Dierde asked, her astonishment slightly masked by her anger.

Terra Mortem

"Exos have lived at the wreck site for hundreds of years," Jarrod said slowly. "Nearly one thousand."

Dierde's mind reeled and she almost lost her balance. She had been told that the *Shrike* lost its coordinates and crashed on AE625 only three hundred years ago, and that her colony was the only surviving population. In a few seconds her life had been turned upside down. "That can't be right."

Jarrod stared at Dierde quizzically. Her firm statement made the man question her origins.

"You've never seen the original settlement? Or at least known about its existence?" he asked, raising one eyebrow, and his numerous piercings shot into the air before resuming their normal position.

"My colony is the remaining survivors of the *Shrike* wreckage. I was told there were no others, and that we wouldn't be able to return for another two centuries," Dierde said warily and Jarrod laughed.

"You are part of the Hydra movement?" He bit his lip in amusement and Dierde watched as one of his rings slipped behind his teeth.

"The what?" she demanded angrily.

"A group of Exos left the Original Settlement in search of water three hundred years ago, believing that the spring beneath the *Shrike* would be tainted by the fuel that leached into the ground upon the wreckage, and that the water would run out and we would die of thirst. They set out with meager supplies to hunt for alternative sources of water and lived as nomads. A representative from the Hydras comes to visit the Original Settlement every year with a copy of the map you produce. *Shrike* civilians, or Shrikers as we call them, visit the springs you find and harvest the water for use at the Original Settlement," Jarrod explained plainly. "You are being used."

"You swear this is the truth?" Dierde said, while behind her Dierde squirmed restlessly.

"I'm an exile, why would I lie to you?"

"Why were you and your people exiled?" Dierde asked and her eyes narrowed suspiciously.

"That is a story for another time," Jarrod said firmly, his eyes set like granite. "Will you return to our camp with us tonight?"

"No. I must go back to my camp and warn my people," Dierde said and turned to leave.

"They will never believe you. The leaders and elites of your community already know the truth. If you stay the night with us, we can travel to your camp with you and give your story more credibility," Jarrod said kindly.

Dierde thought of Rio and how anxious he would be if she didn't return, and then she eyed the stranger and felt her stomach churn lustily. "I will eat with you tonight and return to find you tomorrow," she said coming up with a compromise.

Judging by the look in Jarrod's eye he had the same desires. He barked an order to his clan of exiles and they began setting up camp where they stood. The tents were more lean-tos, supported by the three poles in the center of the tent and pinned down with heavy stakes to prevent them from being torn from the ground by the vicious winds. The sun wasn't yet beginning to set and Dierde knew she had plenty of time to return to the camp before stirring anyone's suspicions. All the exiles retired to their own tents and Dierde decided that on AE625 community meals were not a tradition. She slipped into Jarrod's tent and saw that he already had a pot of boiling water with something cooking in it. It smelled good, but Dierde the goni floated near the top of the tent, even though it was only five feet tall. The snuffling creature was staked outside.

"So, how long have you lived in exile?" Dierde asked, avoiding making eye contact with Jarrod, instead staring awkwardly at the walls of the tent.

"Idle conversation isn't why you wanted to stay for dinner, now is it?" Jarrod asked, his eyes locked onto Dierde's.

She swallowed hard and shook her head. Jarrod moved across the tent sinuously despite the limited amount of room. He held Dierde's face with both hands and pressed his lips against hers firmly. She kissed him back fervently and felt his body against hers. She fumbled with his belt and slid her hand down the front of his pants and was relieved to find him more responsive than Rio. She hesitated, and Jarrod sensed her trepidation.

"You haven't ever done this before, have you?" Jarrod asked, and Dierde demurely bit her lip and shook her head. Jarrod chuckled and moved a little more slowly after the admission. Above the pair of sinners, Dierde brooded angrily.

When Dierde and Jarrod finally extricated themselves from one another, they were both glistening with sweat and spunk. Dierde let out a sigh of relief, and at once felt guilty. She turned her mind to food to alleviate her conscience.

"What's for dinner?" she asked, reveling in the delicious odor filling the tent.

"Goni," Jarrod said and moved to stir the pot.

Neither he nor Dierde had dressed yet and now she felt her skin crawl once more, though this time in revulsion. "What?" she demanded, pulling her clothes on as swiftly as she could.

"Try it, it's a delicacy," Jarrod insisted, but instead Dierde fled from the tent, pulling her backpack on, Dierde flying behind her, matching her urgency.

On her way out of the camp Dierde kicked the snuffling creature, understanding that it was what led the exiles to her, following the scent of her goni. If Dierde had stayed, her goni no doubt would have ended up in a stew.

Chapter Six

Dierde's feet kicked up a torrent of dust behind her as she left the exiled Exos. Beside her, Dierde floated along easily, but her master could sense her seething rage. The goni was furious that Dierde hadn't listened to her warnings, even though she couldn't fully express them. Once they were far enough away that they could slow down, the goni landed on Dierde's shoulder and nipped her ear hard.

"Ow! I know, I know," Dierde exclaimed. "I should have listened."

The goni purred smugly. Dierde felt her stomach drop as realization poured over her. Eventually she would have to confess to Rio what she had done. Their relationship was the only kind like it in the colony, and Dierde knew that she jeopardized it. Rio would at least be understanding, but that didn't mean he wouldn't be hurt. Each step she took in the direction of camp, her dread built. She didn't even know if she could look Rio in the eyes. Her pulse quickened with anxiety, and on her shoulder Dierde squawked in alarm. She could sense her master's unease but couldn't detect the real problem. The human Dierde cursed her foolishness and resolved to not worry about it anymore until the time came to admit her wrongdoings. But if things were different between her and Rio it would never have happened. She just needed to experiment a little. Her transgression had no effect on how she felt about Rio, other than that she felt like scum at the moment.

Wrapped up in her thoughts, she returned to the colony before she had realized it and was standing before the central tent. She reported her lack of findings, much to the chagrin of the Elders. She took their disappointed looks with a grain of salt. After the day's revelations she was no longer impressed with them. She perceived them to be just as dastardly and treasonous as she was. Dierde heard the familiar footfalls of Rio behind her and focused on maintaining a cool composure. As Rio checked in with the Elders he linked pinkies with Dierde, and she felt her pulse pound with guilt. Rio was against any form of public affection and often seemed cold and distant to those who didn't know him well. The light touch of his littlest finger was the most physical attention he would give Dierde outside the privacy of his tent.

"Find anything today?" he asked her, and in her mind she imagined how her confession could go. She quickly dismissed the thought and lied.

"Nil," Dierde said, tight lipped.

"Same here." Rio sighed and shouldered his pack, after showing the Elder's that he indeed had nothing.

Together Rio and Dierde exited the tent and headed back to Rio's tent. Once safely inside, Rio told her of his discoveries for that day.

"I think I found something, it may be nothing…or it might be just what we need," he said in an excited whisper.

"You found enough water for three of us to escape?" she said in a hushed urgent whisper, thinking of the nomadic exiles who might be arriving at their colony the next day.

"I'm not sure, but I think there may be a fissure in a cliff caused by a spring of sorts."

"Could we leave tomorrow?" Dierde asked with a dangerous gleam in her eyes.

Rio shook his head. "It would be risky. There might be nothing more than a trickle."

"When was the last time anyone found enough water to refill the holding tank? It's been months and we've been surviving on mere mouthfuls. It might be the only chance we get for another year," Dierde argued.

"We have nothing but time, but in all honesty, I would be willing to give it a shot. After all, what is the difference between dying today and dying tomorrow. We are living like ghosts, repeating the same task day in and day out," Rio said, and on the last sentence his voice turned sour.

"Perfect, when Yuto returns we will come up with a concrete plan," Dierde said. Her nerves began to tingle with anticipation, and her stomach tightened. She would finally be leaving the colony.

Rio agreed with her and went about extracting molla out of the dried caps he had in his pack. He shoveled a tiny amount into his nose and passed the cap to Dierde. After she had insufflated a sizeable pile she began rolling the cap between her fingers, crushing it into a fine powder to be smoked. She breathed in the first hit and exhaled just as Yuto burst into the tent. He tore his goggles off his face, his hair disheveled and grimy with sweat. His eyes shone with excitement in the dark living quarters.

"We're leaving tomorrow!" he crowed, albeit it was hushed.

"We just decided that, actually," Rio said with a smirk.

"You found water too?!" Yuto whispered and his excitement grew.

"Well, maybe. But we decided to chance it," Rio explained.

Yuto shook his head humorously. "We aren't chancing anything. I found several underground, man-made aquifers. I am positive that the Elders use them. I backtracked some of the previous sites I've found to see if any of them had refilled enough for us to leave, and I found four aquifers," Yuto breathed, and took the pipe from Rio after he took a hit and inhaled one of his own. "We are going to rob the Elders and return to the Original Settlement!"

Dierde's eyes darkened as she began to understand the implications. Perhaps the exiles she had encountered were also raiding the aquifers. In that case she and her friends might face some opposition. "We should take weapons. Better to be prepared than to be caught off guard."

"You think other people are also involved in this?" Rio asked.

"Maybe we aren't the only people who survived the crash. After all, who built the aquifers? The Elders didn't do it. And everyone else in camp is accounted for during the day, unless hunters are the only ones out of the loop. And if that's the situation, we are all getting shafted." Dierde's own conspiracy theory grew in her mind. The Exiles surely hadn't built the aquifer, but someone had to. *And how did they avoid detection?*

"Should we warn the other hunters?" Yuto asked, and Rio answered before Dierde had time to blurt out "No!" The two were in accordance. Yuto furrowed his brow. "Why not?"

"Wouldn't we hear from other hunters if they spotted a crew with machinery moving around away from camp? We all have specific perimeters that we are assigned to search to prevent overlap. Maybe the other hunters are helping the Elders?" Rio said suspiciously.

The fact that the three were smoking molla probably wasn't helping their burgeoning sense of paranoia.

"But I found them in my field of operation," Yuto said, and at the same time six eyes narrowed.

"What the hell is going on?!" Rio exclaimed, almost a little too loud.

"There are others," Dierde said in a hoarse whisper. Her blue eyes darted behind her dark lashes. "There's no other explanation. Everyone has been drinking the piss water in this colony. There's no way the Elders could make it out into the desert every day and take enough water in secret. What if the water is for someone else?"

"So our goal of finding the Original Settlement may not be the best idea?" Yuto asked and took another hit and blew out a cloud of blue smoke to fill the already hazy tent. "We might receive a hostile welcome from its inhabitants."

"Whatever we do, we should proceed with caution. And we should leave soon. It may not be safe for us here anymore," Dierde said, proud that she was able to make the information she had learned from Jarrod sound like pure speculation. Perhaps she would be able to keep her secret, but only if they moved fast.

"Tomorrow it is, then." Rio agreed with Dierde's demand for haste and Yuto nodded in affirmation.

Chapter Seven

The next morning the three would-be-saboteurs rose in the dark and prepared themselves for the long trek across the forsaken climate they lived in. They took extendable spears fashioned from tent poles with jagged scraps of metal welded to the topmost piece, crude machetes, and whatever knives they had available. They quietly moved about the camp stealing any spare water canteens they could find, along with any waterproof fabric they could use as canteens. In only a few minutes the other hunters would rise to find they were missing three of their own. Yuto would lead them to the nearest aquifer and they would take as much water as they could before setting off in the direction of the *Shrike* wreckage.

Before they left camp, they saw a flame flare to life on the edge of the colony. It was held aloft on a torch, whose light illuminated a pierced face and a snuffling creature. Behind the figure of the man several more Exos could be barely made out in the dark. Jarrod saw the three conspirators and made his way towards them, the familiar he held on the leash wrapped tight around his knuckles beginning to snort in excitement. The gonis Aileen, Herma, and Dierde stirred angrily and rose into the air hissing.

"Rouse your camp," Jarrod commanded, and Yuto and Rio bristled, while Dierde froze in fear.

Ethan Proud

"And who are you to be commanding anyone?" Rio demanded of the stranger.

"I can be your messiah, if you have the wisdom to listen," Jarrod answered presumptuously.

Yuto snorted in derision. "We have no need for a savior. You would do best finding another colony to plague."

Jarrod's eyes landed on Dierde and flickered with recognition. "Ah, so she hasn't told you the truth of your desperate situation."

Rio and Yuto looked at Dierde in unison.

"I might have met him yesterday," Dierde admitted, looking directly at her boots. Her face flushed red with shame, but no one could see it in the dark.

All around them, Exos began exiting their tents to see what the commotion was outside. Rarely did the hunters make a sound in the mornings. As the crowd gathered, Jarrod waited patiently and smugly.

Finally the Elders hobbled from their tents and a man by the name of Rumo exclaimed loudly, "What is the meaning of all this? We have a busy day ahead of us. Too busy to be causing this ruckus!"

"I assume that you will be very busy," Jarrod said coolly, and watched with pleasure as Rumo and the other Elders' faces blanched.

"Who are you? And where did you come from?" Treya, the old crone who checked in Yuto's molla count two days ago, croaked out.

"You know good and well where I came from, but as far as formal introductions go, I am Jarrod. And I have been exiled for believing that the Original Settlement should recall the Hydra colonies so they may live in luxury with the rest of the Shrikers," Jarrod said theatrically and slowly rotated, arms spread, so he could see each face in the colony. Murmurs spread quickly through the colony, and Jarrod's eyes flashed, he wasn't done. "Your efforts and poor living conditions are not suffered for your survival. You suffer so that the original colony can have a constant supply of water. This is orchestrated by your Council of Elders. You have been duped!"

"Is this true?" Taiga exclaimed angrily.

The Council of Elders attempted to sputter out a response, but their old minds were too feeble to fabricate a lie swiftly.

"It is, I backtracked to some of my previous sites and found aquifers had been built to draw water to the surface," Yuto said solemnly.

Taiga stormed over to his side. "When did you discover this?"

"Yesterday." Yuto braced himself for the sting of a slap but nothing came.

"Why didn't you tell me?!" Taiga's nostrils flared with anger. "You planned on leaving, didn't you?"

The accusation went without saying, and when Yuto didn't answer, Taiga slapped him. She stormed away from him and disappeared into the crowd.

"Did all three of you plan on leaving?" a hunter, Lepiro, asked in confusion.

Luckily, before Rio, Dierde, or Yuto could answer, Jarrod intervened.

"I believe that you are losing sight of the problem. There is corruption running rampant in your colony. We must recruit the other Hydra colonies and save them from their inevitable doom," Jarrod said, and Dierde found it hard to believe that he had the best interests of the colony at heart. She halfway suspected that he came to the Hydra colonies to find gonis to eat.

"But if you were exiled for wishing to bring us back to the Original Settlement, why would they accept us?" Dierde said in an attempt to deter the rest of the colony from joining someone just as crooked as the Council of Elders.

"I'm glad you asked, little bird," Jarrod said and grinned with half of his mouth. The gesture wasn't lost on Rio, who bristled. "The engineers and scientists at the Original Settlement believe they have found the source of the water, and that if we follow its path, we may find salvation."

"And how are you privy to this information?" Lepiro demanded from the crowd.

"I was an engineer," Jarrod sneered. "And in my day, I have built many of the aquifers and found water by following the maps you have produced."

"He's lying, we need to leave," Dierde whispered coarsely.

"What if he's not?" Yuto countered.

Dierde said nothing, but neither did Rio. None of them made a move.

"Then lead us to this promised land," Taiga demanded as she emerged from her tent, a pack slung over her shoulder. She looked around before her eyes widened. "Where are the Elders?"

A commotion came over the camp as Exos began craning their heads back and forth, yelling angrily as they realized the Elders had slipped away unnoticed. Jarrod raised his hands as an order for silence.

"Settle down, they are no longer our concern. We must find the other Hydra colonies and recruit them to our cause before we find our oasis. We must be swift, however, for some from the Original Settlement may be seeking it as well," Jarrod said, commanding the attention of the colony.

"Screw them! I say we go now!" a voice yelled from deep in the crowd.

"And subject them to the same misery you've been living your entire lives? I think not," Jarrod snapped angrily, and the naysayer was silenced. "Now gather your belon-"

Before he could finish, he was cut off by a hissing sound as a canister flew through the air. It exploded in a shower of sparks and smoke before it hit the ground, and then three more followed. Not all of them detonated while aloft, some landed heavily before sending shrapnel and sand hurtling through the colony.

Ethan Proud

"Shrikers!" Jarrod yelled and pulled a long, tubular weapon from his pack. He crouched down and scanned the area for assailants. It didn't take long before the dark figures began swarming the colony, holding the same type of weapons. From each weapon, a spark and loud percussive sound was ejected. Each time it sounded a colonist dropped.

"Now we need to leave," Dierde said flatly and began to sprint into the darkness.

Yuto followed her wordlessly, but Rio hesitated a second too long. Something struck him in the leg with incredible force and he fell to the ground. His ears were ringing, his vision blurry. He coughed in a plume of smoke and tears streamed from his eyes from the corrosive fumes. He reached down and touched his thigh to feel gushing blood and a fragment of metal sticking out of his leg. He knew better than to pull it out, but he also knew there was no way he could keep up with Dierde and Yuto now. He would have to fight. He drew his machete and rose to find a man sprinting towards him, one of the exploding sticks in his hands. Luck was on Rio's side, however, as the man didn't see him before he stood and didn't have time to level the gun at him. Rio slashed as hard as he could at the man's torso and the machete tore a ragged opening in his rib cage and mutilated the organs in his thoracic cavity. He coughed, a liquid, laden sound, and a second later Rio was bathed in blood. Rio yanked his machete out of the man's body, and the assailant crumpled into a spasming pile of limbs on the ground.

Rio stooped down and took the rifle from the man, he didn't know how to use it, but he would learn. He limped into the skirmish, painfully aware of the metal in his thigh and the blood gushing down his leg. Rio saw a Shriker aiming a weapon similar to his and firing it at a Hydra Exo. He noticed that the man made a small movement with his hand that seemed to trigger the explosive projectile to fly from the barrel. Rio leveled the weapon the way he saw the man do it, but failed to find the trigger. He looked at the weapon in confusion and ran his hands over it experimentally.

Sure enough, he found the trigger and sent a bullet launching straight up into the air. Rio jumped in alarm, before he regathered his senses and aimed the weapon again. He pointed the weapon at one of the Shrikers, and pulled the trigger. The gun went off and rammed the stock into his shoulder painfully. Of course he missed, but he didn't let it discourage him, he took aim again and pulled the trigger. Click. Nothing. He had run out of ammunition. He cursed his luck before he ran into the melee. He didn't discard the gun, as it could be useful later if he survived.

He fought, swinging the gun similarly to his machete, and it proved to be useful. He swung it in a vicious arc and it connected with the back of an unsuspecting man's head. The Shriker crumpled to the ground, and the Hydra he was engaged with nodded with appreciation at Rio. It was Taiga, her face soaked with blood, but it wasn't hers. She fought with two small knives, and once the Shriker went down she pulled a smaller gun from his thigh holster. She didn't know how to use it either, and she wasn't about to try to learn on the fly. But much like Rio, she wasn't going to let an opportunity pass her.

"Where's Yuto?" she yelled to be heard over the din.

Rio didn't grace her with a verbal response. Instead, he tightened his lips and looked right into her eyes. She understood.

"He left," Taiga said too quietly to be heard, but Rio knew what she had said. He also knew that she didn't particularly care, but perhaps she had expected more from him.

Their moment was cut short as a loud screeching whistle sounded. The Shrikers turned mid-combat and disappeared just before the sun began to creep over the horizon.

Rio looked around and saw that their colony's population had been decimated. There had been nearly one hundred and fifty of them, but now it looked like less than half of them had survived the attack, if even that. In the middle of the camp, Lepiro hovered over the prone form of Jarrod.

Chapter Eight

"Where's Rio?" Dierde said as the sun began to crest over a sand dune and bathe the desiccated landscape with its burning rays. The gonis lazily flapped circles around the pair. Yuto ran his fingers through his hair in frustration.

"He didn't make it. He didn't..." Yuto choked on his own voice before he turned a steely stare over to Dierde. "Why didn't you warn us about the exiles? We could have left at night instead of waiting until morning. Rio's death is your fault."

"We don't know if he's dead!" Dierde screamed in response but didn't defend her actions. "We should go back for him."

"And die ourselves? Our entire camp was destroyed, I've never seen weapons like that before. We didn't stand a chance against them. Don't be thick," Yuto snarled.

Above them, Aileen and Dierde exchanged confused glances and flapped down to the head height of their masters and stared balefully.

"I can't just leave him to die," Dierde said, her molla eyeliner beginning to run in thick streams down her face.

"You should have thought about that before you lied to us."

"I didn't lie!" she protested, even though her own false words rang in her ears.

"'There are others. There's no other explanation. Everyone has been drinking the piss water in this colony. There's no way the Elders could make it out into the desert every day and take enough water in secret. What if the water is for someone else?'" Yuto mocked in her in a sing-song voice laced with stupidity. "You knew there were others!"

Dierde sank to her knees in the sand, and barely sobbed out the words, "I am so sorry."

Yuto regarded her coldly, before he began to feel a little guilty for his harsh words. "I'm sorry for what you've done as well. But I suppose we have to work together to survive. I'll apologize later if I decide I truly feel sorry."

"What do we do now?" Dierde said, choosing to ignore his last sentence.

"We find the aquifers and hope that nobody beat us to them."

"What if we don't get there first?" Dierde asked, her voice low.

"Then we kill them," Yuto said and patted the machete at his hip with the spear in his hand. "We can't trust anyone anymore. You, least of all."

"I thought you said we had to work together." Dierde rose to her feet and snarled, spit hitting Yuto directly in the face.

"I know, but that doesn't mean I've forgiven you. You killed my best friend," Yuto said, his eyes welling with tears, but he blinked them away.

"He's not dead, don't say that again," Dierde fumed, and Yuto opened his mouth but she cut him off. "Lead the way."

X

Back at the Hydra Camp, Rio, Lepiro, and Taiga stood around the bound form of Jarrod. Rio had removed the shrapnel from his leg, applied an ointment, and now had a piece of cloth tied around his lower thigh as a bandage. The snuffling creature was staked to the ground, but it struggled against its bonds and stretched its greedy, shoveling paws towards the gonis. The gonis shrieked and swooped down and dived bombed the ugly creature, but their gelatinous bodies did little harm.

"What is that disgusting thing?" Lepiro asked, and nudged Jarrod roughly in the ribs.

"His name is Mycka," Jarrod said angrily.

"I don't care what its name is. What is it and why do you have it?" Lepiro persisted.

"It's a sand dingo, and it does the same thing your gonis do."

"It finds mollas?" Rio asked, looking at the odd creature as Herma dove down and spat in its face.

"Er, not exactly. We use it to inoculate our young with the bacteria necessary to survive. It hunts gonis, and then we find the molla caches the gonis have found," Jarrod said reluctantly.

"I'm killing it," Lepiro said and drew a dagger and stalked off towards the creature, which cowered when he approached.

"Please don't!" Jarrod said in a pitiful tone. "The Shrikers killed my men, if you kill Mycka I will have nothing."

Lepiro waved a hand to dismiss him, but Taiga interrupted the would-be slaughter.

"Lepiro, stop. If Jarrod was telling the truth, then he was trying to help us." She turned to the man tied at her feet. "Keep him away from our gonis, or we will kill him."

Jarrod nodded in appreciation of her empathy.

"Why didn't the Shrikers kill all of us?" Rio asked, in the back of his mind replaying his conversation with Dierde and Yuto. He couldn't figure out why Dierde hadn't mentioned the exiles.

"They were hunting my men, not the Hydras. They need you. But your colony ended up being collateral damage," Jarrod explained. He was missing one of his eyebrow rings and an ugly purple bruise was forming around his left eye socket and cheekbone.

"Where are they now?" Lepiro asked as he resumed his place with the group.

"Probably hunting down my men who escaped, if any. Or bringing your Elders back to The Wreckage,"

Jarrod supplied, splaying his hands, an awkward gesture tied as they were.

"Why didn't Dierde tell us about you?" Rio asked, but it wasn't a question.

"You her husband?" Rio shook his head in answer. "Boyfriend?"

"They're the only two who are actually in love in this colony." Lepiro snorted humorlessly. Rio realized that the other hunter was jealous of the relationship.

"That would be why," Jarrod said sourly, looking at the ground.

Rio felt a pang of sadness lance through his ribs and a lump formed in his throat. He understood exactly what the exile had insinuated. Anger welled within him and he slammed his foot into Jarrod's face. Blood gushed from the now broken nose, and the man collapsed on the ground, barely conscious.

"We need him!" Taiga protested, as Rio kicked the slack figure in the ribs.

"I know," Rio growled, tears on the verge of escape. "I'm not going to kill him." The heartbroken hunter paced away from the group and disappeared behind one of the tents that had remained standing.

Taiga ignored the young man and turned her attention back to the prisoner. "If I untie you, will you help us find the source of the water?" She had both hands placed on her hips, surveying the broken and bruised man at her feet.

Ethan Proud

"I don't have much of a choice, do I? But as I said, I came here to help. We need to find the other Hydra colonies first, though," Jarrod said and spat a gob of blood from his mouth. It appeared that a molar was stuck in the congealed mess.

"No. We need to secure the water source first, and then we can hunt down the colonies. If the Shrikers know you have warned one colony, they will undoubtedly try to beat us there," Taiga argued and turned to Lepiro. "Find what we can salvage and how many of our people are left. We leave immediately."

"Look around, we are the only survivors," Lepiro said gently.

Taiga didn't respond. She was staring at the dead and dying that surrounded them. It didn't take Taiga long before she saw the corpse of her father in a puddle of his own blood in the otherwise dry sand. Her only solace was that in his advanced age, he didn't have much time left before the attack. She bit back her tears and scanned the destruction for her mother.

"Search for more survivors," she commanded, and made sure her voice didn't catch in her throat. Without another word she began methodically searching for the last of her family. She did her best to ignore the groans of the dying, and eased the pain of those who were beyond help. Tears slowly tumbled down her dusty cheeks, leaving streaky rivulets from her cheekbones to her jaw. After seemingly searching the whole camp, she noticed a strange lump underneath the crumpled and

Terra Mortem

ruined canvas of a tent. With shaking hands, she lifted the fabric and saw a welcome sight. Her mother was unconscious, but breathing. The left half of her face was coated with blood that no longer ran from a jagged cut on her forehead. Taiga gingerly set her mother's head on her lap and stroked her hair.

"Wake up," she whispered pleadingly, and blew out a sigh of relief when she saw the dark lashes flutter.

"What?" her mother croaked, and Taiga let out a tittering laugh.

"Shh. It'll be okay," she said as a tear dropped from her eye onto her mother's cheek.

"What happened?"

"We were attacked," Taiga said hollowly.

Her mother moved to sit up but stopped as a pain wracked her leg. She reclined back into her daughter's lap and didn't move or speak for a long moment. "Your father?"

Taiga shook her head, and the two of them cried unabashedly as the wind began to whip the sand into a flurry around them, tearing the shattered tent into the air. Several long hours later, her mother died in her arms.

Ethan Proud

Chapter Nine

Treya and Rumo hobbled along at a surprisingly quick pace despite their arthritic joints. They followed the raiding party of the original settlers who had rescued them while destroying Jarrod's band of upstarts. The original settlers simply called themselves Exos or Shrikers and had been in communication with the Hydra Elders for many years. When a Hydra reached a certain age and could no longer perform their duties, they were either elected as a member of the Council of the Elders or were allowed to retire. Molla hunters never became Elders as they would be furious when they learned the truth. Part of the Elder initiation ceremony was a 'trek into the desert' that was allegedly a molla fueled vision quest where they learned the secrets of the planet. However, it was all just a clever ruse and the Elder Initiates were given lavish gifts by the Shrikers and told the true history of human settlement on the planet. After a number of years serving on the council, the Elders would be escorted to the Original Settlement where they could live their final days in peace.

Now it looked as if a war was brewing and Treya and Rumo would not fill the twilight of their years with the wondrous food and sinful indulgences they had been promised. More than likely they would be forced into helping hunt down the other Hydra colonies, since they had failed in their duty as secret keepers and an entire colony's aquifer maps had been lost.

"How much further to the Original Settlement?" Treya asked, her arthritic joints starting to ache, even though they had only been walking for a few hours. Then again, walking through sand was far more exerting than walking on solid ground, not that any of the Hydras had ever seen solid ground other than the rocky formations that jutted from the dunes.

The leader of the raiding party, who both Treya and Rumo assumed was a man, pulled down the scarf covering its face and removed the goggles that protected its eyes. The raiding party leader was a woman, and a striking one at that. She had large eyes that seemed both green and grey at the same time and she had high cheekbones that accentuated her full lips. Her head was shaved close to the scalp, except for the Mohawk that arced bright red eight inches from her skull. She smiled, though it wasn't genuine and revealed three gold teeth.

"The rovers are just over that dune. It won't be long." She gestured briefly before pulling her goggles back down over her face and lifting the scarf back over the bridge of her nose. Rumo and Treya both struggled to see which dune she had been referring to. There were an infinite amount of sandy humps peaking into the horizon. Treya sighed resignedly. Clearly, they didn't garner the respect they had back in their colony. It would take some getting used to.

Ethan Proud

The ancient Exos shuffled through the sand, each step sending more of the dirt tumbling down their boots and settling between the soles of their feet and the arches of their shoes. Their old skin chafed against the irritating eroded rocks with enough friction to create a pearl in the mouth of an oyster, though the Exos had never heard of an oyster, and their feet only produced sweat which would never yield a jewel. Finally, they crested a ridge and saw the dark metallic forms of the rovers. Treya and Rumo had seen the vehicles on several occasions before, but were still awed by the machinery and secretly wondered why the Shrikers hadn't sent the Hydras out with vehicles in the first place. Maybe the Hydras had elected to set out on foot in true pioneer spirit. Idiots.

The rover offered little protection from the elements, with sand sucked through the vents and striking the passengers in the face, but the lack of side doors allowed for a cool breeze to rustle through their hair and give the illusion of a pleasant atmosphere. As soon as the rovers stopped though, that unbearable, weighty atmosphere descended on the Exos like a blanket of humidity and despair. AE625 was hardly a livable planet. The massive vehicles weren't designed to be driven through sand, and as a result they sashayed over each dune, sending bits of gravel flying with each rotation of the tires. A rooster tail of burning sand kicked up behind the rear tires and the three rovers teetered across the desert like blind mice, nearly bumping into one another, but at the last minute, as if sensing the other's presence, peeled off in the opposite direction.

Rhea, the woman with the red hair, drove expertly. The wheel moved loosely in her hands as the vehicle sank in the sand before popping back up, sending another plume into the air. If she had kept a tighter grip, the rover would have jerked back and forth instead of the smooth (a subjective term) ride the passengers were now experiencing. The sun had since breached its zenith and was now reaching for its nadir far below the horizon. Earth 2.0 followed it dutifully across the sky, despite the unfathomable miles that lay between the star and the two planets. In the distance, barely visible over the horizon, lights began to gleam, casting their radiance over the spine of a dune that jutted into the sky. The fingers of light reached higher as the sun began to melt, and twin moons rose directly where the Original Settlement came into vision, as if its own light heralded the two moons, or the pale orbs were sent from the city itself.

It didn't take much longer for the eccentric woman's expert driving to get the rover through the looming front gates of the *Shrike's* wreckage turned colony. The perimeter fence was fifteen feet tall and made from shrapnel and looked haphazard at best, but the secondary wall had been carved from stone and was forty feet high. Guards patrolled the top of the wall with long barreled guns, gas masks, and night vision goggles. Behind this wall, the ground sloped into a crater, a relic from the impact of the *Shrike*. The ground here was more solid and makeshift roads had been blasted and paved into the crater wall, winding their way down to what was left of the *Shrike*. The ship had been designed to carry 25,000 humans from Earth as part of a mass sojourn to Earth 2.0. As such, everything needed to sustain life on AE625 was easily salvageable: hydroponic gardens, medical supplies, clothing, manufacturing stations, water purifiers, etc. The ship's shell hummed and glowed with pale greenish blue light as it generated the electricity for the blooming colony of Exos. If human life on AE625 went by seasons, it would be late summer or early fall, harvest time, and the Exos were reaping the rewards sown by generations who had lived long before them.

Rumo and Treya felt a slight pang of guilt for their decimated colony of Hydras. None of them knew this lifestyle was possible. Here in the Original Settlement, no one drank their own piss or birthed cold fetuses or spent their entire day searching for water and returning empty handed. The guilt was short-lived, as the elders realized that their colony was dead, and they were here in the Original Settlement. Rhea glanced over at them, read their expression and sneered.

"Just because you are scum doesn't mean you can't enjoy yourself." Her green eyes flashed with derision.

Treya ignored this, but Rumo spluttered for a moment before going silent. Treya's old eyes scanned

Terra Mortem

the walls of the crater where tunnels had been bored into the rock wall and little hatches that glowed with the same light as the ship marked the entrance to an underground abode. The network of roughly circular doors looked like it belonged to insects such as bees or ants, the term colony never more appropriate.

"Where are we headed?" Rumo asked, and half expected a sarcastic answer.

"Tonight you will rest in the palace. Tomorrow you will meet with the commanding family," Rhea answered dully. Despite it being well after dark, she didn't seem tired. Her eyes were bright, though traces of ruptured blood vessels could be seen underneath her dark lashes. Treya looked closer and could see the dark ring that framed the woman's right nostril. Molla. Even in the Original Settlement drug addicts ran rampant, and apparently played a pivotal role in society.

"Where are our gonis?" Rumo asked, and Treya felt her heart sink. Both of the elders knew that the Original Colony inoculated themselves with lab-grown bacteria synthesized from the saliva of sand dingos, and no longer needed the gonis, and hadn't for hundreds of years.

"They are in the rover behind us. But I doubt you will want to see them again," Rhea answered without looking forward.

"So they are dead?" Rumo asked.

Rhea looked slightly annoyed and her answer unveiled just how cold and cruel she could be. "Slaughtered and soon to be eaten."

The rest of the drive was held in silence. Treya and Rumo were escorted to their room, which had been carved into the crater walls, entry gained by opening a heavy stone door. Rhea easily opened the door, but the elders knew that it would take their combined strength to shut it when the woman left. On either side of the door were glass jars, filled with strange mushroom-like growths with long twisting stems and hastate, flat projections growing intermittently along the stem. The strange organism emitted a pale sea-green light. The edges of the glass were covered in condensation. At the end of the stem, a colorful cap pressed against the glass. The cap was divided into five separate pieces, each as billowy as a blouse, yet undoubtedly more colorful. At the center of this mass were five finger-length projections, placed equidistantly around one slightly longer and thicker projection. These projections bent against the glass playfully like a tongue.

"It's a plant," Rhea said, and her face softened when she saw the bewilderment on the old Exos' faces. "Take them inside in the morning or the sun will kill them. We call them Martian Flares. They only grow underground. They are my second favorite thing on this planet. Now rest, tomorrow will be long," she added and smoothly swung the door shut as Rumo and Treya entered their room.

Terra Mortem

Chapter Ten

Dierde and Yuto trudged through the desolate sandscape. The laces of their boots were laden with grit and with each gust of wind, another wave of sand washed over their feet and more particles nestled their way between toes and down to the soles. Blistered feet were nothing new to the pair, but the silence that stretched between them was. Yuto had not forgiven her for 'killing' Rio and Dierde refused to acknowledge that her previous lover was dead. Their gonis seemed to acknowledge the awkwardness and floated together several yards away from the estranged humans.

Ahead of them, the aquifer Yuto had discovered was revealed, a mere fissure in the ground, barely visible as sand whipped across its maw. Yuto led the way and gracefully dipped between the yawning granite and disappeared. He shook his hair free of sand after he was safe from the vicious winds and heard Dierde lowering herself gingerly behind him. She shook her mane of hair to rid the sand from it, same as Yuto…though the two of them could still feel the gravel clinging to their scalps. The gonis illuminated the way before them, lighting the tunnel surprisingly well. Dierde reached out and brushed her hand against the cave wall and felt moisture. She recoiled from the alien feeling for a moment, before reaching her hand out again and reveling in the coolness.

Terra Mortem

After winding deeper through the subterranean refuge for nearly a quarter mile, Yuto stopped and Dierde stepped around him to see a strange mechanism. Yuto had clearly seen this before and figured out how to use it when he initially stumbled across the manmade aquifer. He put a canteen underneath a spigot and pulled a handle. Water rushed out. Dierde gasped in astonishment. She had never seen such a constant stream of water. After filling the water compartments of their packs, and every canteen they had, they began to harvest the molla their gonis were already munching on. Wordlessly, they dug their nails under the caps and snorted the black spores deep into their sinuses. Instantly their bodies felt the cold rush followed by the galloping heartbeats. Yuto glanced at Dierde as she was filling her pack with the mushrooms and felt a pang of excitement travel from his navel down to his loins. Embarrassed, he turned away. This woman was responsible for the death of his best friend and was his best friend's lover. He brushed the dirty thoughts from his mind and harvested more of the mollas.

"There are three more aquifers," he managed to mumble out, his voice gravelly and sticky. He felt awkward. When Rio had been around he never felt an attraction to the female Exo. Sure, he had noticed she was attractive, but he had never *felt* it.

"I remember," Dierde said, sounding timid and meek. She didn't know how to handle herself around Yuto now that he blamed her for the death of his friend.

Ethan Proud

"I wasn't sure," Yuto said lamely and his voice caught again.

This time Dierde looked up at him. "What?"

"Nothing," he said and looked away from her gaze. "We should get going."

Dierde nodded as he turned around and led them away from the manmade water source.

X

Rumo and Treya sat at a small metal table while they waited for the Commanding Family. They had met the family once before, and family was a poor term. Polyamorous quadruple was more accurate. The Commanding family was comprised of two men, Fleet and Kilo, and two women, Mertensia and Aqi.

The Exo Elders stared at the ornate filigree of shimmery material that laced over the table in a webwork of mushrooms, humans, gonis, and sand dingos. The surrounding room was just as ornate with a high vaulted ceiling. Halfway along its length wires and remnants of support beams could be seen where a floor or adjoining wall had been removed after the initial crash to make more room. Small and large tables, seating either six or twelve Exos were scattered around, in a somewhat alternating pattern. No one else was in the room, save for Rhea who stood by the entrance with her arms crossed. Her red hair was now tipped with neon purple, her eyes hidden behind a pair of dark lenses. Between her index and middle finger she held a piece of rolled paper containing molla spores and caps, burning lazily from one end. Periodically she would raise it to her lips and inhale a lungful, before exhaling a plume of scintillating smoke.

The door next to her boomed open but she didn't flinch or move as the Commanding Family entered. They came two by two. Each time Treya and Rumo met the family they had been paired off differently. Today Fleet and Kilo walked side by side while Mertensia and Aqi trailed behind; whether their pairing reflected that week's sexuality, the aged Hydras could only guess. Their median age was twenty-four, though had they been on Earth they would be mistaken for being in their late forties or early fifties. Fleet was the tallest, with broad shoulders despite his lean musculature, short cropped brown hair and blue, narrow eyes. Kilo was shorter and had dark brown skin and his curly hair climbed away from his head in short spires. Mertensia had a demure build and blonde hair that cascaded halfway down her back, while her counterpart Aqi was a tall, willowy woman with almond eyes only a shade darker than amber in the current light, her dark hair even shorter than Fleet's. Her skin was so dark it seemed to absorb all the light around her, giving the air around her the appearance of a halo around a black hole. Her lips were painted gold, as were her eyelashes, and her fingers were adorned with many flashy jewels. As she passed the threshold of the room she looked

Rhea up and down wolfishly. A muscle flexed in Rhea's jaw as she continued to smoke on her molla. Once the authoritative woman passed, Rhea's lips puckered in a cheeky smile.

The Commanding Family sat down at the table with Treya and Rumo.

Fleet was the first to speak. "We are so glad you survived. What happened at Hydra Camp Seven was very unfortunate. We have sent emissaries out to the other seven camps to ensure the elders are warned of the current developments. The work your colonies do is very important," he said in a tone that was nothing if not political.

"We are very aware of our standing with you," Treya said brusquely. It was not openly rude, but her message was clear.

Aqi's eyes flashed dangerously. "You are alive, are you not?"

"Not all of the Council of Elders survived your attack. Yuron, Hugo, and Nitra were struck down by your bullets. We have been deceiving our people for years, believing it was for the greater good, and this is how you repay us," Treya said coldly.

Rumo placed his wizened hand on hers to belay her rising temper.

Fleet waved his hand dismissively. "The policy and procedures on this matter were set long before we came into office and long before you were even born. We simply follow the mandates to accomplish our mission.

If anyone is to blame here, it is the malcontent Jarrod," Fleet explained casually.

"He refused to listen to us when we tried to justify the current situation. His own conclusions were enough for him to start off on his crusade. He rallied some of our best men and women to his cause…" Kilo's brown eyes were pensive as he spoke, as if he was speaking to someone farther away than the two Hydras at the table.

"Yes, we all want to get off this planet and we appreciate your efforts," Rumo started and Treya snorted at his submissive stance.

They were too old themselves to be rescued from the desolate AE625, and their people had been destroyed. They needed retribution.

He ignored her. "But we feel that our colony was needless collateral damage. Enough aquifers have been established that all of the Hydra Colonies could return home."

"I thank you for your opinion, but it is not warranted here," Kilo said coolly. "You may have been leaders in Hydra Camp Seven, but here you will hold your tongue unless we ask for it."

"Now, Kilo that was unkind and insensitive," Fleet said with an easy grin as he held up his hands as if to pacify both parties.

"Regardless of anyone's feelings on this matter, we must move forward and prevent any more casualties of war," Mertensia said. Her voice was melodic and bounced around the tin can that had become the Original Settlement.

"War?" Treya asked incredulously. "It was a massacre. Not an act of war. Hydra Seven was eradicated."

"Not everyone was destroyed. We have reason to believe that Jarrod and some of your hunters survived. If they reach the other Hydra Colonies before our emissaries do, the consequences could be disastrous."

"True, if the Hydra Colonies band together and march on The Wreckage, everything we have worked for could be doomed," Fleet said, his fingertips pressed against each other in a gesture reminiscent of a steeple. "We made contact with Earth 2.0 three years ago. A mission has been launched to rescue us. In three months, they will be here."

"Why weren't we alerted to these new developments?" Rumo burst out.

"The number of errors that could doom such a mission are innumerable. To give the people false hope would be unwise. A party led by Rhea was underway to bring the Hydra Colonies home. However, after learning of Jarrod's deception, we rerouted her to intercept him."

"Why did Jarrod embark on his crusade if he knew that rescue is imminent?" Treya demanded.

The Commanding Family looked apprehensively between themselves.

"The only persons aware of the Earth 2.0 Mission are in this room. The disappointment of a failed rescue would be too much for the Exos," Mertensia said tactfully.

Treya snorted derisively and shared a look with Rumo.

"You kept your Colonists in the dark, did you not?" Aqi said tersely and both Rumo and Treya blanched. "Just as I thought. We are not so different."

"Perhaps not. But I wish we were," Treya said and looked down at her feet.

"No point in dwelling on the past," Fleet said sagaciously. "We can all save our legacies if we act now and serve *all of our people.*"

Rumo nodded in agreement. Treya looked expectantly at Fleet.

"We will be sending out three parties to the remaining Hydra Colonies. You will each lead a party, while Rhea will track down the survivors of Hydra Seven," Fleet said, the last statement sounding slightly reluctant.

"And do what to them? You don't even know if there are survivors!" Treya fumed.

"We can't have any witnesses to hinder our progress. Salvation is on the horizon," Fleet said calmly. He raised a hand to stop any forthcoming arguments. "I know you have your objections, but we cannot sacrifice our entire existence for a few."

X

Late that evening, Rhea was packing her bags and preparing for the hunt ahead of her when she heard a knock at the door. She heard the hinges squeak nearly imperceptibly before her guest entered without waiting to be ushered in. The figure's silhouette was barely illuminated by the bioluminescent plants that lined the entryway. Perhaps it was only because of how dark the woman's skin was. On a dark night, Aqi could travel undetected unless a full moon, or two full moons, revealed her presence.

Aqi leaned her sinuous body against the doorframe that led to the kitchen and living space of Rhea's abode. It was the only room with electricity. In every house only one room was wired to the generator on the *Shrike*, because if any more rooms were powered the generator would kick off, something the original colonists had discovered several times.

Without looking, Rhea said, "Had to see me off?" Rhea's grey-green eyes glinted as she smirked.

Aqi said nothing, but instead flitted over behind Rhea and wrapped her arms around Rhea's waist and ran her hands down the soldier's thighs. Aqi's gold-painted lips teased Rhea's earlobe before her pearlescent teeth bit down playfully. Rhea continued to fill her pack, tossing in a water filter and a mobile cooking set along with bagged dehydrated food, ignoring the other woman's advances. Aqi pulled

Rhea's hips, dragging her away from the task at hand. Despite her thin limbs and delicate structure, Aqi was strong, her muscles powerful.

With a sigh, not of exasperation but excitement, Rhea twisted and planted her lips against Aqi's.

Chapter Eleven

Lepiro tousled his short blond hair and sand came falling across his shoulders and chest. He wore a pair of goggles and a handkerchief tied around his face. Around him, Taiga, Rio, and Jarrod moved. Their gonis floated in the air around them, sometimes squawking at the hideous sand dingo that was at the center of the group. Its snuffling nose and beady eyes were perpetually pointed at the gelatinous forms drifting in the air.

The air was hot and dry, no different from any day on AE625, and the Exos were used to it. Every inch of their bodies were covered, minus the skin between the cuffs of their weathered jackets and the fringe of their gloves, and the tops of their cheeks and noses. Jarrod's head was obscured by a hood pulled tight around his face, due to his short hair that offered little protection to his scalp.

"How do we know he isn't leading us into a trap?" Lepiro's eyes narrowed from behind his goggles, but the gesture was lost on the group due to the tint.

Jarrod opened his mouth, but Rio interjected. "Because the Shrikers murdered his entire company. He has no one to lead us to." Apparently Jarrod's tryst with Dierde had struck a chord with Rio and he wasn't the forgiving type. Jarrod didn't grace the trio of Hydras with a response, but instead looked at his feet.

"Rio…" Taiga said gently. "If he leads us astray you can kill him."

She said it in such an assuring fashion that it took Jarrod a moment to comprehend her meaning. The stranger considered objecting to that fact that he would consider leading them astray, but instead held his tongue. He was no fool.

"How do you plan on defeating the Shrikers if they beat us to The Source?" Jarrod asked, once again trying to force his agenda of uniting the Hydra Colonies before searching for the water.

"You worry about leading us to The Source. Once we get eyes on it, we can form a defensive plan and track down the other colonies. It will do us no good to have an army that is clueless of the terrain if we need to storm a Shriker fort. They clearly have better technology than us," Taiga said in a commanding tone. "We've been living on scraps for years. If we control The Source, we can barter an agreement with the Original Settlement and perhaps avoid being annihilated."

"What if the Shrikers recruit the other Hydra Colonies to their cause and demonize us?" Jarrod asked firmly.

"Silence," Lepiro said coldly. "You are a demon and brought ruin upon our people. Don't let me catch you using collective phrases such as 'we' or 'us' again. You are the enemy, and so are they."

Taiga nodded her assent and Rio bristled, his broad form seeming to rise up several inches. Jarrod knew that if the other two weren't there to protect him, Rio would beat him until all that remained was meat paste and gristle. Despite the impossibility of it, Jarrod felt an icy rivulet of sweat run between his shoulder blades.

"The only way you get out of this alive is if you get us to The Source before anyone else reaches it," Rio said as he turned, drew his machete and ran it through the sand dingo's flank. The creature let out a final snuffle that sounded more like a gurgle and blue, effervescent blood frothed from its mouth. It slumped on the ground and didn't move again. As ruthless as he was, Rio made a direct hit with the thing's heart and it had felt only a moment of pain. Jarrod, on the other hand, let out a strangled gasp and didn't try to hide the tears that rolled down his cheeks.

He hung his head and saw Rio nudge Mycka's body over to him with his toe.

"You can carry it if you'd like, but we need to get moving," he growled through his teeth.

Taiga and Lepiro exchanged a worried glance. Perhaps none of them would be reaching The Source if Rio couldn't keep his anger in check.

The Exile shuffled to his feet, stepped over his last companion's dead body and didn't look back. Rio fell in step behind him, and Taiga and Lepiro shared one last sordid moment of eye contact before following. The gonis around them settled onto their symbiotic's shoulders and seemed smug and at ease now that their predator was a corpse.

The sand whipped into a frenzy as the Exos trudged between the dunes.

X

Dierde and Yuto hunkered down as the sandstorm intensified. They had found a hollow in a rock face that had been eroded just enough to fit the two of them comfortably. Their gonis clung to the ceiling above them. The sand laden wind took on the appearance of a viscous wall as the wind reached dangerous speeds. The two Exos were nestled into the tight space, Yuto painfully aware of Dierde's hand placed high on his thigh. He wasn't sure if it was intentional, and his subconscious response to it definitely wasn't.

Of course, Dierde was aware of the growing situation and she wasn't sure what to make of it. Yuto had hardly spoken to her in days, and yet here they were, both stirring from mild physical contact. Dierde sheepishly looked up at Yuto. She could see the muscle in his jaw clenched, and he was intentionally looking away from her. She wondered what was going through his head, as she pulled away from him and leaned against the rock wall just to the other side of her. It wasn't as comfortable as Yuto's shoulder, but she believed that Rio was still alive and sleeping with his best friend was not a secret she wanted to keep once they were reunited. She already had transgressions to remedy. Yuto flinched and shifted his eyes to meet hers, though his neck didn't move.

"Sorry," she murmured, though she wasn't sure what she was apologizing for...or if it was even meant for Yuto.

The pair didn't say another word, despite the croons and warbles of Dierde and Aileen in the crevice above them. Unlike the gonis, the exos were not enjoying each other's company. As the seconds stretched into minutes and the minutes stretched into eternity, the sand wall before them began to dissipate in long forlorn tendrils as the wind died down to a mere grumble. The last of the sand fell with gravity and didn't move, except for a slight rustle with each of AE625's lonely sighs. Dierde gracefully leaned forward, her knees leading the way, followed by her hips as she propelled herself into a crouched position. With her left hand she pushed against the rock wall and exited the meager cave. Yuto felt his joints protest as he moved to follow his female counterpart. He stumbled and barely managed to catch himself when he felt the pins and needle sensation of a snoozing limb shoot through his left foot.

"Which way now?" Dierde stared at the landscape before her which was nearly unrecognizable from the view mere hours earlier. Before it had been a relatively flat plain that extended for miles in any direction, except for the small crag behind them and two pillars that led to a canyon directly before them, but the pillars were still a half day's march from their current location. Now, a myriad of dunes lay before them, scattered where the wind had deposited the sandy mounds. Some of them stood nearly forty feet high and were nearly as sheer as the rocky cliffs. The two pillars were still visible, though they were only a fraction of the height they had been. The altitude shifted with the winds on AE625.

"That way." Yuto pointed to the pillars. "There was an aquifer at the base of the canyon. I'm sure it's all but covered now. We will have to make it to the third aquifer with the water we have on us."

Dierde nodded grimly. Her eyes met Yuto's own dark orbs for a moment, but little emotion passed between the two of them. It was more of a mutual glower than anything.

"When we find Rio alive, are you going to apologize?" she asked earnestly.

"I will after you apologize to him," Yuto said firmly, and Dierde nearly flinched from the verbal rebuke.

"Our entire colony is polyamorous, and here I am being crucified for my actions. How do you justify that?" Dierde asked, fuming.

"That's not the problem, you kept a secret that nearly killed all of us. Why didn't you tell us the truth? Why didn't you tell Rio the truth?" Yuto asked, his voice almost pleading.

Dierde's chest constricted. "I was too embarrassed," she said sourly. Dierde looked down at her feet and missed Yuto's features softening.

His hand twitched at his side, as if he was about to place it on her shoulder but changed his mind. "We should get moving. We have a long ways to go," he murmured and pulled his scarf up to cover his mouth. He stepped passed Dierde and she fell in line a pace behind. The gonis flipped languid acrobatics around her, like seals in the air.

Blisters formed and popped on their feet as they wound their way between, up, and over dunes, keeping their eyes on the pillars that barely stood above the windswept grit. Each time a pocket of serum, plasma, lymph, and blood was forcefully ruptured it was a small wave of relief as the gnawing pain ceased, before the sweat mingled with the open wound and caused yet more irritation. Finally they breached the threshold of the monoliths and a causeway of gravel spilled between the rocky teeth and filled the canyon nearly to the brim. Dierde and Yuto cautiously traversed the deceptive footing and each step sent a cascade of sand tumbling down the steep incline, fifteen feet to the false canyon bottom. With each movement they felt the ground shift beneath them as the sand settled deeper to the canyon floor. Depending on what rock formations were beneath them, a pocket of air could collapse and they would be sucked beneath the surface.

"How deep was this canyon when you found it?" Dierde asked as the ground hissed and filled in an air pocket just to her left.

"Hundreds of feet deep," Yuto said, his brow furrowed with concentration.

Dierde didn't say another word, but instead took a mental inventory of the rock walls jutting above them, going higher with each step they took down. The walls couldn't have been more than twenty feet above them right now, and maybe forty feet at the highest. That meant that one misstep and she would be dragged many times the depth of the canyon now, to the true bottom.

The gonis, sensing the danger, squawked loudly and landed before their respective Exos and began taking awkward leaps of several feet before returning to the ground with a soft 'thwump'. They repeated this deeper and deeper into the canyon mouth and sometime their weight would send sand hissing down a fissure, or reveal solid footing. If the ground gave way beneath them they would flap their jelly-like wings until they were airborne, and dive bomb the next proposed footing.

Despite the gonis acting as guides to their Exos, Dierde and Yuto still sank ankle deep in the soft ground they were traversing. With a sudden hiss, the footing beneath Dierde gave way and she felt the suction rush up her calves as the airborne Dierde shrieked in alarm. Yuto dove for his companion, his arms wrapping around her waist and tackling her to the ground, before she slipped into the earth like a needle dropped down a drain. Their bodies lay flat against the sand and slowed their descent, but the ground beneath was still being sucked to the bottom of the canyon after an errant air pocket burst. Like sand tumbling down an hourglass, they were being pulled closer to a widening mouth appearing in the desert.

Yuto kept his right arm wrapped around Dierde and began to slog doggedly towards the rocks that jutted from the canyon's edge. His left arm sank to the elbow each time he planted it and his legs were buried up to mid-thigh as they desperately churned to keep himself and Dierde afloat. Recovering from her shock, Dierde twisted onto her belly and began kicking herself along. Yuto's right arm snaked across her waist as he released her and she felt as though a life preserver had been taken away from her, though she recognized the practicality of the gesture.

Together the two kicked and flailed out of the sand, their bodies thrashing against gravity until they finally reached the canyon wall and clung to it with all the strength their fingers possessed. The sand dragged against their hips and tore at their feet for a few more seconds before ceasing. They were both buried to the navel, but the surface of the canyon was perfectly still. A single grain rolled before coming to rest. Yuto used the rock wall to heave himself out of the sand and felt particles tumble uncomfortably between his clothes and bare skin in places he would rather not have sand. He lent a hand to Dierde and lifted as she pulled herself free of the gravelly prison. Their gonis warbled happily in the air above them before landing on their masters' shoulders, their gooey suction cup like skin squelching as the animals wriggled exuberantly.

"I could use some molla right about now," Yuto said and wasn't surprised when his voice held a slight tremor.

"I have some dried caps," Dierde said and pulled her pack off her back with shaky hands. She leaned against the rocky outcropping and sat down, her feet barely drifting along the ground, the canyon wall looming above the cleft they sat on. She dug a pouch made of a thick fabric from the smallest compartment of her pack and proffered it to Yuto. He opened it and found that the bottom of the pack chock full of spores. He took the end of the spoon Dierde handed him next, dug out a precious amount and held it to his nostril, snorting the black powder back and letting out a little gag as it hit his esophagus. He felt a shudder run down his spine as he handed the pack to Dierde, who took a massive spoonful and inhaled deep enough to pull it all into her sinus in one attempt. She shook her head and made a noise in the back of her throat when the spores slid down her gullet and into her stomach.

"Let's not try to cross that again," she said and gagged a little bit a second time as more molla dripped from her sinus.

"Do you want to try to scale the cliff to get to the plains below the canyon?" Yuto asked, staring down the mouth of the canyon.

"We can probably just slide down the dunes once we get to the end?" Dierde asked, raising an eyebrow.

Yuto imagined it in his head, the two of them sliding down the sand on their rears and he laughed. "We might as well try it. Hell, might even be fun."

Another raised eyebrow, and Dierde clambered up onto the cleft, her booted feet mere inches from what would have been a death defying drop hours prior. Now, it was hardly a three foot drop. The planet AE625 was an inconstant as the seasons on the desolate Earth the Exos had left behind. She searched for a handhold to leverage her weight up higher as she scouted her route up the wall.

Chapter Twelve

Rhea scanned the horizon from behind the wheel of the rover. Her dark goggle rims and the tinted lenses made her grey-green eyes appear ghostly pale. She turned to the soldier in the seat next to her, Gana. His long hair hung to his shoulders, and despite being several shades darker than Rhea, his skin was sallow and appeared pale or yellow.

"There can't be much of Hydra Seven left," Gana stated.

"That's not what I'm worried about," Rhea said casually.

"What then?" Gana asked, his dark eyes meeting Rhea's striking orbs.

"If war erupts, no one will be alive to be rescued," she answered solemnly.

"You are much too dire." He laughed easily. "We will live to see the Second Earth. Right now we can see it in our own sky."

"Optimism is a luxury," Rhea murmured and pressed her right foot down on the accelerator while her left worked the clutch. Out of her peripherals she could see the rooster tails of sand behind three other rovers. She crested a dune and saw four silhouettes on the next ridge over. It was impossibly steep, and it crested into a vertical lip the last twenty feet or so. The Hydra Seven refugees sure knew how to pick the high ground.

However, they had never encountered high powered rifles until the downfall of their colony. Rhea slammed on the brakes and seven soldiers tumbled from the rover, landing nimbly on their feet, guns in hand.

X

Taiga turned, her mousy hair whipping across her face when she heard the sounds of engines. "They found us," she whispered, audible only to her companions. The gonis in the air let out a skree of dismay. Taiga pulled a long knife from her belt and yanked Jarrod towards her by his bound wrists. She sawed the knife between his hands deftly, severing the rope. Rio made to squabble, but Taiga interrupted him.

"We need to run. Feelings aside," she said brusquely and Rio couldn't tell if she meant it as a slight. Without further ado, they bailed down the opposite side of the sandy ridge, their feet sinking into the earth to the ankle. It was more of a carefully conducted slide than an outright run, but nevertheless it was quick.

X

Rhea blinked as the figures ghosted from the view of her scope.

"They won't make it easy," Gana said and grinned.

Rhea glanced at him. If she had been a different persuasion…and he less bloodthirsty, she may have been interested in him.

"Get back in the rover," she barked. "We can't lose them."

The last of the soldiers was barely in his seat before she peeled out. She headed towards the tail of the dune where its expansive flank finally began to dip down, while in the other direction it traveled upwards for miles and miles.

"Gana, make sure that you see them before they see us," she said without looking.

Wordlessly, he moved his left foot beneath his body and stood upright, gripping the roll cage as he lifted his torso out of the gap in the roof, his left arm tucked over the frame, his right arm nestling the stock of his rifle. He checked to make sure the safety was off and rested his index finger outside the trigger guard. No point wasting a spray of bullets every time Rhea jostled him on the uneven ground.

Rhea twisted the steering wheel, cutting a bumpy course up the dune, her foot applying even pressure against the floor of the rover. Gana adjusted his stance and tucked his leg on the headrest of his seat behind him, keeping his body more level as the incline increased. Rhea crested the hill and grimaced when she heard the rat-a-tat spray of bullets. She wasn't a pacifist and her grimace was because she knew Gana had missed his shot. The puffs of sand that accompanied each retort let her know that. Above her, the soldier howled with fury as the last head visible amongst the gritty sea disappeared into a fissure between two rocky outcroppings. The Shrikers could only hope it was a shallow one.

X

Rio cocked his head when he heard the tires of the rover roll to a stop on the rock above them. He turned an eye on Herma, its bioluminescent body shimmering like a damning signal fire. His injured leg protested with each step he took, but he had been through worse.

"We need to move, and we need to hide the gonis." He reached forward, but Herma flitted out of his reach deeper into the cave. He growled before the goni disappeared out of sight, and a smile stretched across his face. The creatures understood the peril and were leading them to safety, or a dead end. He followed the tracer of light his goni had left, a trick of the mind, and found it floating in the air waiting for him. It banked a wide turn and led him through a twisting corridor of rocky granite.

A glance over his shoulder showed him that Taiga and Lepiro were following their gonis as well. Then he heard the heavy footsteps of combat boots in the tunnel. Herma let out a low warble and sped up. Rio needed no further urging, sprinting after the goni as quickly as he could, his footsteps padding along in the dark. His next step hit something cold, and ankle deep. It was water. He felt elation soar in his chest and wanted to scream for joy even though he knew he couldn't. His next step took him out of the precious liquid and he heard one of his companions splash into the water.

Then the tunnel was lit up with the explosive report of gunfire and he saw a light blink out of existence next to him. He heard the most pained cry he had ever heard in his life as Taiga's goni dropped lifelessly from the air. She caught it in her trembling hands as she collapsed on the ground in agony.

Rio, Jarrod, and Lepiro were frozen in place, the single shot temporarily blinding them so they could no longer see well enough to know where they were running. The surviving gonis were still visible as tiny dots of light, but Rio couldn't tell if the orbs were moving or not. As his vision swam back to him, he saw several dark shapes detach themselves from the walls and dart past him and his companions, towards the Shriker soldiers. If it weren't for the clamor down the hall, the Hydras would have thought the creatures were simply their imagination.

He heard another rifle go off before a female voice ordered a retreat from the caves.

"We need to go, before the soldiers or those creatures come back," Jarrod said hoarsely.

Taiga stood up next to him and nodded wordlessly. She pulled the drawstring tight on her pack, and Rio glimpsed the slowly fading light of the goni's bioluminescent skeleton extinguish.

They took off, following one less glowing orb of light.

X

"What the hell were those?" Gana exclaimed. He held his hand over his right ear in an attempt to staunch the blood. It was barely clinging to his face by a lobe, and three deep scratches left rifts in his cheek. He gasped a little as he ripped on his ear, disconnecting it from his head and gave it a look of disgust before tossing it to the ground. There was no hope for reattaching it in the field. Rhea gestured for someone to bring him a medic kit, but it was unnecessary. A soldier appeared with a bandage and wrapped it tightly around the man's head after applying an antiseptic ointment.

Rhea stared at the opening in the ground and for a brief second she thought she saw the shadows shift. The creatures had been lining the walls but hadn't moved until the goni had been shot. The slashing claws and fierce teeth stood out in her mind, but not nearly as much as the red pupils that seemed the glow eerily from the darkest face she had ever seen. They hadn't been Exos, of that she was sure.

"Were those aliens?" a soldier asked dumbly.

Rhea almost rolled her eyes. "*We are aliens*. This planet belongs to those Greylings. We must tread carefully." Rhea realized that some of her party members were missing. "Stand in groups of four and be quick."

The soldier obeyed, and she counted three groups of four, and one group of three. She had fifteen soldiers left, sixteen including herself. She had lost half of her unit.

"You three," she indicated to the partial group, two young women and a man who looked to be in his twenties (close to an earthling of forty-five in appearance). "Return to the *Shrike*. Report on what we encountered today. The Commanding Family will want to hear about this. The rest of you take the rovers and find the outlet of this cave, or the outlets. Map them and return to me. Gana and I will guard this entrance." Each of the rovers had a map compiled from all the data the Hydra hunters gathered, though Rhea had a feeling that this was uncharted territory. The Hydra Colonies migrated outward from the *Shrike* wreckage in spiraling patterns, as ordered by the Commanding Family, and the Commanding Families before them. However, the refugees had struck out, cutting across the path of Hydra Eight unwittingly. Hydra Seven had been close to the other perimeter and they wouldn't have had to travel far to reach unknown waters. According to the engineer Jarrod's calculations, the source of the water, or at least the largest speculated water source, had allegedly been close to the Hydra Seven camp, which was why he sought them out.

"Respectfully, Rhea," a woman a few years older than the lieutenant started, "you and Gana cannot fight off those Greylings." She was one of the soldiers Rhea had ordered back to the Wreckage.

"We will be enough," Rhea said and lifted her chin while glancing down her nose at the soldier.

The female ducked her head in acquiescence before stalking over to a rover. The woman, Utria, wasn't angry, she walked with purpose and Rhea knew this. Rhea also was fairly certain that Utria was a better shot than Gana. She had considered making Utria her second but Aqi was a jealous lover, and Rhea suspected that she would have ordered her squadron to be comprised of all males if their tryst had been public knowledge. Nepotism would be rather unbecoming of a member of the Commanding Family, and superiors did not fraternize below their rank. Just thinking of Aqi brought a crooked smile to Rhea's lips.

X

Three Shrikers blindly groped through the tunnels, too scared to use their lights. The sounds of the Greylings tearing their comrades' bodies apart and greedily gobbling up the soft flesh still echoed in their ears. Their breathing rattled from their lips as their lungs struggled to slow their respiration down despite their galloping heartbeats. Dermest reached out a hand to feel along the wall and felt something firm, but decidedly not rock. He reached for the pistol at his hip and flicked his flashlight into the 'on' position when he felt the tremor of a breath run underneath his hand. The creature in front of him batted his hand away and shoved him into the middle of the labyrinthine hallway.

He stumbled backwards, raised the gun to hip level and blasted. The ignition of light that escaped the barrel gave him enough light to see more of the animals swarming from honeycomb holes in the ceiling. They landed nimbly and damn near silently and didn't take but a second before they were on the Exos. Dermest fired off three more shots, and another of the Greylings dropped. It wasn't enough though and feeling claws rip into his chest he fired another three shots at point blank range into his assailant's stomach. The creature stumbled back and Dermest shouted to his companions but didn't hear a reply. He turned to see the other two soldiers lying on their backs as the bloodthirsty creatures began feasting on their innards.

It took less than a fraction of a second to decide which fate he preferred. With one bullet in the chamber and an empty clip, he turned the gun on himself.

X

The three Hydras and the Exile stopped when they heard the eight shots ring out, all in a span of thirty seconds.

"Why haven't they attacked us?" Lepiro asked.

Rio knew the answer. He had seen the pairs of red eyes blink into existence before winking out a moment later. Herma had illuminated a few faces that seemed too human for his liking. The creatures hiding in the dark had no quarrel with the Exos, but apparently had a special relationship with the gonis. When Taiga's familiar had been killed they took vengeance for the slain goni. One glance at Taiga and Rio knew it wasn't time to voice his hypothesis. He did speculate that if he hadn't killed the sand dingo the creatures would have set upon them instantly.

The patter of many footsteps heralded the approach of the cave denizens. Wordlessly, the Exos took off down the tunnel, not trusting stealth or the goodwill of their saviors. Even over the sound of their feet, Rio swore he could hear three other churning hearts above his own. The gonis easily kept pace in front of them, lighting the way. Despite the danger, the gelatinous creatures were making a gentle humming noise that was unmistakable excitement.

Suddenly the gonis dropped from the air and began feasting ravenously. Even in the dark, the mass of pale mollas was visible. Rio fished the headlamp from his pack and flicked the button, lighting up the cavern wall before them. It was covered with bumpy protrusions, ranging in size from a fingertip to the size of a human skull. Black exudate dripped from each of the caps, forming a puddle on the floor. In the middle of the fungal growths was a bare patch of rock, covered in a fingerpainted mural. Handprints stood out as unblemished granite, surrounded by a splatter of color, presumably molla, judging by its dark color. Other crude figures were drawn, bipedal animals which looked like Exos, except for the dark red eyes penciled in. The number nine was written over and over and over. Rio's eyes moved hardly two feet before seeing the integer repeated. In the middle of the mural was a giant goni devouring a ship. It was the only part of the cave art obvious to Rio. The ship was the *Shrike.*

He turned to look at his companions to see their reactions, as no one had said a word. Rather, he saw that Taiga and Lepiro had their own headlamps on, projecting light out into the cavern. It was covered in molla, some as tall as he was. Paths were cut between the molla and peering out between the stalks were a myriad of blood red eyes and dark skin. He didn't bother trying to count the encroaching Greylings. This encounter could only end poorly for the Exos.

Chapter Thirteen

Treya stared at the camp before her. Hydra One had at least twice the number of inhabitants than her colony. She turned her eyes to the man driving the rover. His name was Toledo and he had greasy skin, and a disagreeable smell to him.

"This should be simple," he stated confidently.

Treya hid her disgust. They had been traveling for several days, and his arrogance was reducing her patience at an alarming rate.

"Quite." Her reply was terse, but he still bobbed his head like a fool. Treya looked back at the camp and saw the forms of many Exos gathering in the center of the camp, no doubt discussing whether or not the new arrivals would be friendly.

The rover dipped its headlights over the crest of the dune and slid more than drove down the incline of sand. Treya placed both hands on the dashboard to ensure that she didn't crash into the windshield. She held a sour expression as she bounced back and forth in the seat, her swollen knuckles painfully aware of her grip on the dash.

Toledo laughed easily. "Use your feet to brace yourself and lean back. It's easier."

Treya's feet barely touched the floorboard beneath them, there was no chance that she would have any additional purchase if they were extended. She ignored her guide.

She felt her heart beating harder and louder, and in her old age nerves rarely accelerated the beat. The Exos in the camp were becoming more visible and she could make out individuals. She recognized the mixture of distrust and fear on their faces. She was able to determine which ones were the Hydra One Council of Elders, though there were only three of them and two didn't fit the 'Elder' bill. These three individuals looked very aware of the situation at hand.

The rover continued slowly until it had passed thirty tents and was at the center of the camp. The three soldiers in the back seat were silent. The partially filled rover was all the Commanding Family had sent out with Treya as bodyguards. Whether they thought she was unimportant or did not care for the fate of the Hydras, it was hard to say, though she was technically a Hydra, so the latter was more likely.

The Elders approached the rover as Treya stepped onto the sand.

"Who are you?" they asked in unison in mock confusion. The poor bastards.

"We are Shrikers, from the Original Settlement," Treya said slowly. Her entire speech was scripted, the next line to be *'Can we speak in private, this is a lot of information to process at once. It would be best if you relayed it to your people.'*

"The Original Settlement?" one of the Elders asked, once again faking his lack of understanding.

"Can we speak in private?" Treya stuck to the script, obedient to the end. "This is a lot of information to process at once. It would be best if you relayed it to your people."

"Of course." An old woman smiled through pursed lips. She turned on her heel and led Treya and the Shrikers to the water and molla collection tent.

Treya couldn't help but notice the three large holding tanks, two water tanks full to the brim with cool liquid, while the urine tank was decidedly low. Treya had never seen a tank so full, let alone two.

They were ushered into the tent, and when the flap closed Treya began her speech.

"The Commanding Family has determined that enough aquifers have been located and all Hydra Camps should return to The Wreckage," she said.

The look on the old woman's face showed her true emotions. "Oh, the Commanding Family has finally permitted our return!" She glanced cynically at the other two 'Elders'. One had purple hair and the other the mottled complexion of vitiligo. Neither were old, they looked like soldiers. "Finally, we are deemed worthy of luxury."

Treya's head spun, her speech didn't count on this type of encounter. She glanced at Toledo's hip and noticed glumly that he hadn't brought any weapons

Terra Mortem

with him, and the other three soldiers were still at the rover.

"The Commanding Family has toiled over this decision for many months now. The policies set forth before them did not allow for the return of the Hydras for another two hundred years." Treya folded her hands as she spewed the next piece of political trite.

"I won't toil over this decision though," the woman said coldly, and three hunters stepped into the tent, machetes drawn. "Kill them."

Treya's eyes bulged from their sockets as Toledo spun to face the assailants.

"Wait! Why?" the Hydra Seven Elder sputtered dumbly.

"Since my rise to power on the council, we have been falsifying our maps to the Original Settlement and stealing water from their aquifers. When we found Hydra Camp two, we slaughtered their Elders and welcomed them into the fold. The *Shrike* will be ours once we find the other Camps," the woman said coldly, and Treya felt ashamed that she herself had not thought of this scheme.

The molla hunters moved in closer once their matriarch finished speaking.

"A rescue mission from Earth 2.0 is on its way!" Treya shrieked and the woman held up a hand to stop her men.

"Excuse me?"

Toledo looked on in shock, he had never even heard a rumor of rescue. "My camp has already been brought back in, I volunteered to find the other camps," Treya lied and the woman placed a hand on her chin pensively.

"Then we shall let you live, if you are truly looking for the other colonies. I regret to inform you that your men by the rover have already been killed. The two of you will have to find Hydra Three alone." She turned to the hunters. "Remove the radio from the rover."

The men with dark molla stained nostrils nodded and exited the tent.

The old woman smiled warmly. "My name is Ellie. If either of you return to The Wreckage before the remaining six camps, we will do what we must."

X

Toledo and Treya returned to the vehicle and stepped over the dead bodies of the Shrikers. Turning the key in the ignition, Toledo started the engine and peeled through the sand, without waving back at the genial figure of Ellie, who might have been blowing kisses. Treya couldn't tell, she had to grip the dash to avoid being tossed into the sand. She could hear the man next to her grinding his teeth in agitation. A muscle flexed on and off in his jaw like a switch. After fifteen minutes of silence, and three sand dunes later, he stopped the rover.

"A rescue mission?" he asked. His demeanor was awkward, almost as if he didn't know if he should ask.

Then it dawned on Treya, he was hoping or praying that it wasn't a lie. Discussion of being rescued from the planet was taboo. A false hope, like Fleet had said, would be devastating.

Looking at the hope in the young man's eyes—anyone was young compared to Treya, but Toledo was not young—she couldn't dash this glimmer of excitement.

"Three months," she murmured.

Toledo slumped in his seat in what had to be pure relief. He punched the steering wheel in excitement and the horn honked back in answer. "How do you know this?"

Treya almost rolled her eyes. She considered keeping quiet, but there was a chance that she wouldn't live for another three months anyway. "The Commanding Family told Rumo and I after they slaughtered our colony."

Toledo nodded and started the rover back up. He pulled out the map and determined the location of Hydra Three. Treya could tell that he was disappointed he had not been trusted with this information as he chewed on the inside of his lip and pointed at their destination.

"And you controlled one of these tribes that have been wandering the desert, finding water and food sources for The Wreckage?" He continued with his barrage.

"Yes," Treya answered simply.

"Are you really savages who drink their own urine when water runs out, and eat dead babies?"

The bluntness of the question stung like a slap. Treya had allowed her people to live in squalor, all for a city they had never seen and people who had no right to her allegiance.

"...Savages," she repeated hollowly. The Commanding Family even made the Hydra Colonies sound like lesser peoples.

"And the Elders are in on it? That's why that woman killed the Hydra Two Council?" Toledo fired off another question. His dark brown eyes revealed a high level of intelligence, despite his lack of hygiene and Treya felt guilty for judging him so quickly. She wondered how many friends the man had, or how many of his peers had treated him poorly. Yet, he had worked himself to a high enough rank to be leading a mission like this. Unless...the Commanding Family truly didn't care about the Hydras.

"What is your rank, Toledo?" She added his name to make the question softer.

"Scout Team Lieutenant. Before this mission I just did recon as a scout, but I got promoted for this mission," he said proudly.

And Treya groaned inwardly.

Terra Mortem

"Congratulations," Treya said, as she thought of an accompanying sentence.

"I don't think it was based on merit," Toledo admitted. "I think it was because I am expendable. We were given four soldiers and an emissary to bring back six camps, which must be at least six hundred people."

"We only have to bring back One through Three. Rumo's team is bringing back Four, Five, Six, and Eight," she said, though she didn't know why that information seemed important and was sure Toledo had been told that during his briefing.

"I think we should intercept the other Hydra Camps on their way back to the *Shrike*," he said as he put the rover in gear and pressed on the accelerator. "The Commanding Family sent us out here with very little regard for our well-being or return. Rhea had thirty-one soldiers in her squadron."

Treya felt her breath catch in her throat from raw excitement. She was positive that she knew what Toledo was implying.

"A coup," she breathed.

Toledo shot her a sideways glance and grinned as he shifted into a higher gear.

Ethan Proud

Chapter Fourteen

Rhea and Gana sat outside the fissure waiting for the rovers to return. Rhea eyeballed the bloodstained rag tied around Gana's head, impressed that the man hadn't complained about losing his ear even once. Neither of them said much, they were professionals, and had not been bonded in combat yet. The Wreckage Army policed the city and ran drills constantly. The only threat to the establishment was the possibility of a Hydra Revolt. Rhea scoffed at the idea. They were so busy drinking piss and desperately hunting for water that they had little time to dream of a shining jewel in the desert that benefitted from their endeavors. Even if they did, they had no guns and no hope of overthrowing the Commanding Family.

"Rhea," Gana said a little too loudly, and Rhea realized she had been daydreaming. She sighed, her thoughts had been on the verge of turning to Aqi.

"Yes, Sergeant," she said, twisting to face him.

"Warchieftain," he began, and Rhea had to laugh to herself. He thought she called him sergeant to be addressed by her rank. In truth, she cared little about the formalities of rank. Anybody who insisted on being addressed by their rank was insecure. "I think I hear something in the tunnel."

Rhea craned her neck and positioned her ear towards the slit in the earth. She didn't hear anything. Wordless, she made eye contact with Gana, who understood what the look meant. It was pity. He clasped a hand over his left ear. The sounds he heard had been nothing more than his blood moving within his skull, amplified by the piece of cloth and the trauma of losing an ear.

"My apologies. I shouldn't have said anything." He looked down at his feet.

"It is better to be hypervigilant than lax," Rhea said, then added, "You will get used to it."

Gana didn't answer but nodded, and began to fiddle with his gun. Rhea smirked at a typically male inability to express his feelings. Maybe someday he'd learn. Then she heard a scuffling against the rock. Gana looked up in time to see her shoulder her rifle.

"Don't shoot it unless it attacks," Rhea commanded. "I want to see what it looks like."

The Greyling emerged from between the two rocks, and Rhea almost dropped her gun. Its eyes were bright red, with pupils so large they threatened to take over its entire eye. As the light struck it, the pupil shrank to a pinprick. The creature had sharp exaggerated teeth, and its posture revealed that it was built for climbing walls and crawling through tunnels. The only clothing it wore was a bag slung over its shoulder that was bursting with molla. Its fingertips were flattened, and a curved claw protruded from each digit. Tapered ears extended past the back of its skull and its nose was flattened. The entire creature was covered in coarse, blueish hair. It looked back and forth between Rhea and Gana, sizing them up, but did not have an aggressive stance. The Greyling emanated hatred, but it did not appear aggressive.

Rhea wasn't trusting by nature, however, and placed a bullet square between its eyes. Then a screeing call echoed from the mouth of the tunnel, followed by two more concussive calls that had the same two-toned, metallic quality.

Both Rhea and Gana had killed enough gonis to know what they sounded like. However, the small animals did not make any noise loud enough to shake the bones of those who heard it. The two Shrikers kept their eyes trained on the fissure, knowing the owner of that voice could not fit through the gap in the rocks.

Chapter Fifteen

Using their feet to slow their descent, Yuto and Dierde slid down the dune on the seat of their pants, hands working like rudders to keep them straight. The sand slid with them, like an avalanche flowing down the mountainous dune, accumulating beneath their bodies and elevating them as if sitting on a throne. They were both laughing while their gonis happily warbled above them, though the humans were also experiencing a level of terror with their exuberance. They sledded down the incline for several hundred feet, kicking up particles that bounced against their goggles and scarves. Despite enjoying themselves, perhaps truly for the first time in their lives, they were terribly aware of the fact that if they lost control, they would log roll to their deaths.

At the base of the dune, and the mouth of the canyon, Yuto and Dierde extricated themselves from the pile of sand they had dislodged. They shook each of their limbs one at a time, to rid the sand that had seemingly crawled up their sleeves and into their pockets. Dierde pulled her goggles onto her forehead and turned to Yuto.

"Is the second aquifer covered?"

He looked around, and likewise pulled his goggles up and tugged his scarf below his chin. He surveyed the canyon walls and observed that the flood of sand had indeed covered the cave entrance to the spring he had found.

"It is," he answered. It was glum, but he was smiling.

Dierde still had her scarf over her mouth, but her blue eyes did not conceal her excitement. "Where is the third?" she pressed, and Yuto slung his pack off and found his map.

He pulled a mapping compass out, not the directional compass he had received from his father, and began tracking the path. After carefully measuring the distance using crudely drawn landmarks he answered, "It's, uh, twelve miles..." He quickly took inventory of his surroundings before pointing. "That way."

Dierde and Aileen flew lazy circles around the two before landing, their bodies covered in a thin layer of grime.

"It looks like we will have to wait until these two shed," Dierde said as their familiars closed their eyes contemplatively while their cellular waste hardened on their skin.

"Have you ever thought of scraping it off?" Yuto asked. It was a question that always burned in the back of his mind, but Aileen was always in such a great mood when she finally wriggled free that he didn't want to disturb her ritual.

"Not once," Exo Dierde said, and goni Dierde opened one eye at her master's voice. She reached out a cautious hand and grabbed the slime and was surprised by the surface tension. The goni shook as firmly and violently as her soft body could and pulled free of the shell of stain. The dark blue goni took to the air and completed three flips before roosting on Dierde's head.

Yuto laughed and followed suit. Aileen regarded him a moment, unsure of what he was doing. He lifted on the sticky substance, and Aileen went slack for a moment before popping free of her encasement. She sang a few notes before shaking herself from nose to tail in midair.

Yuto grabbed his canteen from his pack and gave it an experimental shake. It was nearly empty, barely a rattle of fluid within. He had another completely empty canteen, one full, and still had water in the specialized compartment. Years of trekking across AE625 in search of molla and water had taught both of them to conserve water at all costs.

He took a swill of the water and swished it around his mouth, not enough to slake his thirst, but just enough to trick himself into thinking he had. He passed his canteen to Dierde, who accepted it even though she had her own. Perhaps it was a peace gesture, he wasn't sure. He knew he was watching too closely as she brushed a handful of stray hairs away from the corner of her mouth, and he averted his gaze. Awkwardly. He mentally cursed himself.

Dierde noted it but chose not to comment. When they found Rio alive she was sure that Yuto's lingering gazes would cease. She stoppered the bottle and handed it back to Yuto and the two began walking purposefully in the direction of the third aquifer.

The sun beat down on their backs and they could feel the rays heating their skin despite the layers of clothing. Perspiration beaded on their necks and shoulders as they continued their brisk-near-jog pace. They could easily cover twelve miles in one day, but if they dawdled they would be exposed to the heat for longer and their water wouldn't last them. They said nothing, the fabric tied around their face muffled their voices, and to remove them would mean inhaling sand and other particles.

Though Yuto and Dierde had put Rio's death and the deceit leading up to it behind them, it still weighed on both of their minds. When Yuto wasn't trying to squash his newly discovered primal feeling for Dierde, he considered throwing rocks at her. Not hard enough to kill her, just to sting a bit. She would have taken it stoically, too. But it was not Yuto who needed her apology and she knew it. She had omitted information, but she hadn't betrayed him. She tossed her head, physically shaking her guilt from her mind as her hair bounced on her shoulders. She reached back and tied it up behind her head in a ponytail and didn't bother to meet Yuto's stare. She knew he was looking. More than that, she knew that he didn't want to.

Chapter Sixteen

Rio stared at the many faces before him. Each of them held a knapsack full of harvested molla. Several of the Greylings were armed with spears, clearly they guarded their kin while the mushrooms were collected. Rio gripped his machete in his right hand and flicked the spear in his other, extending it to its full length. The guardian Greylings didn't brandish their weapons in a likewise fashion, but the Exos weren't taking any chances.

Taiga gripped the handgun she had taken from the dead Shriker, Lepiro held his spear aloft, and Jarrod looked ready to bolt—no one had thought to give him a weapon. Rio considered giving him the rifle in his pack, he hadn't learned to use it, but he had killed the man's pet. He cursed himself for his stupidity, but it was hard to think with a mind clouded by rage. Killing Mycka had made him feel much better though, and he was no longer gnawed by the urge to kill the Exile.

One of the harvester Greylings stepped forward and made a come hither motion. None of the Exos moved, but they shared uneasy glances. The Greyling repeated the gesture.

Lepiro lowered his spear and took a reluctant step forward.

Taiga sighed and holstered the gun in her waistband.

The Greyling nodded and cooed encouragingly.

Rio sheathed his machete and collapsed his spear. Jarrod hissed in discomfort, a low enough sound that the natives wouldn't hear it, and his Hydra companions, no, captors, ignored him.

The Greyling turned and began leading them past the towering molla.

Rio looked up at the many gills, reaching radially away from the stalk. Between each of the gills he could see gobs of black spores, staining the porcelain flesh of the mushroom and littering the ground with piles of spores that would eject their own mass of hyphae and bolster the subterranean farm. He felt his insides constrict with excitement and a phantom buzz in his brain. Despite his psychological hunger for the drug, he could still rationalize his thoughts. In order for the gargantuan molla to grow in such abundance, there had to be a massive body of water in these caves. His heart began doing a light two-skip murmur of excitement. They were near The Source. Or enough water to rival The Source. He knew that his fellow hunters were having the same thoughts. In the same order as well.

The Greylings fell in around the Exos, forming a perimeter around them. Rio tried not to look around too much, but he counted at least eight of the creatures without looking over his shoulders. He did catch a glimpse of Jarrod and felt pleased that the dark bruise around the man's eye had not healed in the slightest and a bloody rent on his brow stood as a testament to a missing piercing. The Shriker truly looked wretched. Like a haggard dog. His face reflected his defeat and his dark, sun damaged skin looked slack. Rio didn't feel any pity for the man, but a lump did form in his stomach when the mental image of Jarrod and Dierde flitted through his mind.

Time underground meant very little. Whether it was day or night was impossible to determine and Taiga was unsure if they had been below the surface for minutes, hours, or days. It was all very surreal. She stood next to Lepiro and the two brushed arms briefly. They had hooked up once. A brief affair, but beyond that they had little interaction. Taiga's heart was galloping in her chest now, she was fearful of where the Greylings were taking them. She knew that the other Exos felt the same way, her thoughts confirmed when Lepiro gripped her hand out of nowhere. It wasn't unexpected, and it offered some comfort. Except that if she needed to run, she'd have an anchor.

She looked past Lepiro and could barely make out two dark forms immediately to his right. Running wouldn't do her much good. Her thoughts turned to her dead goni, Hysco. A feeling akin to being doused by ice water enveloped her. If these Greylings had destroyed the men who killed him, then they would be her allies. Assuming that they could communicate. Then she remembered the 'nine' she had seen repeated on the walls. Perhaps it was a coincidence and it was only a sacred symbol to these strange beings. A coincidence seemed unlikely, though, the number 'nine' was a fairly basic shape.

Taiga looked up at the chitinous organisms that grew from every crevice in the caves, and felt an itch growing in the back of her mind. The cravings for the mollas felt no boundaries. She glanced over at Rio, the brownish blooms on the bandage around his thigh were spreading and it would probably need to be changed soon. Depending on their captors' generosity, he could die from an infection. Before the destruction of their colony Taiga hadn't felt particularly close to either Rio or Lepiro, but with the death of her parents and her missing husband a surprising bond had grown between the surviving Hydras. She even felt somewhat responsible for Jarrod, though if Rio killed the man it would be justice in her eyes.

The creature leading them deeper into the tunnels began crooning again as it picked up its pace, as if urging them to stop dawdling. If Taiga had known how to operate the handgun in her belt she would have considered using it to drop the alien beings. The Shrikers who had attacked had fired in rapid succession, but she didn't know where the ammo for the weapon came from, let alone how to load it. Whatever ammunition in the weapon was all she had.

The Hydra refugees were led deeper into the tunnel, and Rio was partially in awe at the sheer depth. He had never found a cave or fissure that led deeper than one hundred feet below the surface. He was sure this one was beginning to measure in miles. The only light available came from the two gonis, which reflected off the pale caps of the monstrous mushrooms, amplifying the effects of the bioluminescence.

The first Greyling turned and pointed to an opening in the ground several feet ahead of it and gestured to the Exos that they would be descending. Before waiting to see if its signaling had been accepted it clambered down the chimney while the other creatures waited for the Exos to follow suit. Taiga was the first to crawl down the chute, her only guidance her sense of touch, blindly groping for the next handhold. She didn't know how many feet she climbed, it could have been less than two feet or more than ten for all she knew. Finally her feet touched solid ground beneath her, and the rock above her was illuminated as Lepiro began his descent, guided by his goni. Once Lepiro was clear, she could see the rest of the cavern they had entered as his familiar floated in the air right in front of them. The only textured parts of the subterranean realm they had just entered were the walls and the ceiling. Several stride-lengths ahead of them, the ground became an expanse as smooth as marble, but as inky black as the molla spores. Not a ripple disturbed its surface, and though the Exos had only ever seen a limited supply of it before, they knew the underground lake was water.

How far the lake extended, they couldn't tell, but judging by the numerous hollowed molla caps along the shore, they would be crossing it. Though they had never seen a boat, they knew the purpose of the mushroom caps were to float across the water. The closest noun the Exos had to describe the canoes was ship-based on the *Shrike*. Ironic, considering these paltry vessels were nothing compared to an Earthling ship meant to sail the seas. The molla caps had been taken from the largest of the mushrooms, the gills and stems removed, and the cap transformed into an oblong shape, using cords made from the stems wrapped several times around the cap, folding it, and then more cords used to bind either end so that the stern and bow were held out on the water. The scaly skin of the mollas was extremely waterproof, and the boats surprisingly buoyant, only dipping under the water a few precious inches when the live cargo was loaded.

The Exos uneasily crawled into the canoes at the Greylings' wordless bidding. The footing was strange, and the Exos sat down awkwardly in the middle to avoid rocking and ultimately capsizing the craft. The Greylings emitted a sound similar to a chuckle before nimbly joining the Exos and paddling. The paddles were shaped like flattened ladles. A molla cap the size of Rio's chest was tied to a shaft of braided molla stems, and the Greylings expertly maneuvered the canoes by alternating strokes on either side of the prow. The only sound to break the silence was the rhythmic dip of the paddle.

Rio let his hand hang over the edge until the tip of his fingers touched the surface. He met the gaze of his ghostly reflection and wondered how far he would sink before touching the bottom. He imagined himself peacefully floating an immeasurable distance as bubbles escaped his mouth and cold enveloped him. His fantasy turned ghastly as a ghostly tail the length of a school bus, which he had never seen, passed mere inches from his face. He shook himself free of his reverie and pulled his hand back into the safety of the boat.

He continued to stare at the flat surface of the water as imperceptible ripples permeated from the boat's wake. Whether it was a morbid or childish daydream, his eyes convinced him that the ethereal glow of a goni skeleton, near twenty feet long, resided just beneath him. For the remainder of the crossing he kept his eyes forward and his hands in his lap. Herma landed on his shoulder, its cold suction cups sticking to the side of his face as the creature sang playfully. The sound echoed across the cavern ceiling and was amplified when it returned. Rio closed his eyes and forced the idea of a monstrous goni from his mind.

Mere minutes shy of an hour the boats began to approach a tunnel mouth on the opposite shore. The tunnel mouth was alight, a glowing orange blaze making an eerily bright stencil of the rocks. The light seemed to be shifting or dancing. The molla craft shuddered as they scraped bottom before jolting against the ground. The Greylings easily leapt from the craft and offered their assistance to the wobbly Exos, who were attempting to make their exit.

The orange blaze was, in fact, millions of little grubs, each soft segmented body covered in long hirsute projections tipped with a globe that gave off a faint glow. Around the immature insects, the adult versions, free of their chrysalis, flitted around at head level. Taiga reached her hand out and one of the moths landed on her outstretched fingers. She couldn't help but laugh at the feel of its fuzzy feet. The long feathery antennae probed the surface of her skin inquisitively. The creature had two sets of wings, completely black, save for a single strip of orange. It had a second pair of antennae as well, that lacked the feathery apparatus for detecting the pheromones of potential mates but were longer and curled backwards at the tip.

Quick as lightning a barbed tail whipped over its thorax and head and sank into the fat-pad of Taiga's hand. She let out a yelp of pain, which was followed by a whimper when the insect's proboscis sank into the webbing of her fingers. She clapped her hands together and the exoskeleton crunched followed by burning ichor that pulsed onto her hands. She ran back to the water and dipped her hands below the surface and vigorously washed her skin clean. She felt the welts of blisters already forming on her rough calloused hands, let out a brief sigh and looked at the flat surface of the lake. Except it wasn't flat. A lump was distorting the plane, and the lump was letting off a faint turquoise light. She blinked quickly and turned without waiting to confirm what she had seen. Gonis simply did not grow that big. She chided herself for her foolishness. She was surprised to see Lepiro only a few paces from her. Apparently he had been concerned, the expression on his face a funny one, but Taiga doubted it was from the same specter she had just witnessed.

"Are you all right?" he asked, escorting her back to the rest of the party.

"I'm fine. The bastard just bit me. I wasn't expecting it," she reassured him.

"I didn't just mean about the little demon," he said slowly.

Taiga felt her throat constrict and screwed her eyes shut until the tears dissipated. *Hysco*.

"I will be fine," she said determinedly.

They returned to the tunnel to find Rio, Jarrod, and the Greylings waiting patiently while Herma and Lepiro's Goni, Icharus, chased after the flying little demons-imps as Rio called them and occasionally landed on the cave wall to gobble up the caterpillars or their pupating cocoons indiscriminately. The sounds of the insects crunching and then spurting their innards echoed across the cavern walls and in minutes the imps had fled while the grubs crawled away in a panic on numerous chubby legs. The cavern was slowly growing dark as the immatures disappeared into crevices or holes bored into the rocks.

Ethan Proud

The gonis flew from the tunnel in a frenzy and for a moment the tunnel was pitch black, until Herma and Icharus returned, each with a pair of wings protruding past their grins. Compared to the desolation on the surface on AE625, the caves were brimming with life. Lepiro mused over this, wondering if perhaps the imps were edible to the Exos as well. After all, the only reason the first human beings to land survived was because the gonis accidentally shared their bacteria with them, therefore it made sense that they could feed on whatever their extraterrestrial companions did. Then he remembered the blisters on Taiga's palms and decided that it wasn't worth trying.

A diet diversified from the staple food source often emerged in the back of his mind. In truth, Lepiro would eat a rock if it tasted well enough to be a reprieve from the never ending monotony of molla stew. His stomach rumbled and he began to wonder how long it had been since he had eaten. Surely it had been at least three days. He pressed his hand against his stomach and it felt concave and stretched against his ribs. He had a lanky, yet athletic build so it wasn't as if he was starving or at death's door, but he was simply hungry. Two meals a day in the Hydra Seven Colony was a good day, and it was commonplace to go at least one day without food.

While his mind was elsewhere, his next step took him ankle deep into a puddle. He was startled back to the present and looked in astonishment at the near perfect circles that pockmarked the floor, each one full of water. He felt a stray drop land on the tip of his nose, and looked up in time to catch another drop right between his eyes. Tiny stalactites were forming on the cavern ceiling, the pockmarked pools the receptacles for the leaching water once it broke free from its granite cage.

Lepiro stepped another foot into the pool and reveled as the wetness seeped into his boots and meandered between his toes before filling the sparse empty space that existed in his well-broken-in boots. Showers and baths were foreign to the Hydra Colonists, their concept of bathing was rubbing fine silt against their skin and through their hair to exfoliate dead skin particles and to absorb the natural oils their skin and follicles generated. The sensation of being submerged, even if it was just his feet, was a novel one.

He paused slightly as he lifted his foot and heard the squelch of a gelatinous body behind him, but decided it must be his foot and set it down and felt the water squish between his toes. The sound that echoed down the tunnel, however, did not come from within his boot.

Chapter Seventeen

The rover cavorted over each rise and jolted with every indentation, but it never tipped, no matter how uncomfortable the angle made Treya. She watched as Toledo expertly shifted gears and listened to the engine respond to each change. Despite being double the man's age, she had no idea how the vehicle worked or what it ran on...though the only logical explanation was sand. She hadn't seen him fuel up, and both molla and water were too precious. Or perhaps it filtered the air. Being raised in a Hydra Colony she had never learned the periodic table of elements and had no idea which molecules were found in the atmosphere of AE625. In fact, she didn't even know what an element was in the sense of chemistry.

"What does the rover run on?" she asked when the curiosity became too much.

"What do you mean?" Toledo asked. "What powers it?"

"Yes?" Treya asked, though she wasn't entirely sure if that was what she was asking.

"See that dark grid on the hood?" He pointed, and Treya nodded as she observed the shiny black surface, lined with silver circuitry. "That is a solar panel, however the sun in this solar system is much closer than it was to Earth, so it had to be modified to only run for one hour before shutting off or it would generate too

Terra Mortem

much energy that would be released as heat underneath the hood. We also have a reserve tank filled with rocket fuel, in case we have to drive far distances at night."

"Rocket fuel?" Treya asked.

"Yes, it powered the *Shrike*. We don't have much of the fuel left though, and we have to use it sparingly. But having not made it to Earth 2.0, we have enough to run a generator in The Wreckage and enough to fuel the rovers," Toledo explained. He had taken an interest in being a mechanic before he became a soldier, but failed the chemistry portion of his test and when dealing with a civilization built upon a dependency on hydrazine, an understanding of the field was necessary. Not to discredit soldiers, but it required a different mindset.

"How long have we been on this planet?" Treya asked next.

"Nobody knows. The day lengths here are different than on Earth. The original crash survivors tried to keep track of time using the Earthling calendar, but the number of days in a cycle around the sun are different and there are no seasons. We've lost track. The engineers and scientists estimate at least one thousand years. But using our generations as indicators, I think it's closer to eight hundred. But in Earthling years, nobody knows… not that it matters anymore," he added.

"Eight hundred?" Treya asked. She had been told it had only been three hundred years. More than double that, though?

Ethan Proud

"I'm the thirty-second generation of Exo in my family, fifty years each, give or take. Some more, some less, bearing children between twelve and twenty. Eight hundred years." Toledo sighed. "Too long to be living on this blasted planet."

"How do you know all this?" Treya asked, scrutinizing the man some more.

He glanced at her from the corner of his eye, the sun reflecting on the sheen of the bags above his cheekbones.

"Do Hydras not attend school?" he asked, though it was more out of surprise than judgment.

Treya only shook her head in answer. She didn't even know what school was. Hydra children learned by helping their parents with their chores, and by exploring in small bands, usually supervised by an older hunter. Their education was imitation, but then again the last Hydra child born in Colony Seven had been Rio, a little over fifteen years ago. As such, his mentor had been the last.

Treya tried to remember the man's name, but it escaped her. The hunter disappeared while searching for water and mollas, but his corpse had been found four days later, desiccated and mummified by the scorching rays and brutal winds of the planet. Rio took it especially hard, he had only been about nine at the time. Reminiscing, Treya thought it was then that Rio and Dierde forged their deep connection. She pondered why the two had not declared marriage or tried for children, but their reasons were beyond her. Thinking back on her colony, she felt ashamed for leading them astray. She wished she had the same foresight and courage as Ellie. Instead, she had selfishly inflicted a life of servitude upon her constituents. She blinked quickly to prevent the tear from rolling down her cheek.

X

Across the desert, an immeasurable distance if judging it solely by the horizon and landmarks, a single rover putted along. A similar band to Treya's, though it still possessed all four soldiers and a grouchy Rumo, cut a path across the burning sands. Having already contacted the fourth colony, a dismal affair, they were now in pursuit of Hydra Colony Five. The fourth colony had begrudgingly accepted the information relayed by Rumo. Judging by the looks the Elders received from the colonists, they would not be making it to the *Shrike* alive. Rumo found it hard to believe that any of the Elders would survive long in the Wreckage. If their own people didn't kill them the Commanding Family surely would. The Elders were a liability, the rulers of the ruined ship had to know this. The Hydra Colonies themselves were a threat. They were savages compared to the civilized folk, and seeing the glory of the Original Settlement could only incite anger in the nomads.

Ethan Proud

Looking briefly at the soldiers in the rover with him, he began to wonder if they had orders to kill him after making contact with the rest of the Hydra Colonies. Or perhaps the colonists would be slaughtered before they reached the *Shrike*. As long as all the malcontent exiles were destroyed, there was little reason for the Shrikers to accept these new barbarians into their midst. Sighing, Rumo decided that the outcome had little bearing on his conscience. These people were not his concern. His survival was his only priority.

"What is it, old man?" the driver asked brusquely. He was a rude young man. He had dark skin, a sort of sunbaked brown. The sides of his head was shaven short and the top styled upwards and forward, a chunk of it dyed bright green at the front. His ears were gauged and his lower lip pierced right in the middle. His lean arms were bare and covered with scars, little muscles flexed each time he corrected the course of the rover. Had Yuto been raised in The Wreckage, he might have looked similar to this man, Rumo mused.

"Nothing," Rumo said, equally as coarse.

"If you don't have any questions, comments, or corrections, then you can ride in silence." The young man's name was Lago.

"How'd you get promoted to your position if this is how you act towards your elders?" Rumo asked tersely. He was used to being in charge, not ordered about.

"By acting like this towards my elders. Now quiet, old man." Lago smirked but his eyes glared at Rumo.

The Elder settled in his seat and resolved himself not to make another sound. The rover purred a guttural sound only a machine can make as it made it over the next rise and Lago applied pressure on the brake when he saw a myriad of tents.

"Is that Five or Six?" Lago said, pulling out a map from between his seat and the gun holstered next to it. The map had all the movements of the Hydra Colonies on it, and Five and Six were dangerously close to discovering each other.

"I don't know," Rumo answered first. It was a mistake.

"I didn't ask you," Lago said and leveled his dark eyes directly at Rumo's. The ancient Exo looked away.

"Neither, sir. It appears to be Eight," one of the soldiers in the back answered.

"How the hell did we miss Five and Six?" Lago exclaimed and slammed a fist into the steering wheel.

"We will find them, sir," the soldier answered cautiously. He was definitely older than Lago, but seemed wary of the young man.

"We have a map of their last known location. The Hydra Colonies don't move far very fast. They usually stay at one location for months. Do you understand what this means?" Lago spat at the man.

Rumo nearly smiled when it dawned on him. "They've been sending you false reports."

Lago raised a hand to backhand the Hydra but stopped himself.

Ethan Proud

"We have a coup on our hands."

X

The Hydra Colonies Five and Six had indeed been sending false reports to the Wreckage as well as fabricated maps from Hydra Colony Three. Hydra Colonies Three and Six had initially met with hostility and Six was the victor, wiping out their rivals before the Elders could tell them what had been going on. When they discovered Hydra Five, they had been much more diplomatic and freed those they had enslaved from Colony Three.

As the sun dipped below the horizon and plunged the landscape in darkness, except for the light of the stars and the two waxing moons, Treya and Toledo found themselves in the middle of a celebration in the combined camps. Hydra Five, Six and the survivors of Three called themselves the Wyrms, after the mythical creatures the gonis were rumored to resemble. The two Exos held a bowl containing a molla broth, though it must have been cooked at a lower temperature as it still had fairly strong narcotic effects. What little light shimmering overhead seemed to dance until it touched the ground and the fire built at the center of the throng rose impossibly high until it mingled with the descending stars. A bag of molla spores was passed around, and when it reached Treya and Toledo they paused.

Terra Mortem

"Have you ever done this before?" Toledo shouted to be heard over the singing and the sounds of drumming on baskets with stretched fabric pulled taught across the openings. The sound was like a million heartbeats mingled into one.

"Forty-two years ago, I was ten at the time," Treya said laughingly. She brushed her hair out of her face and dipped a finger into the bag and pulled it into her nostril. "I hated it."

"You what?" Toledo asked, missing her last sentence.

"Just do it. It's…fun." Treya offered and this time he heard. His pupils widened as he insufflated the spores, though they were already huge in the poor lighting. His eyes fluttered from one side to the other before settling back onto Treya's own dilating pits.

"This is awesome." The next second he was gone, weaving his way through the crowd.

Treya laughed and turned her thoughts inward. She was certain she wouldn't survive this little rebellion, but at least she was finally doing the right thing. She felt a weight on her chest dissolving, though the guilt for her own tribe remained. But tonight was for merriment and tomorrow could be for war, regret, and new beginnings. She looked up as a man at least ten years her junior sidled next to her and she blushed, and was glad he couldn't see it. Their eyes met and danced playfully for a minute before their bodies continued the courtship.

Ethan Proud

X

The morning sun rose, and Lago and his crew descended on Camp Eight. The colonists seemed wary of the rover carefully picking its path towards them, but they didn't move. When the Shrikers and Rumo were within ear shot, Lago kicked Rumo out of the vehicle. The old man shuffled towards the Hydras and followed the script provided.

"We are Shrikers from the Original Settlement."

It was the same line Treya had used on Ellie and her insurgents. The Elders approached cautiously, and Rumo started with the next line without being addressed.

"Can we speak in private, this is a lot of information to process at once. It would be best if your people heard it from you."

The Elders nodded and ushered Rumo to a tent.

Lago and the other soldiers remained at the rover, the former reclined against the wheel in the shadow cast by the silhouette. He picked his nails with his teeth and drummed the other digits against his thigh impatiently as he waited for the elderly Exo to finish with his business. He began to count the members of the clan discreetly. It was difficult to get an accurate head count as they kept moving, and he eventually gave up. He had been trying to calculate if there were enough bullets that each Hydra could have one. He had nothing against the Hydra Colonies, but death came to everyone and he might as well be the one to deliver it. He couldn't act out his fantasies in the civilization of the *Shrike,* but here in the desert…he had free reign.

Lago turned his attention to the gonis which filled the air or squawked noisily from the shoulders of their Exo companions. He began to wonder how the newest additions to The Wreckage would take to the Shriker's diets. Saliva welled up between his gums and his molars as he watched one of the creatures float sinuously through the air. Its red skin caught the light and it shone like a ruby. Lago closed his eyes and imagined finding the tip of the tail caught on his spoon in a bowl of thick molla broth. He reached over to his backpack, sitting right beside him, and pulled out a pouch filled with dry meat. Goni jerky was the staple food of traveling Shrikers as it didn't have to be cooked like molla and preserved well, unlike cooked molla.

The Shrikers rarely traveled, unless it was to meet the Elders at specified rendezvous points to exchange maps with small luxuries to make their lives easier on the fringes of society, to gather water from the aquifers in high walled trailers pulled behind rovers, or to build the aquifers. Lago had been on many such missions since he had been nine years old. Now he was twenty and had a healthy sense of disdain for the Hydras and the uncouth manner in which they lived. He also looked down his nose at the societal structure of the Wreckage, yet it was the price paid for decadence. If only he had been alive on Earth to truly know what the word meant.

After satisfying his cravings for the flesh of the scarlet goni with the dried jerky, he fished around until he found a vial of molla spores. He unstoppered the cap, tipped his head back and carefully spouted the narcotic fungi directly into his nose. He snorted deeply, capped the vial and tossed it back into his bag. Even in the blasted middle of nowhere, he brought a little decadence with him. He felt the eyes of the rest of his crew on him and sighed. Reaching back into his pack he tossed the vial of precious spores over his shoulder without looking. The soldier it was headed for caught it easily and passed it around to the other two and the last leaned towards Lago, the glass tube held between his outstretched fingers. It crossed Lago's peripherals and he took it wordlessly and tossed it back into his pouch. Vultures. His companions were vultures and an old man. The Commanding Family hadn't even found it fit to grace them with the presence of a woman. No matter, they would be returning to the Original Settlement soon. And probably deployed shortly after their return with more soldiers to hunt down Colonies Five and Six.

At the thought of another massacre, Lago felt his stomach tighten with excitement. He had been part of the squadron dispatched to track down Jarrod and destroy whichever Hydra Camp he had found. Part of him wished Jarrod had made contact with more colonies, the thought of war made Lago's darkest tendencies rejoice. Ever since he was a child, he had an unnatural obsession with death and violent intrusive thoughts. He didn't call them intrusive though, he called them fantasies. He knew in his youth he couldn't act out on all of his impulses but it didn't stop him from acting out violently towards his classmates. His parents wrote it off as a classic case of bullying, but when they found a dead goni in his backpack and he refused to tell them where he had found it, they grew concerned.

His parents had a conference with his teachers and it was decided that his time before adulthood would be best spent in the Early Entry Scout Soldier Program or EESSP. He had only been four at the time and usually classroom instruction began at seven years old and vocations were chosen by ten, followed by two years of apprenticeship. Vocations were not lifelong positions and could be switched after five years. Lago had found himself being 'tempered' as the EESSP Director referred to it or as he called it 'beaten into submission' when speaking with his parents. It wasn't actual abuse, but he had to be broken down physically and mentally and tested likewise before he would ever be suitable as a soldier, let alone trusted near a gun. Lago didn't resent his time at EESSP or the treatment he had endured, he could only imagine where his fantasies would have taken him if they had not been given direction as a soldier.

After four years his apprenticeship began and by nine he was the youngest official soldier of the Shrike

Colonial Military. His early conscription, he suspected, caused him much grief from the Council of Warchiefs, of which Rhea presided over. The Shrike Colonial Military was made up of four branches, the scouts, police, palace guard, and the infantry. Only the scouts routinely left the safety of The Wreckage. The palace guard did exactly what their position sounded like and the police put down uprisings and maintained peace, while the purpose of the infantry had been a mystery up until now. It was their duty to protect The Wreckage from a Hydra insurgence.

Finally, Rumo exited the tent and Lago pressed his shoulders into the frame of the rover, shifted his weight to the balls of his feet and rose to his full height. He grabbed his pack by the top loop and tossed it into the back of the rover. His backpack was much nicer than those of the Hydras, a textile factory at the *Shrike* recycled old clothes into new fabric, often unraveling the clothes completely, reinforcing the thread with molla and weaving a whole new garment. As a result, little of the Shrikers' clothing was a solid color but was usually mottled. Lago's shirt was a mixture of the pale grey of the molla, a faded maroon, with eclipses of a teal color near the bottom and a different shade of grey near the neck. Hardened leather-like pauldrons of molla caps and pieces of the *Shrike's* parachute were patched together making a tortoiseshell pattern. Another plate of the material covered his chest, and a larger section for his back. His pants were darker than his shirt and were primarily dark grey, black, and what appeared to be purple in the light, at other times green. Boots were harder to manufacture on a less than hospitable planet, and his were covered in wart-like patches. As a result, his feet were callused and rough.

"Are they on board, old man?" Lago spat in the dirt, his saliva tinted grey from the black spores.

"Yes," Rumo said exasperatedly. "They will pack immediately and follow the map I gave them to the Original Settlement."

"Good. Load up," Lago ordered as Rumo clambered aboard the rover.

"Let's make like a tree." Lago smirked and took the rover from park into low gear and peeled away from the camp.

"What's a tree?" one of the soldiers in the back seat asked.

"I don't know. P-p-eople on Earth used to say it," Lago said curling his lip. Idiots. Idiots. Idiots. He had a slight stutter from when he was younger, but for the most part he had outgrown his speech impediment. He didn't duck his head in shame anymore, but rather challenged people to make note of it. It only came out when he was embarrassed, angry, or excited. Luckily, he was none of those very often.

Hours later, and miles away from Camp Eight, Lago spotted two figures at the top of the next dune, their gonis scintillating in the light.

Chapter Eighteen

The Commanding Family, with the exception of Kilo, gathered round the radio that had been salvaged from the cockpit of the *Shrike*. In truth, everything they owned had been salvaged or manufactured with molla. Through the static they could make out the instructions of the woman on the other side.

"I'm…..going…….need….your….coordinates."

Between the static they deciphered what she meant.

"We don't have coordinates. We have generated several maps but nothing that would mean anything to an off-worlder," Fleet said, pressing his fingers against each other in a steeple gesture. It was meant to be pensive, but Aqi knew that it was a nervous habit. He was lacking faith in their saviors.

"That…….problem," the voice scratched back through the white noise.

"Clearly," Mertensia said and crossed her arms.

"Won't…" the woman on Earth 2.0 said back and Aqi swore she heard her chuckle. "We..been…..pping……AE625……you"   Static. "an…identify…..landmar……..should…be able….to…….close."

Aqi smiled. "We will study our maps and find three equidistant landmarks so you can triangulate our position."

She turned to the palace guard member who was positioned near the door. His face was completely concealed with a mask that covered from his brow to the bottom of his nose, and a sheer fabric descended from that and stopped right at his collarbone. Or her collarbone. Aqi really wasn't sure. The guard had a lithe figure and could be a young male or an adult female. Her eyes dropped to the hips, male. Even wearing the body armor, the hips were much too narrow to be a female. "Fetch us the maps."

The figure nodded and left the room. As he exited, Kilo entered with Utria in tow. Her clothes were nearly completely sand-bleached, and small particles fell from her shoulders with each step.

"We have a development," Kilo said.

The other three rulers turned to the radio, but the woman on the other side had heard.

"Take…..are….of…it. ontac….me…..when….you….have….your location."

They heard a click as the transmission was ended.

"We found The Source," Utria began. "It is guarded by monsters."

Aqi's mind raced, but she knew she couldn't ask about Rhea's whereabouts. However, she did feel Fleet's eyes on her, monitoring her expression. She gave nothing away.

"Bring back all of our units. The Source is not our concern, rescue is mere months away. We can subsist off the resources we have," Aqi commanded.

"Not with the influx of the Hydra Colonists," Fleet began. "We should be prepared for the worst and at least take The Source. How many units would you need to remove the natives?"

"Two hundred soldiers," Utria said confidently.

Kilo sucked in air between his teeth. "That is a third of our force. We wouldn't have enough to quell an uprising."

"There won't be an uprising," Aqi stated. "The promise of exodus will be enough to stop any rioters. We should go public."

"And if the attempt fails? The populace will be at our throats without warning," Mertensia hissed.

At once, all eyes landed on Utria. Her expression was stony but her eyes glimmered with hope. "My attention lapsed, forgive me."

The Commanding Family looked inward and nodded, they could trust her not to say anything. Fleet turned back to her once they had wordlessly vouched for the scout in their midst. "Go, make the preparations necessary to establish a foothold at The Source."

Once she had left, Fleet addressed his co-leaders. "We cannot fail, or our people die on this planet."

X

Yuto and Dierde stared at the rover as it climbed the dune towards them. Everything around them was a blanket of desert, wrinkled with the massive dunes.

Terra Mortem

They couldn't outrun the rover—trying to sprint down one of the eroding hills would result in a tumble to their death or an injury that would halt their flight. And down was the only way for them to go right now.

"If we cooperate, we might make it out alive," Dierde said, though her words stuck in her mouth.

Yuto only nodded.

The vehicle came to a rest twenty feet from them. The driver said something to the passenger, who seemed to disagree before a few hand gestures convinced him to exit the rover.

The Hydra Seven survivors recognized him immediately. Rumo approached with his hands held out in a peaceful sign. He took slow steps, either because of his arthritis or because he was treating his renegade wards like wild animals. No quick movements.

Yuto snorted. "Come to make your apologies?"

"Not quite. I come to offer you a place on the rescue ships," Rumo said hesitantly, which both Yuto and Dierde noted.

"Rescue?" Dierde asked hollowly.

"Yes, the Commanding Family made contact with Earth 2.0, we are going ho-" His words were cut off as Yuto's fingers clasped around his neck.

He easily forced the older man onto his back and let a flurry and punches fly from his right arm. The old man coughed, wheezed, and bucked but his feeble attempts were for naught.

Dierde hadn't moved. The thought of stopping Yuto hadn't even crossed her mind. Her gaze traveled from Rumo and Yuto to the rover, none of the soldiers had gotten out to intervene. She squinted, was the driver pumping his fist in the air? She saw the flash of white teeth and was instantly confused.

X

"Now this is what we're h-here for!" Lago crowed. His fist struck the windshield twice accidentally, and a little spider-web crack appeared. He ignored it, just like he ignored his stutter.

"Are we not going to stop this?" a soldier asked as he fingered the rifle in his lap.

"Fuck the old codger," Lago spat. "The Commanding Family doesn't care if he comes back."

"They said that?" the soldier piped up.

"It was implied."

X

Rumo's face turned purple as Yuto's grip on his windpipe tightened. The man ceased squirming and his pulse weakened, but Yuto knew better than to release him just yet. Once he could no longer feel a heartbeat throbbing beneath his thumb he sat back on his heels. He pulled Rumo's belt free of its loops and wrapped it around the Elder's neck, just in case he didn't finish the job. He rocked back onto his feet and stared at the rover—nobody moved for a second. Then a dark skinned soldier with a ridiculous patch of green hair got out of the driver's seat. He held the rifle in one hand, pointed skyward and away from the two Hydras, but his finger was on the trigger.

"If you don't make a fuss, we will take you back to The Wreckage unharmed," he said with a charming smile.

Dierde felt the same sensation as when she saw Jarrod run from the back of her skull to the base of her spine. She silently cursed herself.

"Is it true?" Yuto asked, wiping the blood on the back of his hand on the side of his pants. Rumo's face had been a myriad of cuts and ugly purple welts from Yuto's fist before he finally expired.

"Why would I lie?" Lago asked, smiling deceptively.

"Only liars have to ask that. But I wasn't referring to that. Is what he said true?" Yuto pointed to the corpse next to him.

"I don't know what he said," Lago said dismissively.

"Are we being rescued?" Dierde asked abruptly.

Lago let the gun slip a little in his hand. "Rescue?" The Shriker's eyes narrowed.

"By Earth 2.0," Yuto offered.

Lago's demeanor shifted completely. He bristled and raised his rifle and pointed it directly at Dierde's chest. "On the ground now!" he barked.

Yuto complied but Dierde hesitated.

"If we cooperate, what is going to happen to our gonis?" Dierde demanded, her voice not breaking or wavering despite her fear.

"We'll eat them," Lago snarled and pointed the gun towards the airborne Dierde.

"No!" The shriek came at the same time as the report of gunfire, but the goni dropped a few feet in the air unharmed and nosedived down the dune, Aileen right behind her. When they neared the bottom, their wings spread out to slow them down before they agilely changed direction and turned a corner out of sight.

Dierde felt a pain in her chest, knowing she would never see the creature again as long as she lived. Not of her own accord, she lunged and tackled Lago to the ground. He pulled the trigger two more times by accident as he fell before he dropped the weapon and grabbed Dierde by the hips in an attempt to thrust her off him. Screeching, no, roaring like an animal, her fist rammed into his nose and mouth, and blood filled both. Her next attack sent a fistful of claws towards his right eye. Lago felt it tear under her fingers and his right field of vision flooded with white light. Before she could do further damage, he launched his fist into her stomach. She gasped as the air left her lungs and rolled off him. For good measure, he kicked her in the ribs.

The two soldiers flanked Yuto, both with their guns leveled at his face.

"Cuff and gag them," Lago ordered, and spat a gob of bloody saliva inches from Dierde's face. He pulled a pair of handcuffs from his belt and roughly twisted her hands behind her back. With one hand he pulled his belt free and used it to prevent Dierde from speaking. He made a new notch with his knife and fastened the belt there. She still lay on her stomach, so he grabbed a fistful of her shirt back and hefted her from the ground. Her feet dragged through the sand as he marched her to the rover and tossed her into the backseat.

"I t-trust you'll behave now," Lago said with mock politeness. His right eye was mangled and didn't look in the same direction as the left. In fact, it barely moved other than in little circles while it stared despondently at the ground amid its bloody socket.

Dierde swore she could see something reflective in the back of his eye from a small tear right above the iris.

Lago growled when he noticed Dierde staring at his now useless eye. He tore a length of fabric from the bottom of his shirt and wrapped it around his head; if there was any chance of salvaging his vision, sand would ruin it. Yuto was dragged to the rover and similarly shoved into the backseat.

"You know, a team was sent out to dispose of the rest of your clan. Perhaps you should show a little more gratitude." He leered at Dierde with his good eye and slapped her cheek in a mockingly affectionate gesture. Three of his fingers were evident in the welt rising on her cheek. Neither of the captives protested against their gags. Lago turned to his men. "Make sure they don't fall out, we return to The Wreckage."

Terra Mortem

Chapter Nineteen

The refugees of Hydra Seven followed their captors, or saviors, the distinction wasn't clear yet, deeper into the subterranean realm. The Greylings ahead of them didn't so much as hesitate at each fork, and easily traversed the world the Exos had never encountered. Jarrod shuffled along behind the silhouettes of Rio, Taiga, and Lepiro. He would have run and tried to find the surface, but the three creatures behind him gave him pause. He knew that he had no allies if things took a turn for the worst. He also hadn't forgotten Taiga's promise to Rio. But they had found The Source. He was no longer necessary. If they survived this first encounter, would they spare his life and accept that he had been honest with them, or would they still hold him responsible for the destruction of their colony?

His thoughts turned from such a grim subject, and he began studying his surroundings. Pinky sized molla caps burst from hairline fractures in the rocks and clustered around the bases of much larger fungi. The small fiery caterpillars grubbed along the caps like spots of molten rock. The air felt wet. After living on the surface for his entire life, Jarrod had no idea what humidity was. Other than uncomfortable. He knew that he disliked how his clothes stuck to his body and the clammy air pressed in against his face. If it had been much thicker, he could have chewed the air. He felt tiny droplets run down his temple like beads of perspiration. In the tunnel before them, an archway was hewn roughly from the rock. Motifs of gonis, molla, and humans littered the stone threshold. At its zenith was an object that Jarrod recognized immediately. After spending his entire life in its shadow, he would never forget what *The Shrike* looked like, no matter how crude the rendering. On either side of the arch the number nine was engraved. The gears began spinning in Jarrod's brain. His hypothesis, though, was impossible. He glanced at his companions and decided to keep his mouth shut, they hadn't much appreciated the last time he shared his insights with them and their kin.

Rio ghosted up next to Jarrod and surveyed the monolithic art. Jarrod felt Herma's eyes boring into the side of his head, yet Rio spared him no notice. Jarrod winced as a flashback delivered him the image of the blade piercing Mycka's side and his fists clenched. Rio felt the man tense and glanced down at the white knuckles.

"Consider us even," Rio said, and turned to look Jarrod squarely in the eyes.

"How?" the man hissed, his purpled skin making his left eye all but glow.

"You…slept with Dierde." Rio ground his teeth and started to turn.

Another flashback sent Jarrod to his tent at the moment he realized the Exo woman had never been with a man before.

"I did. Why didn't you?" Before his smirk could break across his lips, a fist rammed into his nose and blood spilled after a loud pop. He doubled over in pain, cursed, and spat out one of his front teeth. He ran his tongue along the gap and discovered it was the left fore-incisor. He straightened and tried to ignore the pain coursing through his cheekbones to the back of his skull.

The Greylings around them bristled, clearly disturbed by the transpired events. The short dusting of hair that covered their bodies stood on end and they recoiled from the group, chattering, and crouching down. They tamped their legs as if ready to spring and Taiga raised in her hands in a universal peace gesture.

"You fool, Rio." Lepiro swore and followed Taiga's example.

"I-" He was cut short as Taiga let out a curt whistle between her teeth.

"Silence." Her bobbed hair barely touched her jawline, and Rio could see the muscle clenched behind the curtain of hair. Both he and Jarrod followed her example and didn't hesitate when she slowly lowered herself onto her knees to ensure that she was shorter than the Greylings.

The creatures chattered back and forth, their red eyes darting between their companions and their prisoners.

Rio felt every hair on his body raise when he caught one word of the gibberish. *Geelum*. It sounded dangerously close to "Kill them".

One of the creatures, perhaps a leader of the foraging party, had the last say. It raised its hands and waved them towards the ground, as if to say "stand down". It shook its head and barked out an order before stepping forward and helping Taiga back to her feet. Four other creatures stepped forward to help the Exos back upright, two attended to Rio. A look at the hominid faces revealed apprehension. Taiga couldn't blame them. She had always known Rio to be reserved, mild mannered, and completely devoted to Dierde. Being her husband's best friend, she had known him reasonably well. Almost as well as she knew her husband. For a moment she mused over why she had never been with Rio.

Yuto had his time with most of her friends (she blinked back tears at the thought, all of them were dead now) and sometimes they were even invited back to the tent. Yet she had never had a chance with Rio. Maybe that had been what Earthling Marriage had been about. Needlessly shackling yourself to one sexual outlet for the remainder of your life. Taiga pursed her lips. She shouldn't be bothering herself with thoughts such as these. Not out of consideration for Yuto, she could only guess what he and Dierde were doing right now—she had witnessed their flight from the camp—she needed to focus on survival.

They were led past the archway and down a series of steps roughly hewn into the rock. The igneous stairwell twisted around the edge of a shaft the plummeted straight down into the abyss. The Hydras had never seen a staircase before, had they been raised in The Wreckage they would have found its placement rather peculiar. Jarrod, on the other hand, jotted this occurrence down as more evidence to support his hypothesis.

After descending nearly seventy feet, the stairs leveled out and became an archway, cutting through the chasm towards a plateau of gleaming light. As they got closer, structures became visible. Hundreds of molla huts with rocky foundations were placed at intervals, forming a geometric pattern. Cages lined streets and were placed in front of each house, full of the glowing grubs which inevitably escaped and Greyling children would gather them back up with joyous choruses and return them to their lantern-like abodes. Small gardens of molla grew in mock planters in front of some of the homes, while others had what could only be interpreted as lawn ornamentations, weirdly shaped rocks, dried mollas tied together like a ristra of peppers, even beds of sand framed with smaller rocks and littered with lines and patterns drawn with an idle finger. Gonis of varying size floated lazily between the houses, singing their metallic songs. Herma and Icharus stared after the foreign gonis longingly, but settled on their masters' shoulders nonetheless.

The Exos' eyes grew wide as they were led past row upon row of houses, the level of civilization and luxury here surpassing what they experienced in Hydra Seven. After what seemed like close to an hour of walking they found themselves in the center of the colony. A bubbling spring was surrounded by nine buildings, larger than any of the other homes they had passed. The underground spring was more of a lake or massive pond, at least a half mile wide and more or less circular. A crowd of Greylings gathered around the lake chanting, their crescendo growing louder as the bubbles burst on the surface at a more frenzied rate. The chattering suddenly stopped as did the bubbles. The surface tension of the pool flexed and a massive creature breached the surface in a spray of droplets.

Herma and Icharus took to the air, screeching.

Chapter Twenty

The sheets and blankets on the massive bed were crumpled and in no particular order. The duvets had originally belonged to the pioneers on the *Shrike* and were a patchwork of original threadbare fabric and molla. In fact, they were more molla than anything else. On the blasted planet of AE625, there were few resources to go around. It was a miracle the Earthlings had even survived.

Lying on top of the sheets, with the exception of a stray leg or arm, were three of the Commanding Family members. Aqi was absent. A sheen of sweat glossed over the chests of Fleet, Kilo, and Mertensia. Fleet lay in the middle, while the other two flanked him. The bed was circular, made up of several cots that had been butchered and combined to make a much more accommodating sleeping arrangement. In the early days after the wreck conventional human pairings had been dominant, but slowly disintegrated as the outlook for their survival grew bleak. Before a random group of scouts returned after finding a second spring miles from the settlement, orgies and hedonism ran amok and the precious booze aboard had been drained in less than two weeks. It may not seem like a long period of time, but the 1,400 barrels of whiskey had been meant to last until a new mind altering substance could be brewed or synthesized on Earth 2.0. Fleet often wished he had been alive for that bender.

"The Hydra Seven Elders should have arrived by now," Mertensia said and idly pulled at a strand of her long blonde hair until her arm could stretch no longer, yet there were still inches left on her mane. She let it fall onto her breast where it stuck to the sweat, and grabbed another errand strand. She did this several more times, before sitting up and pulling it all back behind her head and twisting it into a knot on top of her head. "Where has Aqi been?"

"Aqi has other interests now," Fleet muttered somewhat distastefully. It had been two weeks since she last shared their bed, and she had always been his favorite co-leader.

"Other interests?" Kilo asked and sat up.

Fleet waved a hand dismissively. "No time for us. I am sure she is simply waiting for the return of the rovers."

It was a pathetic attempt at a lie. He knew Aqi had taken a liking to Rhea, but whether or not she acted on it was a different matter. Any Commanding Family guilty of fraternizing with anyone outside of the family was punished by death. It was not a light accusation to make, thus Fleet kept it to himself, however bitter it made him.

"Perhaps we should be attending to such affairs rather than frolicking as we have been," Kilo said and rose from the bed, in search of his clothes. He pulled on a patched pair of pants, and Mertensia followed suit.

"Must you two be so dull?" Fleet jabbed jokingly and gestured back to the bed. "We are in a game of hurry up and wait. In mere months we will be rescued from this damned planet. We might as well enjoy it before we are forced to adopt their cultural norms."

With that gentle prodding, the two standing members shimmied out of their pants and crawled towards Fleet. He grinned. Aqi was missing out.

X

Aqi was not missing out. Nor was she engaged in such activities, but her lack of longing made it clear. Instead she was waiting in the banquet hall, which doubled as a meeting area… typically used as such as there were few occasions worth celebrating on AE625. The holiday feasts and parties were few, and rather ironic. The first was the Celebration of Landing, which took place over three days with molla wine (tea is a more accurate term) consumed by all residents of The Wreckage, not just the addicts. The second was called the Days of Desperation, dedicated to the two weeks in which the original survivors drank whiskey while they hastened to their deaths. This celebration lasted six days, molla tea was also a staple, as well as massive orgies, held in the banquet hall. During these six days Commanding Family members could engage in sexual activities with those below their caste. Two years ago, Aqi had met Rhea at one of these celebrations. They had met only two hours in and hadn't been seen for the rest of the holiday.

Across the table from her was the lead medic, Abstor. He was an aged man, nearly as old as Treya. As such, he officiated over all the surgeries, but rarely participated. Most medics stopped practicing at thirty-six after arthritis set in. Their apprentices did most of the precision work until they too took on apprentices. Medicine on AE625 was largely holistic, and based on the properties contained in the molla, gonis, or sand dingoes. The antibiotic properties of one of the creatures was usually enough to treat most ailments caused by bacterium. However, sometimes the patient died before the proper cure was utilized. Luckily, bacterial infections were rare. Viruses could be ridden out by the patient, but for sexually transmitted diseases such as herpes and human immunodeficiency virus, which had persisted since the Human Days on Earth, there was no cure. Sexually transmitted diseases such as these though, had almost been removed from the population by confinement. In the worker classes, such as farmers and maintenance crews, the diseases thrived.

"We need a system of screening the healthy population prior to rescue to ensure that we do not expose ourselves to a pandemic aboard the vessel," Abstor said pensively.

"Are you suggesting we leave them behind?" Aqi said suspiciously. She saw the wisdom in this, though the very concept was repugnant.

"Unless the ships from the Second Earth have adequate quarantine procedures. If not, we might as well remain here or arrive at our new home as lepers."

Aqi curled her lip in disgust.

Abstor raised his hands defensively, palms facing the dark woman.

"I see the merit of your plan. And I'm afraid that we will have to utilize it," Aqi said before he could justify himself. "It doesn't mean I like it. Try to locate the burrows with the highest incidents of contagious infections. Perhaps we can remove individuals from the population and quietly leave them behind if need be. We do not need any riots."

"I will be discreet," Abstor said and left Aqi sitting at the table. He could sense her disappointment, but it wasn't as if he didn't feel his own. At his core, he was a pragmatist and the survival of the colony was more important than the feelings and lives of a few.

He headed to the medical bay, which still remained attached to the *Shrike* though it had been detached and set level on the ground some years ago and welded back to the ship. Much of the life support equipment wouldn't have survived without being powered by the mainframe of the shuttle. He passed the hydroponic farms, the main dietary staple that took up the bulk of the massive room. The mycelium of molla was pressed against the glass walls of the hydroponic tanks, the gossamer fibers impossibly white and stinking of decay. Occasionally a stray body part of a sand dingo or goni pressed against the glass. The cryptic fungi acted much the same as they did on earth, perhaps they had been stowaways on the *Shrike,* and decomposed the deceased readily.

The gentle trickle of water belied the sinister nature of the hydroponic farms. On a resource scarce planet, anything of nutritional value had to be utilized. The deceased Exos were blended into a slurry and poured into the center of the tank, this way a stray finger or eyeball would be unlikely to find its way to the edge of the glass. However, there were always urchins, eager to be seen by their living counterparts. As he passed through the row upon row of molla tanks, he reached the Earthling relics. These plants had been some of the most decorated and adored crops on earth. Soybeans, corn, potatoes, squash, and tomatoes. They were only eaten during a harvest time, which coincided with their holidays. Only a portion of the fruits and vegetables could be eaten, the seeds were collected while the meatier portions would be devoured. He looked longingly at a plump red sphere, catching the artificial light and gleaming like a ruby. On Earth it had been called an 'early girl'. Why, Abstor had no idea. He broke his gaze when he felt the hardened eyes of the farmers. Their faces were dirty, though actual soil didn't exist on AE625 and they were growing hydroponically. The farmers often had the highest rates of bacterial infections due to the special ingredients used to offer nutrients to their food sources. The pumps in the vegetable gardens were more robust than those in the molla tanks, as they supplied partially decomposed gonis, sand dingoes, and humans. But the plants the Exos ate doubled as their waste removal system. Human shit was pumped into the vats and the plants greedily absorbed it through their roots. The potato beds were especially vile, they did poorly submerged in water as the tubers became soggy and rotted quickly. Rather, they were planted directly in dung. In order to be harvested, the starchy roots had to be excavated.

Abstor pushed the door open and left the fetid air, breathing a sigh of relief as fresh clean air rushed through his nostrils, cleansing him of the filth. He was still three corridors from the med bay, so he hastened his step.

X

Treya and Toledo entered The Wreckage at the front of the combined colonies that made up the Wyrms. Both Treya and Toledo were in the rover, along with the man Treya had bedded. His name was Cain, and he had hardly left the old woman's side since they first met. An alarm was blared upon their arrival, a loud siren. Though its sound was dissonant, it didn't warn peril as it did on Earth. The single blast was a welcome and meant to alert the Commanding Family. Two calls, however, meant to rouse the Shrike Colonial Military. Treya allowed herself a smile, the Shrikers had no idea they had just greeted their enemies as friends. Surely she would have to meet with the Commanding Family first, then she would seek out Ellie.

The entirety of the Original Settlement lay before her. The *Shrike* was located centrally, to its left the goni breeding facilities. On the other side of the shuttle were the sand dingo rearing pens. To the far right were stone quarries, where machinery moved large blocks of rock and stacked them to the side. The Shrikers weren't mining for mineral resources but digging to find water. On the other side of the crater were huts, some used the stones from the quarry as a foundation and the rest were made from scavenged materials from the ship. Barely visible from behind the *Shrike* were row upon row of outdoor crops, their yields not nearly as productive as the hydroponic gardens, but space was limited and had to be utilized.

The pealing laughter of children could be heard as the toddlers ran from hut to hut, holding whatever object they deemed suitable for a toy that day. Seeing so many children was strange to Treya, Rio had been the last child she had seen in fifteen years in Camp Seven, with the exception of the stillborn fetuses. She tried not to imagine the younglings running around simmering in a broth. Before they made it very far, they were approached by a soldier.

"Treya, the Commanding Family thanks you for your service. Your presence is requested. A chaperone escort is waiting for you at the palace. I will make sure the Hydra refugees are quartered and fed." He had strong features and was taller than Toledo by at least five inches. His skin, hair, and eyes all matched. Dark.

"Thank you." Treya smiled kindly and said her farewells to Cain and Toledo and made her way briskly to the palace. By the time she reached the airlock doors, which hadn't been operational for centuries, she was breathing heavily. As promised, a chaperone was there, who waited patiently and offered her a glass of water. She graciously accepted it and followed the woman to the banquet hall, where Aqi had just met with Abstor. The other three family members joined her now, apparently they had concluded their cavorting.

"Thank you for completing our task so expeditiously," Fleet said with a patronizing smile. "Your loyalty to the survival of our kind is to be commended."

Now it was Treya's turn to smile. "Yes, I am relieved that our internment on this prison of a planet will be coming to an end. My only regret is that I will likely pass before I lay eyes on our new Eden. You will have to enjoy it for me."

"We will recognize your efforts, and the efforts of all the Hydra Clans. Without you, AE625 would have killed us long ago," Mertensia practically sang in her melodic voice.

Treya nodded slightly at the acknowledgment, however thin it was. She knew the perception of the Hydra Colonies among the Shrikers. She wouldn't be surprised if war broke out before she could put her rebellion into action.

"We need an emissary to the clans, I'm afraid we would not be well received among the desert dwellers," Kilo said and Treya balked at the slight. Desert dwellers. As if all of AE625 was not a desert. Fleet saw her reaction and placed his hand on Kilo's forearm.

"That is the kind of language that would get us stoned," Fleet said cajolingly.

Kilo pursed his lips in what looked like agreement.

"And that illustrated our need for an emissary such as you, if you would accept?" Aqi asked, her dark eyes showing little amusement. In fact, it seemed like her thoughts were elsewhere.

"I would be honored. My goal has always been for the greater good of our civilization." The answer was facetious, but Treya doubted that any of them would guess her ulterior motives.

"You may go now," Fleet said politely. "I'm sure you would like to rest. The chaperone you met at the door will take you to your accommodations."

Treya departed, though she wouldn't spend much time resting. She needed to find Ellie.

Chapter Twenty-One

Out of the dark waters of the lake rose a massive creature. Its gelatinous skin stretched across two sets of wings, the widest being nearly sixty feet in length. From nose to tip it was roughly forty feet long. Its crescent shaped head swayed as its dark eyes surveyed the newest additions to the Greyling colony.

It let out a call of metallic discord, which Herma and Icharus mimicked several decibels lower. The monstrous goni glided over the surface of the water and stopped mere feet from the Exos. From the cavern ceiling above, the sound of many wings filled the air. Gonis the size of eagles and larger, some as big in length as a horse descended like a flurry of bats.

The gigantic goni's luminescent skeleton glowed red, its slimy skin a slate grey color with blotches of black scattered over its body. Each of the suckers that lined its underside was the size of dinner plates, and pulsed, as if hungry to latch onto something. Its immense weight prevented it from rising into the air, but it moved fluidly in the water. It leveled its head at the Exos and let out a steamy puff of air that blasted them in the face. Its mouth, lacking teeth, was covered in knobby ridges that could undoubtedly crunch through bones with little effort. Its gaze settled on Rio last before it turned and splashed back into deeper water, its tail whipping through the air behind it. In unison, the Exos let out a sigh of relief.

The Greylings began tossing some of their molla harvest into the dark waters, and the airborne goni began dive-bombing the water. Each one struck the surface like a bullet and emerged with a cap held aloft in their jaws before retreating to their roosts. One of the larger gonis broke the surface empty handed and, on its ascent, snapped up one of the smaller gonis which let out a squeal as it was gobbled up.

Rio held his hand over Herma's eyes. She let out a coo of concern and Rio felt his stomach churn at the thought of what would become of them among these aliens. Abruptly, he felt a fist slam into his stomach, and an empty molla sack was thrown over his head before another fist rammed squarely between his eyes and his world went darker than it already was.

X

Treya found Ellie standing in front of a wire cage, two stories high. Inside were the fluttering wings of hundreds of gonis. Their suction cups squelched to the thin metal wires, threaded in hexagonal patterns too small for even their heads to fit through; on Earth they called this chicken wire. The bottom of the cage was littered with remnants of molla caps and the hardened cellular waste exoskeletons that the gonis wriggled free from every few weeks.

Without looking over Ellie said, "It's sick that they eat these beautiful creatures."

"I think they find our way of life equally as disgusting," Treya said with a sigh. Her mind wandered back to her goni, Copri, who had at least gotten to experience the wild before being made into a stew.

"If you want to defend them, I am not sure why you came to me," Ellie said, not hostile but not friendly. Contemptuous, maybe.

"I do not. But I am disgusted at myself for supporting them. If I hadn't, perhaps Hydra Seven would have survived." Her voice held a tone of rebellion. She felt Ellie tense next to her.

"Well, maybe this is your shot at redemption," Ellie mused.

"The Commanding Family needs to be removed," Treya said, just as a blast sounded off on the other side of the pen.

It was a small explosion, but the two guards stationed near the door took the brunt of it and dropped to the ground, howling and covering their faces with bloody stumps of fingers. Their ears and noses were mutilated, shrapnel stuck out from their chests, their bodies coated in a thin layer of sand quickly turning red. Six Hydras ran towards the cage. Five set up a perimeter, while the last finished off the dying guards with a knife across the throat. He found the keys and fumbled with the lock before he located the correct one and flung the door open. He leapt out of the way as the first of the gonis to notice barreled towards the exit. The rest of the flying creatures took heed and like a flock of birds or a school of fish fled from the enclosure. In perfect sync, they rose up into the air, twisting like a giant snake before darting for the horizon.

Treya looked at Ellie in amazement.

"You're late to the party." The other woman grinned and offered her hand to Treya, a silent pact of rebellion. Treya took it.

"Then I have catching up to do."

X

The rover rumbled into the Original Settlement and slowed to a stop at the barracks entrance. It had been the workers' quarters on the *Shrike* and was positioned 90 degrees from the hydroponics. Lago turned to his men. "Take the prisoners to the holding cells." These were located near the sand dingo enclosure, but also within the *Shrike*. Lago needed to get his eye checked out by Abstor's apprentices, but first he needed to find Rhea.

He showed a metal ID badge with his rank and name engraved into its surface to the soldier on duty. He was allowed to pass. Lago strode down a dimly lit hallway, row upon row of doors on either side, which led to wide open rooms filled with six beds each. Most of the soldiers only had enough possessions to fill the space directly beneath their bed. Past the barracks hall was the Council of Warchiefs' offices, and beyond that, their lodging and the armory. The only person in the offices was Utria. And Lago knew that she was not on the council.

"Where is Rhea?" Lago demanded.

Utria regarded him coldly, she was his elder and he was acting like an upstart. "Still at The Source. As if that is your business. Who might you be?" she ordered back.

Lago's ego was undiminished, nonetheless he saluted her. "Scout Team Lieutenant Lago. And I have Hydra Seven prisoners." He brought his hand back down to his side.

"You were supposed to kill them," Utria stated bluntly. She didn't quite have the official authority to punish him, but she was acting in Rhea's stead...

"The male of the pair killed the Elder who was serving as my guide and emissary to the errant Hydras," Lago explained and watched the wheels turn in her eyes. She raised an eyebrow for him to elaborate. "That means that they have reason to suspect the Elders, and that Jarrod told them the truth of the situation before their camp was razed."

"And what bearing does that have on us?" Utria asked, her eyes narrowing.

"Who did we just bring into our city in droves?" Lago pursued his train of thought. Just then they felt the explosion from the goni cage vibrate their shins, through their spines and up until it chattered their teeth.

"Hydras," Utria growled.

X

Taiga, Lepiro, and Jarrod sat in the blackness of a windowless room. Had it not been for Icharus, they would not have been able to see each other. Where Rio had been taken, or if he was still alive was a mystery to them. After being assaulted he had been gingerly carried away, in stark contrast to the beating he received prior to unconsciousness. The remaining three Exos had been escorted away in the same friendly beckoning manner the Greylings had assumed since their first meeting. However, that didn't mean they wouldn't abruptly turn on the Exos.

It was unclear if they were permitted to leave. Their thoughts were preoccupied with the gigantic goni that dwelled in the lake. Or the semi-massive ones clinging to the cavern ceiling. All eyes were on Icharus as he flitted along the single circular wall. Would he grow to such an immense size? Was he the same species as the lake monster? How long would it take for him to grow the length of a bus? Surely the Elder's gonis should have grown larger?

Or perhaps the creature in the lake was older than centuries and had seen the birth of AE625. Undoubtedly it was ancient. A sentinel of time itself.

"Is Rio alive?" It was Jarrod who asked. His cheekbones and nose were swollen and shiny with blood and lymph just below the surface. His nose was no longer sharp, but looked more like a molla cap placed on his face for comedic effect. His eyebrow had just started to heal, and now his face was littered with more blood, bruises, and cuts. Taiga was certain he was regretting his noble mission to save the uncouth curs of the Hydra Camps.

Lepiro snorted. "You better hope he's dead. That was some move you pulled back there."

"He brought it upon himself," Taiga stated simply. She did not want to rile emotions while they were in such close proximity, in the middle of a hostile city.

"How?" Lepiro asked, baffled.

"There is no love on AE625," Taiga murmured. "Their ideals were bound to be shattered eventually."

"But do we think he's actually dead?" Jarrod asked his question again, the words coming out stuffy.

"If we manage to escape, we should assume as such. We can't pull off a rescue and an escape successfully," Lepiro suggested.

"How can you say that?" Taiga asked incredulously. "Rio wouldn't leave you here to die alone."

"He'd leave me," Jarrod said with a plaintive shrug.

"There is no love on AE625." Lepiro stretched out his legs in front of him, pulled his hood down over his face, and closed his eyes. He attempted to block out the high pitched scream that seemed to shake the walls of the entire cavern. Icharus landed on Lepiro's chest and mimicked the cry in a much smaller voice.

Lepiro opened one eye to regard the little animal. Then he sat bolt upright.

"They're going to feed Rio to it."

He wasn't wrong.

Chapter Twenty-Two

The Wreckage was in absolute turmoil. Soldiers flooded from the barracks, and the plebeians ran back and forth from their huts, trying to figure out what was going on. Ellie, Treya, and the Hydras, however, were mobilizing, calm and collected despite the adrenaline coursing through their veins. This civil war would ensure that they never taste an early girl tomato, but they couldn't miss what they never had.

The Hydra and Wyrms were busy creating a protective perimeter from dismantled huts after they had driven the residents away, or recruited them to the cause. They were surprisingly efficient, and also used the tents and water holding tanks from their colonies to set up a defensive position.

"Won't we be backed into a corner here?" Treya shouted over the din of clattering metal and booming voices. She turned her attention to the battle raging on the inner stone wall. The sentries were standing their ground, but the rebel soldiers were slowly picking them off. Some of the water colonist soldiers had acquired guns, and this leveled the playing field.

"This isn't our entire force. But we need to draw them out of the palace first. We will never get to the Commanding Family in an all-out assault," Ellie said with an air of confidence. The two Elders and their escort reached the just-erected wall and as soon as they were safely on the other side, the gap was sealed. Two workers with solar powered drills fastened scrap metal bars in place with screws for reinforcement.

Both Toledo and Cain were safely behind the wall and greeted Treya when they saw her. Toledo looked as greasy as ever, if not greasier, and Cain's eyes wept with relief at seeing his newly assimilated lover.

"What's our plan?" Treya asked once she caught her breath.

"We draw their fire until our men can get inside the palace and assassinate the Commanding Family," Ellie said simply and called for two of her soldiers to her side. One was a striking woman with wide hips and bright purple hair, the other a short stout man who had broad shoulders and a mottled complexion. These two had been with Ellie in the tent when they first met, perhaps they were co-leaders or bodyguards.

"Do we have a backup plan?" Treya asked timidly.

"We blow the hydrazine," Ellie said with a devilish grin.

Treya clamped her teeth together to prevent her jaw from plummeting into the sand. From what Toledo had explained to her, setting off the unstable chemical would incinerate everyone in the crater and probably send the *Shrike* back into orbit.

Ellie turned her attention to her two bodyguards. "Asia and Jackson, we will draw their fire, and you two will circumvent the *Shrike* and enter near the sand dingo pens. Find some Shriker peasant clothes and get ready."

"I'll go too," Treya volunteered. "I've been inside the palace."

Ellie nodded, and Toledo also suggested he join the party.

"That's perfect. Once inside, separate. I don't need anyone recognizing you and getting my Wyrms killed," Ellie said brusquely.

Treya and Toledo exchanged a glance and shrugged, loyalty meant something after all.

Without further conversation Treya took off for a heap of possessions. When the Hydras built the defensive wall they had spared little sympathy for sentiment. The belongings of the previous occupants had been dumped on the ground unceremoniously. Treya found a set of women's clothing after skimming off the top of a pile and wasted no time in shrugging out of her clothes and into the stranger's misappropriated wardrobe. After she was dressed, she saw other Hydra insurgents setting up water tanks and molla caches. Ellie had planned for the long haul.

She caught a glimpse of more Toledo than she ever wanted to see as he pulled on his pants and tightened a belt. The two reached Asia and Jackson at the same time and Ellie smiled broadly.

"You two haven't disappointed me. Good luck." She pulled open a panel and Asia and Jackson darted out without a word. Treya and Toledo were right on their heels, albeit Treya not so fast. A percussion of bullets sounded from the Hydra post and was returned from the trench just before the palace. It had been dug in an extremely short amount of time and was lined with the barrels of many guns.

Treya's legs were burning like they hadn't burned in years and her lungs were aching like old bones before a storm. When they were finally far enough away that they could act like scared commoners, they slowed and the pop of firearms faded only slightly. Treya didn't stop to catch her breath, despite the other three assuring her there was time.

"Once we are inside we can rest for a moment with the other citizens seeking asylum. If we act easy out here, any soldier watching will know we are Hydras. We need to still be panicked and hurried."

She pushed past them, and they fell in behind her. Her heart began galloping faster than it had before as they neared the sand dingo pen. The ugly snuffling creatures gripped the fence with their large hooked claws and their beady eyes followed the foursome unwaveringly as they approached. The dingos made a strange whistling noise of excitement as the Hydras walked within spitting distance. The creatures ran clumsily along the edge of the cage, tripping over each other as they vied for a closer position to the humans. Treya would have found them amusing or even cute if their sole purpose wasn't for hunting down gonis.

Two soldiers urgently waved them over, clearly a gesture for more haste on their part. The four Hydras broke into a run and were unwittingly accepted past the threshold of the palace as frightened refugees. The soldiers pointed them down the long hallway and told them there were blankets and plenty of water for everyone, food as well. Treya kept her face blank as she hurried in the direction she had been beckoned to.

The hallway was surreal. Women, children, and men not fit for war, or too cowardly, were huddled against the wall, clutching tin cups full of water and wrapped in blankets despite the scorching heat of the planet. They truly looked pitiful. No one in a Hydra colony would ever act so helpless or destitute. Hydras had scratched out a living among rocks, all the while providing for these pathetic people. Treya felt disgusted at the thoughts that flitted through her mind, but she knew they were accurate, which made them all the harder to block out. The report of gunfire sounded outside, wove its way into the *Shrike* and echoed from wall to wall as it traveled across the ship. It was then that Treya realized she had brought no weapons with her. She cursed her stupidity. She knew Asia and Jackson were well prepared, and inferred that Toledo being a soldier would not overlook such an important aspect. Nonetheless, she felt foolish. She was ancient, a crone, her ability to plan stunted by the thrill of the moment. She would make do though, she just needed to be more aware.

Those were her thoughts when she saw two familiar faces being taken down a hallway. Both forms were unconscious, and the Shrikers were literally dragging them but their faces were visible. Not for a second had Treya thought she would ever see her fellow clansmen alive. Yet here were two of them. Yuto and Dierde.

She tugged on Toledo's sleeve and broke away from the rest of the group. Toledo wordlessly followed.

X

"Utria should have returned by now." Rhea addressed Gana and the other fourteen remaining members of her unit. They had three rovers, it would be more than enough to transport them back to The Wreckage.

"You think something ill befell them?" Gana inquired, twisted towards her so his good ear could catch her voice.

"No, I think something ill befell the *Shrike,*" Rhea said. The radios had run out of batteries yesterday and were now charging on the roofs of the rovers, but the wind constantly tipped them over or blew them off the hood. It was slow going. But the radios could be damned. Something happened to their city. Which meant something happened to Aqi.

The three rovers ripped through the sand a moment later, leaving at least one radio battery-pack behind in the sand in their haste to depart.

X

The lights flickered overhead and abruptly went out with a static pop. A moment later, the generator whirred and the lights came back on. The entire hallway was bathed in a harsh fluorescent light. Not a single Shriker had spotted Toledo or Treya as they ghosted after the Hydra Seven captives. They made certain not to follow their quarry too closely lest they were spotted. Their footsteps echoed faintly against the metallic floor, just decibels below those of the guards.

The sound of scuffling footsteps reached Treya and Toledo's ears as one of the captives stirred. A moment later, the sound of a fist ramming into flesh was followed by a grunt, then silence. Judging by the voice behind the guttural noise, it was Yuto who had regained consciousness, albeit only momentarily. Several times the footsteps halted, and Treya was certain they had been discovered. Before she knew it, however, she heard the sound of bodies slumping, doors clanging, and keys jangling.

"We're going to have to kill them," Toledo whispered as he looked about the hallway. He was familiar with the prisons. The corridor they were in led to a T junction, and to the left was the prison, while the right led to a control panel. After they freed the Hydras, the panel could also be destroyed to further the rebellion.

"I don't know how to use a gun," Treya said, before admitting, "And I didn't bring one."

Toledo only smiled. "There's too high a chance of ricocheting in here. We can't use guns."

"I didn't bring a knife either," Treya said perhaps a little too loud.

Toledo pressed his finger against his lips and drew a kukri from a scabbard across his lower back. He pressed himself back against the wall as if trying to become absorbed by the metal, his body flatter than Treya thought possible. She heard the guards approaching when she realized she was standing in the middle of the hallway. She moved to dart towards the wall, but ended up tripping and falling splayed out across the floor.

The Shriker soldiers rounded the corner and started with alarm upon seeing the woman. The soldier closest to Toledo grunted audibly as the blade slid across his midsection, opening up his guts, which splattered as they unraveled like a spool of yarn before hitting the floor. The second barely had time to react before the blade pierced his abdomen and traveled upward into his heart. Both men died with hardly a sound.

Toledo offered his non-dominant hand to Treya, which thankfully wasn't covered in blood like the right, and hoisted her to her feet.

"Now to save your friends." He smiled grimly.

"I don't think they'd call me that," Treya said as she hurried around the corner.

Terra Mortem

"If they don't thank you, we can leave them in the cells," Toledo joked, but Treya ignored him.

Thirteen doors lined the halls, each cell designed to hold forty humans. The door to the cell had a circular window with safety wires crisscrossing the pane. Little did she know, but there hadn't been prisons on the *Shrike*. Nonviolent criminals worked in the boilers, machine rooms, and performed janitorial services, while violent criminals were executed. Each of these rooms had been classrooms. Reproducing on the *Shrike* in flight was a privilege and each family could have one child every six years to not overcrowd the ship. Hardly any of the cells were occupied, as criminals could not be tolerated in a society of rock scratchers. They needed every body available and little was illegal on the lonely planet. Only two of the thirteen rooms had penitent Shrikers and the third (though the cells were not abutting) held the Hydras.

"The keys?" Treya asked, and Toledo cursed and jogged easily back to the fresh corpses and snatched the key ring. He ran back without even a catch in his breath. He was sorting the keys when Yuto pressed his forehead against the glass. Dierde stirred behind him. He smiled, despite his black eyes and bloody teeth, but it wasn't a comforting smile.

"I killed Rumo. And I'll kill you next." He jabbed his index finger against the glass and Toledo paused, the correct key clutched between his index and thumb.

He glanced at Treya, at whom the threat was aimed.

"We probably deserve the same fate, and you can give it to me once we overthrow the Commanding Family," Treya said evenly.

Toledo turned so his back was to the door and the prisoners couldn't read his lips. He mouthed, *We don't have to open the door.*

But Treya shook her head. "Free them."

Yuto stepped back from the door so it could swing open without clocking him in the face. The lock clicked and Toledo twisted the handle and pushed the door open, his kukri still gripped firmly in his right hand.

Yuto caught the door and tensed, ready to spring. He recoiled slightly when he saw the blade before going slack.

He sneered at Toledo before facing Treya. "Is this your prize for selling us to the Original Settlement?" he rebuked her, but she remained stoic.

"My prize is my guilt," she said simply.

"That's rich," Dierde said, rubbing a hand against her temples as she brushed by Yuto. He really needed to learn to live and let live. Survival was at stake and he still wanted to be childish. That didn't mean she forgave Treya, but she could be pragmatic. "Why are you here?"

"To rescue you," Treya answered.

"Why, though?" Dierde said with a roll of her eyes. "I do not believe that you did it to clear your conscience. Something is at hand."

"You are correct. We are rising against the status quo. There is a mission from Earth 2.0 en route to AE625 to take us to our promised land." Treya said grandly. "The current Commanding Family will not be boarding."

Dierde snorted. "You've got to be kidding me? In the autumn of our society you decide to lead an uprising and jeopardize our chances of escape. You might as well have doomed us all."

"Being a Hydra Seven member, you would have been executed. The Commanding Family will allow no witnesses to the massacre to survive, let alone spread rumors in their new home," Treya said bitterly.

"It's true, it's doubtful that any of the Hydras would be allowed to live. The laws of the Second Earth might demand punishment if their injustice was revealed," Toledo supplied helpfully, his knife still trained on Yuto.

"I suppose we don't have much choice, other than to follow your ploy…not much has changed," Yuto spat out. "What next?"

"We disable the power in this quadrant of the ship. There are four main generators in the *Shrike* and in each sector is a control panel which contains breakers. Most of the wiring has been spliced too many times and the breakers are near irreparable. The *Shrike* is running low on supplies and the maintenance crew will not be able to replace the breaker with a spare. The colony is on its last legs," Toledo explained and gestured for Yuto and Dierde to walk towards the panel he spoke of. He pointed with his blade, but never took his eyes off Yuto.

The two Hydras crept slowly down the corridor, wary of more soldiers, though when they reached the junction, Toledo pushed past them and found the control panel easily. Surprisingly, there was no lock on the panel door. He found the range breaker and yanked hard but it refused to budge. He looked closer at it, seeing that it had been melted into its socket by a welder or conductive heat. He growled and examined the grip of his kukri; the handle wasn't metal, and hopefully wouldn't electrocute him. He jammed the blade into the box and sparks flew from the panel before it let out a gust and flames erupted. The generator whirred again, the lights flickered, died, and this time they stayed off.

Chapter Twenty-Three

In the subterranean realm of the Greylings, the light of the surface was a distant memory for the Exo captives. Rio most of all. With the exception of Herma, he was completely isolated. Unlike his companions, he wasn't even in an earnest dwelling. He was in a natural alcove that had been transformed into a cage by placing a large rock at the opening. The boulder could only be moved by pulleys from the outside as it fit into a cleft in the cave floor that was three feet deep. Rio could stick his fingers out from gaps between the makeshift door and the entrance of the cave, which earned him a quick rap across his knuckles. Try as he might, he could not get the boulder to budge, and after hours of throwing his weight into it, or kicking it, all he succeeded in doing was wrenching his knee and nearly dislocating his shoulder.

The cave walls were slick with moisture too, which he had reveled in at first, but now it chilled him to the bone. His clothing had been designed to keep the sand and sun off his skin, not wick moisture away from his body. Out in the desert heat, the sweat trapped between his skin and the first layer was a welcome relief. Now he shivered, and his teeth clattered in their sockets. Herma languidly swam in a pool of water. It had tried to comfort Rio at first, but now resigned itself to floating laps, its body flat against the water. Only

Herma's tail moved, like a little propeller. The sight would have been comical if Rio wasn't sure this would be his deathbed. He had explored every crevice of his confinement, but there were no cleverly hidden outlets, rubble piles to be dug through, or underwater passages. He was trapped. Together man and beast languished in their confinement, waiting for the end.

X

In an undetermined location within the Greyling City, Taiga, Lepiro, and Jarrod sat in relative silence. Since Lepiro's hypothesis, none of them had much to say. Lepiro and Jarrod were still on board with leaving the fourth member of their party, though Taiga alone objected.

"How are we going to get out of here?" Taiga asked in the dark room. "Once we cross the lake, I have no real recollection of the path we took."

"Not to mention the molla farmers," Jarrod said sourly. "Do you still have the pistol?"

Taiga somehow knew that he was referring to the weapon tucked into her waistband. "Yes, I do. But I don't know how to use it."

"It's not difficult," Jarrod said, and it seemed that his answer was good enough for her.

"What is it? Other than a pistol." Lepiro had to ask, his curiosity piqued.

"It's a gun, a .40 caliber. But none of that will mean anything to you. If we make it out, and the clip is full, I can give you both a brief lesson." By his answer, Jarrod did not think that their escape was likely.

"If we get to the tunnels, Icharus can lead us to the surface," Lepiro said, looking at the creature curled on his chest, fast asleep. The little animal was snoring peacefully, and once again Lepiro began to wonder why the monster in the lake had grown to such a size. If Icharus stayed underground, would he too become immense?

His musing was interrupted by a terrible keening, that started out low before transforming into a wail that shook the foundations of the very cavern they were trapped in. Taiga leapt to her feet and pressed her face against a small window and took in the spectacle taking place on the streets. Greylings of all ages lined the streets, all of them wearing headdresses of molla, rock necklaces, and body paint that glowed orange.

A parade was winding its way down the wide street. Each of the Greylings in the procession wore long cloaks that trailed on the ground and were bound to their wrists to appear as if the marchers could fly. The artificial wings were made from the bodies of many of the scorpion-tailed moths from the tunnels, stitched together so that the strip of orange on one set of wings matched that of the next set. Their bodies, however, were painted with a faint blue-green gel that was probably extracted marrow from the bones of dead gonis. The Greylings danced through the streets, their arms outspread and cloaks shimmering as they raised their hands skyward or swooped close to the ground, the rustling of the exoskeleton cloaks heard even by the Exo prisoners.

As the goni dancers passed, the groan of wheels and creaking of planks could be heard. Three massive goni sculptures, made of a scaffolding of dried molla stems, were being pulled on carts. The keening call of the Greylings became more unified, until it became a chant, "GONI, GONI, GONI."

"At least we can agree on one word with them," Lepiro said dryly. Jarrod thought back to the paintings he had seen in the tunnel and the repeated number nine. He briefly toyed with the thought of sharing his theory, but quickly shot it down. These people would not appreciate it.

"Do you think we are next? After Rio?" Taiga asked, her skin, even in the limited light clearly pale.

"We may be sacrificed right next to him," Lepiro said without taking his eyes off the symbolic parade.

"Sacrificed?" Jarrod piped up. "To what?"

"The goni, are you dense?" Lepiro jeered, though his voice cracked and Jarrod could tell his bravado was false.

"Obviously, but for what purpose?" Jarrod elaborated and Lepiro shrugged.

"Protection, a good harvest, prosperity…victory in a coming war," he supplied. "What would you petition the gods for?"

"The gonis are their gods?" Taiga asked incredulously.

"Our god was water, whether we knew it or not. Or perhaps the Original Colony. At least this civilization lives among theirs," Lepiro said and tickled Icharus under the chin. The creature screed excitedly.

"Can you imagine being devoured by your god, or seeing your children devoured?" Taiga asked in disgust.

"I think the term you're looking for is ecstasy," Lepiro said and snorted, fascinated by the culture he was witnessing. Momentarily, he forgot that he was a prisoner.

"Rio will be able to tell you soon." Jarrod's wry answer garnered him a half-hearted kick across the shin from Taiga.

Before anything more could be said, the door rattled to reveal an incredibly tall Greyling. His molla headdress rained spores down on his shoulders as he ducked to enter the small hut. The orange scorpion-moth ichor was painted in three vertical lines beneath his lower lip and one line from the bottom of his left eye to his jawline. On his chest, the number nine was painted three times, one large integer in the middle, and two smaller at the junction of his pec and deltoid. Other than the headdress and a necklace of molla caps, he was completely naked, not that the Greylings ever wore clothes to begin with.

He smiled broadly and proffered a rock bowl to the Exos. It was full to the brim with molla spores. The Hydras greedily dug their fingers into the bowl, and insufflated the black powder, but Jarrod refused it politely and attempted to hand it back to the Greyling. The creature was clearly offended and held its palm out in a stop gesture and indicated that Jarrod partake. With a sigh, he dug one finger into the bowl, and half-heartedly snorted the spores. The high hit him immediately and he stuck his face into the bowl and inhaled deeply. The Greyling chuckled heartily and this time received the bowl and motioned for the Exos to follow him.

Unsure of what they were getting into, Taiga, Lepiro, and Jarrod stepped out into the ceremony, almost deafened by the sound in the streets. The walls of the hut had offered some insulation against the decibels, but out here the cacophony bounced from crag to crag and back into the colony amongst the dancers. Woodwind, or mollawind instruments made an unlordly wailing that had an undeniably catchy beat, but perhaps that was the understated drums rattling in the background. Orange flitted through the blackness, as painted bodies moved to and fro. The luminescent ichor gave off enough light that it seemed a predawn grey was overtaking the cavern, soon to give way to the sun.

Terra Mortem

Taiga tried to peer past the Greyling bodies but did not see hide nor hair of Rio. Their Greyling guide led them behind the procession until they reached the edge of the lake. The three wicker gonis were placed in a triangular pattern on its shore. Nine poles were erected on the outside of these in a misshapen circle, with two ropes attached at the top of the posts on a large ring. At the opposite end of each rope, it split into two strands that ended with a piece of what looked like bone that had been whittled down and sharpened. A female Greyling stepped into the middle of the circle—she alone lacked any body paint—and held a massive molla cap, upturned. Eighteen male Greylings approached, dipped their hands into the gills of the mushroom and took a whiff of the spores before smearing their fingers across their faces, chest, shoulders, and stomachs. The black streaks were visible along the glowing body paint, applied earlier.

The Greylings paired off as they approached each of the totems, where one of each pair scaled the pole, wrapping their legs tight as to not slide down, gracefully grabbed the sharpened bones and ran each through the skin of one of their pecs before leaning back so that their bare feet were braced against the pole. Their bodies stuck out horizontally, the only force keeping them from dropping to the ground the pressure of their legs against the totem and the rope secured to them, only by skin.

Ethan Proud

The crowd cheered raucously, and the instruments blared as the second of each pair agilely leapt onto his partner, grabbed the opposite rope, and pierced the bone through his own chest. The crowd yelled again, even louder, as the second Greyling leaned back and fell into the air, his weight moving him pendulously. The first Greyling crouched and leapt into the air; at his zenith the rope extended perpendicularly at full length. At the Greyling's nadir, their feet landed solidly against the totem, before they launched themselves outwards again. The two creatures were always opposite of each other, and how they managed not to get tangled amazed the Exos.

The flesh of the Greyling's chests oozed blood from the wounds as they stretched open by the sheer weight of being at the end of the rope. Each of the eighteen Greyling's faces was the image of pure ecstasy. The molla smeared on their faces and chests mingled with their blood and dripped onto the ground beneath them, intermixed with the ceremonial paint. Beneath the aerial dancers lay a spatter of orange that inevitably contained molla and blood. Greyling teenagers, and younger, ran up beneath the totems, their heads barely avoiding being smacked by an ankle or wrist by mere centimeters. They crouched down, like greedy demons, dipped their fingers into the puddles of gore and licked their them without regard to their parents and peers in the crowd. Not that any of the other Greylings cared. They were busy dancing, playing music, or imbibing molla. In any event, more were likely to join the adolescents in their dark behavior.

Taiga, Lepiro, and Jarrod stood in shock as the events before them unfolded. It was both barbaric and beautiful, but for the Hydras it seemed less foreign than to Jarrod who had grown up in the cushy atmosphere of The Wreckage. However, he drew many parallels between it and the Days of Desperation. He looked around, surprised by the lack of orgies, though perhaps that would come later. Or maybe these people were less carnal than his own. Jarrod found himself back at his hypothesis for their origins. That was what they were, people. Not aliens. While he pondered his theories, he wondered whether or not Exos and Greylings could interbreed. All evidence he had seen thus far was in support of it. He brushed the thoughts away before they manifested into something more explicit and less scientific in nature.

Taiga glanced around nervously once she had been able to break the spell woven through the very air. Still no Rio. Had he already been sacrificed? Or killed? Was she next? How much did a monstrous goni need to eat? Lepiro seemed to be enjoying the revelry immensely and had just been given a cap full of spores from their Greyling Guide. It appeared that the two were trying to communicate with extremely vague hand gestures accompanied by sentence fragments from Lepiro and gibberish from the Greyling. Taiga glanced over at Jarrod, completely absorbed in his own thoughts.

Ethan Proud

She was shaken from her observations of her comrades when she noticed the blood drinking youths climbing into the wicker gonis. They filled every inch until they were crammed in at impossible angles. Heads and feet stuck out from beyond the scaffolding and it was impossible to tell where one child ended and the next started. They merged into a single amorphous goni, or rather, three amorphous gonis. Taiga strained her eyes to try to discern what was going on, when she heard the hungry roar of fire. Three women Greylings parted the crowd, each holding a blazing torch aloft. As they passed, the crowd became prostrate on the ground, eyes upturned to behold the spectacle. This continued until only the three Exos stood, but their guide gestured frantically for them to follow suit, so they did.

The aerial dancers continued to spin, while even more Greyling children clambered into the wicker gonis, trying to squeeze themselves into the frames. The low crackle of flames transformed when the women touched the braziers to the objects of their idolatry. The flames leapt to the top of the cavern in an instant as both molla and Greylings caught fire immediately. The sound of combustion drowned out any other sound in the cavern. Even the cries of the dying couldn't be heard, but the smell of burning flesh and hair was unmistakable. The pyres grew as the hungry flame consumed more, but in mere minutes, the tongues stopped lapping at the rock ceiling and began to dwindle and inch by inch, receded. However, the fire was still large enough to illuminate the entire city and the surface of the lake. Gonis could be seen clutching stalactites and surveying the Greylings beneath them, but none were bold enough to leave their rookery.

At the center of the lake, a turbulent mass of water could be seen making anxious laps. The tip of the tail alone broke the surface of the water and slapped loudly in agitation. Then the gigantic head breached and let out an earth shattering squeal. Rocks rained for but a moment after being shaken from their formation.

The lake goni abruptly ceased its laps and began swimming towards the shore in a serpentine, winding pattern. It had been called. And it was hungry.

Chapter Twenty-Four

Lago and Utria were in the Halls of the Commanding Family when the lights went out. Had the lights stayed on, they would have seen paintings and statues of the previous families lining the corridor. As it was, they were in complete darkness. Simultaneously, they produced flashlights, and two identical beams shone into the hall, the click of the buttons sounding at exactly the same moment. Despite the turmoil raging outside the tin can of a ship, the corridor seemed unnaturally quiet. Of course, the two Shrikers could hear the muffled sounds of conflict, but the darkness brought a heaviness to the air. A moment later, the sounds of their boots clacking down the hallway broke the surrealist moment. Lago reflected on the loss of power; since he had been alive he had experienced only a few blips in the power grid and nothing that lasted longer than a millisecond.

They reached the door to the Commanding Family's chambers and Utria pounded on it with a fist. Three strikes, each one with authority. The door opened a moment later. Aqi stood in the frame, her molten brown eyes surveying the two of them.

"Come in." She stepped from the frame, and the soldiers entered. Martian Flares in glass terrariums lighted the room, as well as a flashlight placed in a glass bowl. "We have surmised the reason for your visit," Aqi continued.

"The Hydras," Fleet interrupted, which earned him a glare from Aqi.

"It is our understanding that two members of Hydra Seven were found in the desert and you brought them in," Mertensia stated, or perhaps she asked.

"T-that is correct."

Four heads cocked when they heard the stutter. Luckily for Lago, his flushed cheeks were hidden by the darkness and his own skin tone.

"Where are they now?" Fleet asked, and gracefully ignored the impediment.

"In the cell block with the other prisoners," Lago answered, carefully enunciating each word this time.

"I believe there is a breaker in that hallway," Kilo supplied. "That is where the energy breach must have occurred."

Fleet nodded. "Then the prisoners are no longer our prisoners."

"Kill them," Aqi lilted. "Before they escape the compound and meet up with the other insurgents."

Utria and Lago both dipped their heads in a shallow bow and turned to depart.

"Wait." It was Fleet.

The soldiers turned in response.

"Collect an engineer on your way to repair the breaker."

Fleet's order was met by an incredulous hiss from Aqi. "We will send an engineer. Focus on killing the Hydra Seven survivors."

Mertensia and Kilo nodded in agreement and Fleet seethed internally.

Lago and Utria turned and this time left without further interruption. The sounds of their boots against the metal floor was the only sound as they navigated towards the jail cells. They had barely made it past two junctions before they spotted two lower class citizens walking with purpose towards the Halls of the Commanding Family. One was a woman with purple hair, and the other a dark skinned man, his face littered with asymmetrical patches of white. Both were striking individuals and didn't carry themselves like the plebeians.

"Those seeking refuge should head for the lower levels," Utria said in a steely tone.

Lago could tell by her voice that she did not trust the two individuals in front of them. Her suspicion was proved prudent a moment later when the woman lifted a gun and leveled it at the Shrikers. She didn't offer any warning before squeezing the trigger. Luckily, Lago and Utria had caught the movement and dove into the adjoining hallway. Both of them clicked their flashlights to douse the damning light. Lago pulled the strap of his rifle over his shoulder and ducked back into the hallway to return fire, but it was empty.

"Were those the prisoners?" Utria asked huskily.

"I've never seen them before," Lago answered as he stalked into the hallway. He primed his ear for the sound of footsteps but heard nothing of the sort. The Wyrms, Asia and Jackson, were still in the hallway.

"They're after the C-" Utria's sentence was cut short by a clap of gunfire. The shooter had aimed for her voice, and the bullet ricocheted off the wall the Shriker stood tucked behind.

The bullet bounced off the wall and grazed Lago's tricep and part of his back, but he made no sound. He had seen the flash of light from the conflagration of ignited gunpowder. Quick as lightning, he fired his own shot and heard a muffled cry in response as his bullet struck Asia. He dropped to the ground before his enemies could employ his own tactics.

Utria stepped from behind the corner and leveled her gun in the direction Lago had fired. Taking a risk, and putting faith in her comrade, she illuminated the hall with the flashlight. She heard a report of two gunshots, and fortunately didn't feel the teeth associated with the sound. Instead, she saw two slumped figures, the man with a rose of blood spreading across his chest, the woman with a rivulet of it running down her nose. Utria scanned the hallway without detecting Lago, before he stood and intercepted the beam and flicked on his own light.

"Good work," she complimented him. He nodded in answer, but she could tell by his smug look that his ego was swelling. "Now to find the rats you brought in."

His expression darkened and Utria allowed herself to smile this time.

Together they set off down the hallway like lions after a zebra. Lago was already at a deficit in the dark hall, his right eye clawed out by Dierde. He cursed himself for not having his way with her there and slitting her throat after. His weakness had always been beautiful women. He was aware of the sound of blood dripping from his arm and back and the soft patter as it hit the ground, accenting every so many strides. They descended two flights of grated stairs and crossed three sectors of the ship to reach the ground level.

The flashlight beams fell on the figures of a multitude of refugees, huddled in blankets in the dark tunnels. Voices of soldiers could be heard outside as gunfire continued to rain down. Occasionally the ping of metal on metal sounded as a bullet hit the exterior of the *Shrike*. Utria and Lago entered the cell block five minutes later and found the open door Dierde and Yuto had escaped from. Lago turned to one of the locked rooms still occupied and produced the key set from his belt. The first key was wrong, but the second unlocked the door. Each soldier in the Shrike Colonial Military had three keys, one to the barracks, prison block, and the armory.

Before he opened the door he gripped the light between his incisors and drew his gun. He pushed the door open and fired off three shots, killing the occupants. This earned him a disgusted look from Utria.

Terra Mortem

"What?" he demanded.

"What the fuck was that for?" the woman growled.

"We already have two escaped convicts. We don't need to add to the number. These already had a death sentence," Lago explained and turned down the hallway to resume the hunt.

The escapees would not be headed out past the refugees and would need another exit. His first assumption was past the hydroponic gardens and med bay. Either could have disastrous effects. If the power outage plagued the hydroponics as well, then the survival of the *Shrike* was already at stake. At least the molla could survive in the absence of photons.

When they arrived at the hydroponics, they found that it had not lost power. They also discovered that Lago's assumptions had been correct. With her molla darkened eyes, Dierde stuck out like a sore thumb. Yuto, Dierde, and Treya were nearly past the rows of stinking manure and the potatoes it grew when they heard the party crashers.

"I thought there were only two?" Utria asked as she leveled her gun at Yuto.

"Doesn't matter, the old bitch is complicit," Lago muttered as he too raised his rifle.

Before either of them could get a shot off, a body crashed into Utria, knocking her from her feet and knocking Lago off balance. His rifle skittered across the floor. Lago turned to confront the assailant, pulling a knife from his boot, when he recognized the man as one of the other Scout Lieutenants.

"Toledo?" he exclaimed, eyes wide with shock. Then he grinned a shark-like grin. "I'm gonna murder you."

Terra Mortem

Chapter Twenty-Five

The flames of the wicker gonis were nothing more than faint tongues of blue, clinging to the ashen mantle that once contained the bodies of many Greylings. The worshippers were nothing but mounds of dust and a few recognizable pieces that survived the fire's hunger.

The aerial dancers now barely moved, their arms outstretched and covered in a sheen of sweat while their eyes lolled listlessly in their sockets, looking everywhere and nowhere at once. Their legs pushed off the totem lazily and the blood no longer ran from the piercings on their chests. Instead, it was congealing and slowly dripping to the cavern bottom like thick teardrops. The music had ceased and the kowtowing Greylings turned their faces towards the floor and took up a rhythmic humming that reverberated against the rock.

The Exos dared not look up more than they already were, but they sensed that something terrible was about to happen. The air was tangible and carried an acrid taste. The beat of the drums slowly returned, though it was barely audible over the pounding of pulses in the throats of the trio of Hydras.

X

Rio came to suddenly when he heard the rock being lifted from his cage. He leapt to his feet, thinking to make a quick getaway, but the first light he had seen in days blinded him. To his light deprived eyes it seemed like the entire city was ablaze, though in truth it was only the hemoglobin of the impish moths. His view was obstructed by three of the largest Greylings he had ever seen. The first one struck him in the head with a club, rendering him gasping and barely conscious on his knees. The other two lifted him by the arms and hauled him to a hut on the edge of the city. Inside, were two more Greylings. The inside of their mouths and both eyelids glowed orange. Next to them sat two basins full of black spores. Herma floated in the air behind Rio, its distress apparent and very painful to its master. Despite his own dire circumstances, he hated to see the goni in this state.

The Greylings stripped him of his clothes, and he felt ensorcelled by the cold air in the room. Every hair on his body stood on end as gooseflesh rippled across his chest and arms. The Greylings that had brought him in began lashing his arms to his side with thick cords before he could protest. He turned to run, but fell to the ground as another length of rope was wrapped tightly around his thighs. He began to panic as Greyling hands started to rub molla spores over every inch of his body, feeling vulnerable as they applied gobs of the stuff indiscriminately. Rio thrashed against his bonds, but within minutes the drug had been absorbed into his

Terra Mortem

bloodstream and he felt oddly at peace. At least physically. His brain still struggled to understand his predicament. He was rolled over onto his stomach as his captors continued to slather him. He attempted to inchworm his way towards the door as Herma began to dive bomb the Greylings. They paid the creature no heed. One of the Greylings chuckled as Rio nosed his way closer to freedom. He felt hands grasp him, and like a felled tree they hoisted him onto their shoulders. Positioned face up he could see nothing of his surroundings, but became aware of a vibrating sound as they brought him closer to the center of the ceremony.

His thoughts inevitably drifted to Dierde. He wondered where she was, if she was alive, and whether or not she would miss him. At this moment he knew he would never see her again and she would never hear him say he forgave her. Tears brimmed and threatened to spill over, but he refused to die crying and blinked them away fervidly. Suddenly he was roughly placed on his knees. His heart hammered against his ribcage when he realized that he was at the edge of the lake. He could see the surface tension threatening to break as a monstrous beast swam towards the shore. Herma landed on his shoulder and he tried to shake the goni off him, to encourage it to fly away. He attempted to vocalize his demand, but his voice caught in his throat. Herma needn't die with him. The small creature met his gaze before staring stoically forward, accepting its fate.

Now tears fell down his cheeks, but Rio didn't care. He followed Herma's example and watched as his doom reared from the water in a spray of droplets. He stared into the massive goni's eyes and felt nothing but coldness. Its maw gaped open widely as it brought its face down to consume man and beast together.

Chapter Twenty-Six

Taiga, Lepiro, and Jarrod didn't bother to remain prostrate now. They rose to their feet, as if pulled by their tumultuous stomachs. They wanted to puke after seeing the gross spectacle. Taiga and Lepiro felt shock and grief mingle through their bodies as they watched the goni's neck bulge and their fellow hunter disappear down its gullet. Jarrod felt an overwhelming amount of pity, but more so, he was afraid for his life. Icharus, on Lepiro's shoulder, let out a warble of terror, and clutched tightly to his master's neck.

"We need to go," Lepiro whispered, and his companions looked around quickly.

None of the Greylings had risen from their positions, but were now murmuring prayers into the godless air. Taiga grabbed Lepiro's sleeve to get his attention and nodded fervently. The hunter turned to Icharus and whispered, "Take us home."

The goni seemed to understand. It took off silently and floated past row upon row of Greylings without making a sound. The Exos crept after it, and within minutes they were stalking through a deserted town. All of its members were paying homage to the beast in the lake. Once they were confident no one would hear them, they took off at a dead sprint. The sound of footfalls echoed a thousand times back at them, but no pursuer ever came.

Icarus' faint light led their way as they stubbed their toes on every rock and crevice fathomable, yet none were bold enough to let a peep split their lips. They reached the stairs without facing any adversary and bolted up the flight into the passageway.

"We need to find a place to rest," Jarrod said, his chest heaving.

Lepiro snorted derisively.

"He's right, if we don't rest now, we will have no energy to run when those creatures find us," Taiga argued.

"We don't even know if they will chase us," Lepiro hissed. "What we do know is that they will sacrifice us like they did Rio if they do."

Taiga closed her eyes and tried not to imagine the sound of Rio's bones crunching as his legs spasmed one last time. "We need to regroup. Even if it's just for a few minutes."

Finally, Lepiro assented. They found a suitable alcove and clambered inside. Lepiro pulled the pack off his back, and ushered Icarus inside, lest the Greylings spot his light. Without him the cavern was pitch black. Lepiro could no longer see his companions, despite the fact that he could feel one of their legs pressed against his. He waved his hand in front of his face, nothing. He moved it closer and closer, expecting to see a faint outline, but instead struck the tip of his nose. The air was musty and warm around him, and he could smell it deep in his sinuses. It was as if his nostrils had opened up more given his lack of vision. He could detect the faint odor of perspiration and differentiate between the scent of himself and his companions. Icharus murmured from within the bag, the noise seeming to echo back several times more than it should have.

Lepiro felt oddly at peace. His chest rose and fell rhythmically, the air tasted much more…flavorful than it did on the surface. Each breath held its own microcosm of tiny organisms waiting to explore a new world. He was amazed that he hadn't appreciated the nuances of this world until just now. It was like nothing he had ever experienced. In the pitch dark, nothing seemed to matter.

Then Jarrod broke the silence. "How long do you think we can stay here?"

"In this cubby, or alive?" Lepiro answered sardonically and snorted at his own joke.

"Probably not very long for either," Taiga said, and though the statement was a dismal one, her voice held a hint of humor.

"You're probably right." Jarrod sounded like he regretted his crusade to save the nomad colonies. "We are being hunted by the Shrikers, and….these other beings." He still wasn't comfortable voicing his hypothesis. A pathetic predicament after the recent revelation.

"If it wasn't for you, we would still be living in peace. Thirsty, but in peace," Lepiro said with a sigh, though there was no friction in his words.

"We would have died after leading a miserable life, without ever knowing that we had been lied to our entire lives," Taiga murmured.

"Our lot hasn't improved." Once again Lepiro snorted at his own joke.

"At least you are being agreeable now." Jarrod sounded truly despondent.

"How have we lived on this planet for three hundred years, and never known another race existed here?" Taiga asked the air, even though she knew it would yield no answer.

"It's been longer than that," Jarrod spoke up. "The best estimates have the *Shrike* crashing onto AE625 nearly a millennium past."

"Nobody knows how long we've actually been here?" Lepiro exclaimed, and his voice echoed back, "here, here, ere…..ere."

"Compared to Earth the day lengths vary with distance from the sun, and how long it takes for the planet to rotate on its axis, the length of its orbit arou-"

"I'm not an idiot," Lepiro growled.

"None of the clocks from Earth tell time accurately," Jarrod supplied, extending his hands to show that no offense was meant, but the gesture was lost.

"…Sorry."

It didn't sound genuine, but Jarrod accepted it.

The sound of dripping water punctuated the short silence that ensued.

Terra Mortem

"We still have to cross the lake," Taiga said absentmindedly. "We'll need to use the boats. If those things come after us, I'm sure they will move them."

"They can't know that we can't swim," Jarrod argued.

"Our faces gave it away, I know it. We were like children discovering something new. And besides, they know what's in the water. They know that we know as well," Taiga said, thinking about the distortion in the surface she had seen after being bitten by the moth-scorpion. Before she had thought it couldn't be a goni. Now she knew it couldn't be anything else.

"I can kill it with the handgun," Jarrod answered, and heard the clatter of metal a moment later. He groped in the darkness until he felt the barrel of the .40. He was amazed Taiga trusted him with it. But after all they had been through, how could she not? Now that Rio was dead, nobody was around to hate him.

He felt a hand settle on his thigh, he could only assume who it belonged to. Then he heard the sound of lips on lips and the hand moved up his thigh. It was the end of their worlds after all, there wasn't much else to do.

Chapter Twenty-Seven

Toledo scrambled across the floor of the hydroponics, trying to find his gun. He chided himself for dropping it.

"Utria, kill the Hydras," Lago hissed as he advanced on the turncoat, a knife gripped in his hand. He hadn't even gone for his rifle, he relished the violence. He pounced upon Toledo, and the knife flashed towards the man's neck, but he flung his head back and the blade cut into his collarbone. Lago raised the blade again while pressing Toledo to the hard metal floor. Twisting his body like a snake, Toledo rammed his knee into Lago's ribs, making him grunt and recoil.

Toledo shot his hand out towards the gun and wrapped his fingers around the grip, finding the trigger as he brought it around. He wasn't fast enough, and felt a boot slam into his face, but he refused to let the weapon slide from his hand. Lago's next move sent the knife slashing across Toledo's right hand, severing the tendons. The gun slipped back onto the floor.

Toledo cried out and struck the side of Lago's face with his good hand. A moment later he felt the knife penetrate his forearm, and all feeling in his left hand disappeared in a wave of pain.

He looked Lago in the eyes and only saw the face of a madman.

"You stupid son of a bitch." Lago laughed and plunged the dagger into Toledo's heart. Lago twisted the blade violently as Toledo squirmed his last. The Shriker stood up and wiped sweat from his forehead. Utria hadn't moved and the Hydras were gone.

"What are you d-doing?!" he exclaimed.

"Nothing. The Hydras have nowhere to go," she stated coldly. "We don't need to follow them into a trap. We need to regroup with the rest of the troops."

Lago nodded in reluctant agreement. Then a realization dawned on him. "Med bay is just beyond this. We can't let them destroy it."

Utria didn't let him finish the statement before she took off, sprinting in the direction the Hydras had gone. Three corridors later, they came upon a dire sight. Sparks flew from severed electrical cords, bags of intravenous fluids (a rare commodity, only to be used in dire situations), and donated blood were spread across the floor. The computer monitoring systems had also been destroyed, their screens smashed in. The current patients were now fit to be fed to the hungry molla. Abstor lay dead on the ground, a metal rod stuck through his neck. The pills manufactured from plant extracts and molla had been taken. There had never been very much of the pharmaceuticals, but they could ease the passing of a terminally ill Exo.

"Those bastards…" Utria breathed.

Secretly, Lago commended the Hydras for the haste of their destruction, though there was no respect behind his admiration.

"They won't be alive much longer," Lago commented and turned back the way he had come.

They came to the hall of refugees and found the army clamoring to prepare for battle. The refugees had long since been moved deeper within the *Shrike* to safety. Kilo stood directing soldiers while unrolling a map of the colony on a steel table. Utria and Lago ghosted to his side.

"Med bay is demolished," Lago said without introduction.

Kilo straightened immediately but managed to keep his shock and disappointment from his face. "We need med bay. Where's Abstor?" he demanded.

"Dead," Utria offered.

"His apprentices?" Kilo continued.

"Presumably hidden or taken captive," Utria answered.

"Find a squadron." Kilo didn't need further information. Once he dispatched the army, he would search for medical students who could tend to the wounded. "We are sending two forces out to flank the Hydras and positioned snipers on the upper levels of the *Shrike*. Panels are being removed right now. The Hydras are hiding in the peasant villages. We need to keep them away from the ship and the sand dingo pens and quarries. They can't ruin any more of our resources. And we'll need the sand dingos to replenish our food source since they released the gonis."

Utria and Lago turned briskly to join the fray.

"Wait," Kilo commanded. "Release fifteen of the dingos. The nomads are oddly attached to the livestock. It may distract them if they see their familiars being devoured."

The soldiers assented and as they exited the ship they opened the enclosure gate and counted the snuffling creatures. Once the allotted number had passed they slammed the entry shut. Lago had to use his whole weight to keep the sand dingos from exiting as Utria fastened the latch. Together they followed the tail of a regiment into the flurry of gunfire.

X

The three rovers came to a halt at the top of a dune. Rhea and Gana surveyed the scene before them. He stood to her right, so he could hear what she said. The *Shrike* was crawling with soldiers and Hydras alike. From her vantage point, Rhea could see both armies moving strategically, though the Hydra 'army' was nothing more than a sham. She could see how disorganized they were. They had never drilled in militaristic formations, and it was showing now. It was truly a paltry attempt at insurgency. Nonetheless, Rhea felt a pit in her stomach. She could only hope that her lover was unscathed.

"Gana, take seven scouts along the wall to the right above the quarries, I will take the other seven to the left. We can't allow them to flank the *Shrike* using the wall," Rhea ordered. "And disable the rovers before you leave them. We can't give the Hydras a way to escape."

"Disable them?" Gana was incredulous. She wanted him to ruin one of the only vehicles they had?

"Temporarily. Pull a main starter fuse or disconnect the battery. But make it quick." She indicated to seven of the soldiers. "You, with me." They loaded into a single rover, several of them hanging off the side in order to fit.

Rhea had supreme confidence in this mission, for none of the Hydras had been trained in using a gun. Facing an army of soldiers who had been using one since childhood would prove fatal.

The rover rendered useless to those without knowledge of vehicle maintenance, Rhea led her soldiers up the wall. Directly to the interior of the gate was a stairwell. It wasn't the best defensive placement, as any invaders who took the gate could take the wall, but by the time the parapets were constructed it was obvious that AE625 was desolate. It was evident now that the danger was their fellow Exos.

Rhea led the charge up the stairs and crested the wall, her gun drawn as she swept from one side of the wall to the next. None of the Hydras had thought to cover the gate, but then again it was doubtful any of them had known that Rhea had her unit beyond the perimeter. She moved silently, though the soldiers behind her made enough noise to grate on her nerves. They weren't loud per se, but loud enough that a trained ear like hers would have picked them up.

Creeping along the wall, her thighs burnt with the slight strain from keeping her head below the crenulations. Following the gently curving path of the wall, she saw the first Hydra, positioned so he could fire at the soldiers below him without them seeing him. She lightly squeezed the trigger before he had a chance to detect the danger. In a spray of blood he dropped to the ground without uttering a sound. Knowing the report from her gun would alert the other Hydras, Rhea prepared herself.

Sure enough, three more advanced on the Shrikers. Seeing their lack of training, Rhea pitied them. Truly, she felt no ill will for the nomads, other than the Elders who had tricked their own people. But Aqi was in danger, and no life was more precious. Before this war, Rhea had only taken three Exos' lives and she hated it every time. She was bound to duty, not violence.

The approaching Hydras fell in a hail of bullets, their bodies flailing from the impact each time. Rhea winced, she had been trained to kill and was good at what she did, but it turned her stomach with each body. She had never thought she'd actually be killing her fellow humans. Still, she had no personal or ethical crises. Whatever it took to ensure Aqi's wellbeing. She flexed her index finger again and another Hydra dropped.

Nine Hydras later, she saw Gana and his team closing the gap, no more adversaries between them. They turned their attention to the ground level and saw several Hydras staring up at them. Among them was Ellie. The look of desperation on their faces was unmistakable. Rhea paused long enough to make an observation. Several Hydras approached the old woman, Ellie, before hurrying back into the battle. She was clearly the leader. After seeing the wall taken by the Shrikers, she had taken cover.

"That lady is the leader. We need to take her out," Gana stated, and Rhea nodded, proud her lieutenant had noticed what she had.

"Leave your team on the wall for cover. Come with me and we will finish her." Rhea continued in a lower tone, "I only trust you with me."

Gana swelled with pride, but he hid it well. To Rhea's trained and calculated eye, it was obvious.

"I won't let you down," Gana said solemnly.

Rhea flashed her gold teeth. "If you do, I won't be alive to let you know you failed."

For that Gana had no answer, but followed Rhea down into the war zone after she barked a short command to the soldiers on the wall. Rhea's eyes scanned the crowd of Hydras as their concern grew. She didn't see Ellie though, and her *own* concern grew. Any threat to the *Shrike* was a threat to Aqi and Rhea's stomach twisted even more. She would murder every Hydra in cold-blood if it meant that Aqi was safe.

Next to her, Gana fired a spray of bullets into the crowd and a line of Hydras dropped. The Shrikers covering them from the wall couldn't deal with threats in their direct proximity for fear of misfiring. Rhea brought herself back to the present and gently squeezed the trigger and felt the recoil against her shoulder. Had the nomads not been leading a mutiny, Rhea might have shown them mercy. Instead, she mowed down another group. That was when she felt a round cut through the air next to her. The soldiers didn't know she and Gana were in the midst of the battle. She skittered to a defensive position behind the metal foundation of a hut. Gana followed her lead.

"Our own men will kill us before the Hydras manage any sort of an offense," Gana laughed. The remnant of his right ear and the scabs on his cheek were festering and oozing pus, lymph, and blood. He would need antibiotics, or more of his face removed to prevent the infection from spreading.

A snuffling creature barreled past Rhea and Gana's hiding place, its snout upturned as it hunted for gonis. There were enough of the symbionts floating in the air to confuse the dingo, but a moment later it took off in the right direction. Several gonis swooped from the air to nip at it, but it deftly flexed it quills and two of the gonis impaled themselves on the hollow hairs. A Hydra, the owner of one of the dead gonis, stepped in and hacked the poor sand dingo in half with an ugly machete. He raised the blade again to do unnecessary damage to an already dead creature when Rhea punched a hole through his chest with a well-placed shot. The man spat up blood for only a moment before crumpling in a pile of limbs next to the dead extraterrestrials.

"We can't let that woman get away from us. If she sneaks into the palace, there's no telling what she'd do in there," Rhea said as she reloaded. She still had plenty of rounds left in the magazine, but foresight is rarely regretted.

"You're thinking of the hydroponics and med bay?" Gana inquired.

"Uh, sure," Rhea said, flustered for just a moment. "Our people are in there too."

"Without water, food, or medicine, it doesn't matter how many we save," Gana said pragmatically.

Rhea chose not to tell him that she only cared about one. She nodded in assent instead.

Gana darted his head out from hiding, before recoiling as a spray of bullets hit the sand where he had just been. "There's a pile of clothes and metal scraps twenty yards we can get to," Gana reported.

"Did you see the woman?" Rhea inquired, her eye on the prize. No point in getting deeper entrenched in danger.

"No. But that's the direction she was headed in."

Rhea exhaled in alarm. "She's cutting around between the *Shrike* and the farms."

"Why would she do that? There's no entrance there," Gana argued.

"She's not trying to get into it. She's headed for the fuel cells." Rhea's eyes were wide as she realized the danger.

"Why would she do that? How would she know?" Gana still wasn't sold.

"She must have been a Hydra Elder. She's been here before," Rhea explained as she tried to formulate a plan.

"So she intends to kill all of us in this crater?" Gana shouted angrily, Rhea's poor prediction meant they would have to cross the entirety of the Hydra's insurgent camp.

"Not necessarily. The *Shrike* sits on the largest aquifer other than The Source. The sand is porous enough that it would suck the hydrazine right down into the ground water. She's planning to poison us all. You need to make it to the palace and make sure we pump as much water as possible so we don't die of thirst here. I'll take care of the coup leader."

"Careful." With that Gana left the protection of the hut and heard the pop of Rhea's rifle as she took out the Hydras close to him. He kicked up plumes of sand with each step, but in no time was approaching the wall. He easily grabbed the top of the barricade and agilely leapt over, hoping that his fellow Shrikers would recognize him as one of their own.

After he had disappeared from sight, Rhea focused on the task at hand. She took a deep breath and hoped the men on the wall would provide enough suppressive fire for her to reach Ellie without being killed.

Chapter Twenty-Eight

The airlock hissed and formed a tight seal. Treya groped at the door, yet it refused to budge. She heard a mechanical click and knew it was no accident. Someone had judicially held up their flight. They were trapped in the *Shrike*.

"What now?" Yuto exhaled, his eyes darting back and forth.

"We have to find another way," Dierde said as panic climbed up her throat.

Treya nodded solemnly and started back the way they had come, when two figures blocked their exit. Aqi's willowy frame stood several inches taller than any of the three Hydras, while Mertensia's shorter frame hovered a few feet back.

"Treya, you scoundrel." Aqi laughed easily, showing off her pearly incisors. "You had to know this wouldn't end well for you."

Like a cat, Yuto's muscles bunched as he prepared to spring. Aqi took another step closer to him before pulling a handgun level with his forehead. "It won't end well for you either if you continue to behave in this way."

"Won't it end poorly regardless?" Yuto growled from deep in his throat.

"We will need slaves to rebuild the damage you inflicted," Mertensia said sweetly. It was no inflection, simply how her voice sounded.

"Haven't we been slaves long enough?" Treya said angrily.

Dierde looked at her with disgust. This woman was choosing to take the high ground now?

"That's rich, coming from you," Aqi said flatly. Treya felt her face flush. "Don't worry though, you won't be around to witness your peoples' servitude this time. You knew of our impending rescue, why now? Why this revolt? It makes no sense. Did you want to inflict your revenge on us for misleading the Hydra Colonies? You have been wandering the desert for far longer than the current Family has been in control. We were making things right."

Treya had no answer this time. Dierde and Yuto felt waves of shock roll through their bodies. The rumor Rumo and Treya had told them, that they initially refused to believe, was true.

"You are so selfish!" Dierde exclaimed, her dark-rimmed eyes flashing dangerously. "You should have killed her, Yuto."

The old woman's head hung down in shame. She had let her people down again, and this would be her legacy. She looked up and met Aqi's gaze. "You are no more innocent than I am."

Aqi raised an immaculate eyebrow. "Even now, you refuse to take responsibility."

The thud of many booted-feet sounded in the hallway as the guards made their way to the airlock. "Cuff them. Once we collect the rest of the Hydras, these two can join them. The Elder is to stay in confinement."

The guards obeyed and Yuto and Dierde cooperated, the memory of being dragged through the halls battered and broken still fresh in their minds. Treya didn't put up much of a fight, what was a woman of her age really to do?

Just then a body slammed into the airlock door and shouted, "Open the damn door!" It was followed by three percussive knocks.

Mertensia glanced at Aqi for permission before pulling a remote control switch from her pocket. She pressed a button and the doors hissed open.

Gana burst in, beads of sweat framing his face. He didn't bother to introduce himself, but burst out, "The Hydras are going to poison the spring with hydrazine!"

"Are you fucking kidding me?" Aqi screamed. "Alert the engineers over the telecom. We need them to pump as much water as possible." In a moment's span she had regained her composure.

"That will cause a panic!" Mertensia countered.

"And panic we should," Aqi said coolly, then she turned to Treya. "You've killed us all."

"You three," Mertensia said, indicating to half of the number of guards they had summoned. "Go stop them."

"Rhea's on it," Gana managed to say, winded as he was.

Treya noted the stricken look on Aqi's face that passed as soon as it came on. Seeing that was almost worth whatever punishment was to come. Then she saw the fire in the woman's eyes and realized she was wrong.

X

The alarm sirens sounded from the *Shrike* and Rhea knew Gana had done his job. She had skirted the Hydra camp successfully and could see Ellie fiddling with the fuel lines on the ship. She leveled her rifle to take aim but cursed the effort. She wasn't a chemist and didn't know how reactive hydrazine was. She did know that within the tank was a mixture of liquid and gas, constantly shifting between one phase and the other, though the majority of it was liquid. The gas was more combustible and she was not trying to massacre the only Exos on AE625. She lowered her weapon and took off at a dead sprint. She could smell the ammonia scent coming from the tank before she saw the fluid spilling from it. Two more lines were severed, and even more fuel greedily slurped up by the sand. She pumped her arms faster, and her legs heeded the demand but it was all for naught. She couldn't see what piece of equipment Ellie had disconnected, but gallons dumped out like a deluge. The sand was transformed into mud.

Terra Mortem

Ellie turned in time to see the butt of the rifle smash into her face. She crumpled to the ground, dead or unconscious, Rhea didn't care. She frantically looked for any way to salvage what little fuel they had left, and to prevent it from contaminating the groundwater. Ellie had done good work and used a knife. Rhea had neither the tools nor the knowledge of how to repair the tanks and lines. She coughed as her throat began to feel scratchy, her eyes itching as well. She leaned over and gagged as bile rushed her lips. A severe pain wracked her stomach and she knew she had to get out of the toxic substance pooling around her. She grabbed Ellie and hoisted her onto her shoulders, ignoring the blisters forming on the back of her hands. She could only imagine what the exposure was doing to her lungs.

She staggered towards the same airlock Gana had entered through, her lungs burning and her legs moving as if tied together. She teetered back and forth, back and forth, on her way to the door. Her breath felt hot and stung her mouth. She tasted blood. She debated dropping Ellie and carrying on without her, but she wouldn't give the woman a chance to come to and escape. Three indistinct shapes approached her as she collapsed. Two of them attended to her, while the third grabbed Ellie by her ankles. Rhea's vision swam as she felt a blast of cool air, she was inside the *Shrike*. She felt familiar hands frame her face a moment later.

"Aqi," Rhea said and smiled, right before she blacked out.

Ethan Proud

Chapter Twenty-Nine

In the control room, Kilo, Fleet, and Mertensia were gathered with the lead engineers. Aqi was in med bay with the surviving apprentices, tending to Rhea's wounds. Fleet noted this sourly, but he had bigger fish to fry. There were six lead engineers. The only one he had ever dealt with was Johan, in charge of the aquifer construction and water works. The engineer's nickname was Drips, referring to the constant shortage in The Wreckage. No matter what, the flow of water ceased in some quadrant of the ship, or at some spigot for the peasants, and only a steady drip continued. As such Johan was not popular with the commoners, despite his irreplaceable nature. Everyone thought they knew how to run the colony, but in truth their ideas were outdated and had been tried and failed. On the other hand, it had been decades since a Shriker died of thirst or fed their aborted fetus to a goni. Fleet smirked, they should try to live with the Hydras for a month and see if they would still carp on about their shining gem of a city.

"What's the status of the water supply?" Fleet inquired, and Johan's face darkened.

"According to these charts," he said, pointing at three monitors, "holding tanks, three, five, and seventeen have lethal amounts of hydrazine contamination at six ppm. Holding tanks one, two, four, and eight are ingestible and have no readable levels of hydrazine. The remaining thirteen tanks are reading four to seven ppm and will be carcinogenic. We didn't get the pumps shut off until tanks three, five, and seventeen were in the red."

"How long can the clean tanks support our population?" Kilo asked from beneath a furrowed brow.

"Each tank holds two hundred gallons. None of them are at full capacity, and we have three hundred and thirty gallons of drinkable water. Our last census counted us at seven hundred and sixty-four, with approximately five hundred Shrikers in The Exodus. If that number is stagnant, which is highly unlikely, then we have twelve hundred and sixty-four mouths to feed, er drink. Everyone needs roughly thirty-two ounces per day to survive." Johan ran the math quickly. "If we supply the Hydras with the water they need… that's one day. We have one day of clean water."

Kilo ran a hand over his scalp in irritation. "You're suggesting we cull the Hydras?"

"It's not off the table," Fleet quickly interjected. He knew that even if the Hydras were removed, they would only have two days of water. "What if we send teams out to the Hydra Spring locations?"

"We don't know how far the aquifer beneath us spreads, they could all be attached. There is a possibility that none of them would be safe in regards to chronic exposure," a different engineer supplied.

"We can't just kill the Hydras. We need to save face. The coup leaders, yes. Public execution." Mertensia began pacing as she mulled her thoughts over. "We can supply the Hydras with the toxic water, distribute the tainted water to the commoners, and stockpile the rest for ourselves, the army and essential personnel."

"Devious, but wise," Fleet said and rubbed his thumb and forefinger across his chin. "But that plan doesn't divert any water for the hydroponics. We will need food, and molla need water. The vegetables we can live without, and our gonis are gone. We will have to eat the dingos and harvest immediately."

"Are the hydroponics contaminated?" Kilo turned to Johan.

"Our charts don't indicate anything of the sort."

"We aren't staying here. We'll die if we do, and every second we stay lowers our chances of survival," Mertensia interjected. "Tomorrow we execute Ellie and Treya, but today we make preparations for the Second Exodus."

"To where?" Fleet bristled with aggravation.

"The Source."

Chapter Thirty

The entirety of the population of The Wreckage gathered in front of the palace. A crude scaffolding had been placed between two uprights and a parallel bar that ran across their tops. Two nooses hung limply in the breeze. The crowd was silent, but the palpitation of excitement ran through them like electricity. The Hydras who had managed to escape the onslaught of the Shrikers were sequestered away from the rest of the colony, their hands and feet bound, while guards patrolled them.

The Commanding Family exited the palace doors and stood on a pulpit next to the gallows, while the Hydra Coup leaders were brought forward by Gana and Lago. Neither of the aged women revealed the fear they felt. They stoically met the gazes of the crowd.

Fleet stepped forward and raised a hand to bring attention to himself. "My people, we opened our doors to the Hydras in an act of hospitality and kindness, and they returned the favor with slaughter. We cannot damn an entire population for the actions of their leaders. However, those leaders responsible for the destruction of our beautiful city must be condemned to death. It is without pleasure that I deliver this punishment. Ellie of the Wyrms and Treya of Hydra Seven, you are hereby sentenced to death."

Terra Mortem

Gana and Lago helped their respective prisoners onto the chairs while lowering the noose over the Elders' heads. Both of them had a sour expression on their faces. Killing in war was different, but this felt wrong and disgusting. But it was the bidding of the Commanding Family and they had to obey. Fleet nodded and the two soldiers exchanged glances, hesitating for a moment. Before either of them could kick the supports from beneath the Hydra women, the chairs screeched backwards as the women tilted forward, choosing to end their lives themselves rather than relegating themselves to the will of the Commanding Family. Gana turned his back to the scene and covered his face with a hand while the crowd roared in sickening appreciation.

The faces of the Commanding Family were stony, their thoughts darkened by the prospect of their colony surviving. They had to march across the desert and fight for the resources to survive. The satellite comms systems wouldn't work if they were pulled from the mainframe of the *Shrike*. The engineers were working on jury-rigging a rover to provide the necessary connection with Earth 2.0, but it wasn't looking promising. In only a few months they would need to send scouts back to The Wreckage to wait for the ark that would bring them to salvation. The fate of the subterranean civilization of Greylings could only be genocide.

X

Dierde and Yuto alone did not see the execution. They were locked up in the same cell they had been in only a day before. Little was said between the two of them as they tried to process the events of the past weeks. They had been duped by their Elders, their colony slaughtered, they had lost their gonis, and now a chance for escape from AE625. Everything they thought to be true, was false. With Treya killed, they were the last known survivors of Hydra Seven. It was a depressing sentiment. And now they were enslaved, technically for the second time, but they had been ignorant of their first indentured status. Yuto flexed his knuckles and heard the satisfying pop. He did it two more times before he heard a sharp exhale from Dierde.

"What?" he demanded.

"Rio used to do that, despite my telling him how much it annoyed me. I miss him." Dierde stared at the ceiling.

"I miss him too. But he's dead. You know that," Yuto said, and watched as a single tear rolled down Dierde's cheek, followed by a steady stream.

She sniffled, but didn't sob. "You know he wouldn't give up on us that easy."

"If he is alive, but we need to focus on our survival now or we'll never be reunited." Yuto decided to go with a little bit of optimism.

"We're about to be enslaved. We need to escape," Dierde said, and was brought back to the night they made the escape pact in the tent. "I wish we had molla."

"That would take the edge off," Yuto mused. Thinking of taking the edge off, he eyed Dierde's long legs stretched out before her. Her well-toned muscles protested against her garment, showing off more of their shape than Yuto could handle. He shook his head, she loved Rio and he had no right to even think those thoughts.

"Where do you think Aileen and Dierde got off to?" Dierde asked, meeting his gaze.

"Probably cavorting in some caves, gorging on molla. I doubt they even miss us anymore," Yuto said with a lighthearted laugh.

The comment stung Dierde a little, she felt like she was missing a part of her soul. "I hope you're right. The thought of them in any anguish is too painful." Another tear rolled down her cheek.

Yuto watched as the droplet clung to her jaw before dropping onto the floor. He felt his own eyes begin to water and tried to blink back the grief. Little good it did.

"How'd we get into this mess?" He laughed weakly before he felt his tears. Dierde returned the laugh and reached out her hand, which he took. Together they cried. They cried for hours, until their bodies had nothing left to give and they fell asleep, hand in hand. It wasn't even midday, but they slept for hours.

X

Across the camp, the other Hydras were not faring as well. They had been corralled into the empty goni pen and meager rations were distributed to them by the guards. They each were given two molla caps and a tomato. The fruit possessed some of the most vibrant flavors they had ever tasted, both tart and sweet, which they had never experienced before and thus could not describe, unless they called it euphoric. At least the Shrike Colonial Military had given them plenty of water. Fifty-five-gallon-drums with the lids removed sat in the enclosure, each one brimming with the liquid. They took turns, greedily slurping from the ladles provided. The water had a metallic tang to it, but nonetheless it was refreshing. All the water in the Hydra Camps was gritty with sand and wore down their molars. This was undeniably clean, the closest thing to distilled water they had ever tasted. Perhaps living in the Original Colony wouldn't be so bad. Sure, they would have work to do, but none of them were unaccustomed to labor.

Despite the baking sun at their backs a chill crept up the spine of every Hydra who partook of the water, that is to say, all of them. It felt refreshing though. Sweat beaded at their foreheads as the fever began to run and the cold dug deeper into their bones. Their eyes itched, as well as their throats down into their bellies,

Terra Mortem

and they coughed up fluid and crawled along the ground with trembling hands.

One man began seizing, his body twisting violently as foam frothed at his mouth. His innards were wracked with another bout of pain and he evacuated his bowels right into his pants. He was dead. It didn't take long before the other Hydras began bemoaning their symptoms, clawing at the cage that trapped them amongst each other.

The guards tucked their humanity away and watched with the indifference of war as the Hydras began dying, some going easier than others. Only the police and palace guards were patrolling the Hydra Pens, the scouts dispatched to collect samples from the Hydra Aquifers, while the infantry was running drills. It wouldn't be long before they were plunged into another war, this one on unfamiliar terrain.

As they had been instructed, the guards made a show of calling the medical teams to check on the welfare of their new slave population. Then they began pressing the spectating Shrikers back, shouting instructions.

"This is a quarantine area!"

"We need to make sure you don't get infected."

"Ma'am, you need to go to med bay."

"Take your son with you."

"You, get away from there."

When the last Hydra stopped seizing and their veins shone blue and their chests settled, masked men began hauling bodies to the quarries and dumping them. Six hundred and forty-eight bodies later, the only Hydras left in the city were Dierde and Yuto. Mertensia's plan had worked, now any Shriker who died of chronic toxicity would blame it on the sickness brought by the Hydras. With any luck, the onset would begin before the Earth 2.0 ship arrived to save them, but after they had taken the Greyling settlement.

The theatrics of the guards and medical staff were truly impressive. They had been briefed on the new mission to The Source, and the sacrifices that had to be made. The only objection to it was from the soldiers who frequented the commoner brothels, though they had the good sense not to mention it aloud. Most of the soldiers at some point had visited one of the establishments, some more often than others.

The shock from the carnage wrought by the Hydras had yet to wear off; add the public execution, and top it off with a mysterious illness, and the result was a population of numb Shrikers. With the looming Exodus and Greyling War, it would be months before the Exos had proper time to process the events and grieve for their old lives.

Standing in the airlock near med bay and the hydroponics, a pale figure stood next to another darker form. Rhea had recovered well enough to move around, though sudden movements still made her nauseous and her breath rattled from pulmonary edema. Her greenish pallor was accentuated by her lover's dark skin. Rhea appeared as the personification of death, while Aqi looked as if a god had graced the surface of the lonely planet. Her arms were bare as she basked in the sun while Rhea was wrapped in an emergency blanket and still shivered. Her Mohawk was messy and hung to one side, both the purple and red washed out and faded, showing her roots and her natural hair color, black. She leaned on Aqi for support.

"You know that the other Family members will be upset if they see us like this," Rhea said as her teeth chattered in their sockets.

"They can pound sand," Aqi said with a smile. "Why should we hide anymore? Our position of power is precarious and you, being on the Council of Warchiefs, have more true power. You control the army. If the army decides that the time of the Commanding Family is over, there is nothing we can do."

"Are you suggesting another coup?" Rhea asked incredulously.

"No, but if push comes to shove, we can insulate ourselves. Our love has never been safer," Aqi said and felt Rhea snuggle closer under her arm. Probably simply because she was cold.

"Even though our existence hinges on surviving a suicidal march across the desert," Rhea scoffed. Always the pragmatist.

"To stay here is suicide. Ellie and Treya managed to screw everything up. I still don't see their end goal. I could see such angsty behavior from the youth but from the Hydra Elders? Ridiculous," Aqi mused.

"The Hydra Elders are scum," Rhea said heatedly. "They've watched their own people suffer knowingly, all for personal gain. The entire Hydra Movement was wrong and disgusting, but for those within the Colonies to subject their people to such miserable lives, it sickens me. I pity the Hydras who didn't know better."

Aqi pursed her lips. Though she knew that it had been centuries before her birth, she still felt responsible for the Hydras poor living conditions. In reality, the Commanding Family could have done something but altering the status quo was always risky. "We are no better. We've all known about the wandering nomads and done nothing."

"Out of sight, out of mind." Rhea laughed. "I never said we were innocent. But we didn't watch it every day with casual indifference."

Aqi squeezed her tighter. Rhea was right, but she was also wrong. Choosing not to help their fellow Exos but benefitting from their pains was equally despicable. Either way, Aqi and the Commanding Family had to live with their choices. Their constituents followed orders and that was it. Jarrod was to be commended in all honesty, he had followed his moral compass and tried to bring the Hydras out of exile. He had a good heart, Aqi realized, despite that the destruction of The Wreckage was a cascade event, started by his good intentions. Aqi snorted humorously.

"What?"

"We should have done what Jarrod did years ago," Aqi said wryly.

Ethan Proud

Chapter Thirty-One

Beneath the surface, the three survivors of Hydra Seven wearily crawled from their hiding place. Their cramped muscles cried out for joy as they finally stretched after what could have been mere hours or days. Without the sun to track it, time meant little. The Exos operated like animals, waking when rested and sleeping when tired. It was a glorious existence, only worried about survival. They didn't need a purpose to justify their existence, the will to be was enough.

Their eyes had only slightly adjusted to the darkness, or at least it seemed like they could detect shapes. Lepiro wordlessly opened his bag and Icharus crooned as he flew out, illuminating the cavern. As he flew, his body was reflected by the lake that spread out before them. The boats still rested on the near shore.

The Greylings hadn't pursued their runaway captives. Whether it was from apathy or an appeased god, it was hard to say. The boats rocked gently as the three stepped in and fumbled around for the oars. The first blade to break the water seemed loud enough to echo back to the Greyling City and herald their departure. Yet after the paranoia of being hunted and the anxiety of sharing Rio's fate subsided, the hair on the back of their necks lay flat and they continued across the lake. Icharus idled just before the boat like a lantern. His small reflection grew in size as something came from the depths.

Icharus veered out of the way and crashed into the water as a goni the size of a horse broke the surface. The molla boat rocked, threatening to throw its occupants into the lake. The goni's skin seemed to swirl like oil and trapped the light within its body. It continued to rise sinuously until its tail flicked clear of the surface tension in a spray of droplets. Lepiro was at the prow of the boat and struck the thing with his oar, but little good it did. The lake goni's eyes settled on Icharus and it gave chase as its much smaller counterpart darted around the boat in figure eights.

"Jarrod, shoot it!" Taiga shouted as the Shriker began fumbling with the .40 cal in his belt. He brought it level and squeezed the trigger. The bullet found its intended target and ripped the creature between the head and the neck, and it fell to the surface with a loud slap. The body didn't sink for several long seconds as water pooled over the flat expanse of its wings. With a gurgle, the corpse was pulled to the benthic.

Icharus wasted no time returning to his companion's side. It wasn't a graceful return either. The frightened creature slapped into Lepiro's face and wrapped his wings around the man's head, nearly suffocating him. Lepiro laughed a muffled sound as he unglued Icharus from his face. He held him in his lap for a second and ran a finger gently from the length of the goni's nose to tail. The creature warbled as its breathing slowed from its frenzied pace. Taiga felt a sharp pain in her chest as she recalled that she would never again share a moment like that with her familiar. A still silence settled over the lake as the echo of the gunshot faded away into nothingness. Not even a ripple remained to bear testimony.

"There might be more," Jarrod said, looking over the water with darting eyes. It seemed like lights had appeared and the surface tension bowed as gonis surrounded the boat. Or were his eyes playing tricks on him. He blinked furiously, trying to convince his brain to show him the truth.

"We need to get off this lake," Taiga said, her voice sticky. The moving lights were not a trick of the mind.

Without further ado, the trio began paddling as fast as they could. They weren't very good at it. The boat would twist one way too far, and then too far the opposite direction. Each time they tried to correct course they nearly capsized. The other lake gonis disappeared only meters from the boat, presumably to fight over the carcass at the bottom. The turmoil of their conflict was evident as waves and bubbles churned. The Exos took advantage of the temporary reprieve and rowed faster than before.

A smaller goni, chased away from the scavenged kill, rose lazily to the surface. Its dark eyes lit when it saw the struggling boat. It slowly propelled itself closer, only the top of its head and spine visible. Jarrod spotted it and raised the gun again. Dipping its head, the goni dove beneath the boat and out of sight. A moment later it breached on the other side, and before Jarrod could aim, it ducked back beneath the vessel. With an experimental bump, the goni sent the craft spinning like a top and thrashing through the water. Its luminescent skeleton was visible just inches below the water. It made a quick circle before heading back to ram the boat just a little harder this time.

Taiga and Lepiro hadn't stopped rowing, and with only two of them it was much easier to keep the rhythm. They could begin to detect the far shore, growing nearer. With their limited eyesight, distance was hard to gauge, but they couldn't have been more than twenty-five feet out. The crack of gunfire sounded, and the goni and its glowing cartilage blinked out of existence. The sound echoed back many times, and with each rebound another goni surfaced. Taiga and Lepiro didn't have to look directly at the gonis to know they were in trouble. So many of the creatures had surfaced that the cavern was aglow. Like alligators surrounding a single pig struggling to stay afloat, the gonis lazily closed in.

Droplets of spray flecked the boat each time the oars dipped into the water and once again when they broke the surface. The boat bucked violently, but on course nonetheless. Jarrod fired another shot and another of the amphibious beings sank. He checked the clip. He had five rounds left. He lurched forward as the prow of the boat connected with solid land and fumbled in the bottom of the boat, looking for the clip he had just held. His fingers closed around it, amid a pool of water. Hopefully the gunpowder wasn't wet, but luck hadn't been on his side lately.

With a scream a goni erupted from the water. Its jaws led the way. Jarrod squeezed the trigger and was greeted with a latent 'click'. A hand closed around the nape of his shirt and yanked him from the boat, and the goni missed and smashed its face against the rock beneath the vessel. Lepiro half-dragged Jarrod to the shore and down the nearest tunnel. Behind them, the lake was a writhing mess of wings and tails as the gonis devoured their injured kin. The Exos had been forgotten for the time being.

The reprieve lasted for only a moment before the screeching of the hunters reached their ears.

Chapter Thirty-Two

"What about these two?" a guard asked and jabbed a finger at the glass window of the cell. "Are they Hydras?"

The Commanding Family glanced amongst their ranks for a brief moment. They had forgotten about Dierde and Yuto when they culled the nomads.

"Kill them," Mertensia said absentmindedly. Her only concern now was reaching The Source and orchestrating the return journey for the rescue by the Second Earthlings.

"Don't be so barbaric," Aqi disagreed. "These two are from Hydra Seven, we massacred their village and they had barely escaped their cells when the rebellion was put down. They can serve us."

"What do you mean?" Mertensia said crossly.

Kilo and Fleet rolled their eyes as the women argued.

"They can literally serve us," Aqi said with a leer.

"Servants. So be it," Fleet said dramatically. Now the other three rolled their eyes. "Put them in restraints and load them into our royal rover."

The guard nodded and the Commanding Family left to oversee the rest of the last-minute preparations.

X

The rover jostled and Yuto's face thudded against the headrest twice. His hands were bound to the roll cage directly overhead. Dierde was likewise indisposed. There were seven available seats in this rover, all facing inward, and all but one occupied, not including the driver and shotgun seats, taken by two of the palace guardsmen. The Commanding Family made light conversation while passing around a large bowl filled with boiled molla caps, tomatoes, corn, and cooked squash. Yuto refused to look at the scrumptious food, despite his mouth watering to the brink of drooling.

"Once you've removed the dark looks from your faces, we will release you and you can partake in this food," Fleet said with a voice laced with generosity.

Yuto didn't grace him with a response.

"If only the same courtesy had been extended to our people," Dierde said dryly.

Kilo chuckled at the comment, which earned him a glare from the Hydranian woman.

"You'll come around eventually," Kilo said with assurance.

Yuto still refused to speak and Dierde gave up. They didn't make a single noise for many more hours. The Commanding Family took no notice.

"Are we positive that none of the radios will work to reach the Second Earth ship?" Fleet asked as he popped a cherry tomato into his mouth.

"Drips assured us that they would not," Kilo answered.

"Don't use such a vulgar nickname. It's not becoming of our status," Fleet said with mock sincerity.

"Don't play coy, when it was you who started it," Kilo said and elbowed Fleet lightly.

He almost dropped the bowl, but instead passed it to Aqi.

"Johan pulled the satellite comms from the mainframe and is trying to boost its signal by wiring into one of the rovers," Aqi answered. "But as he said, without a powerful enough antenna the signal will never leave the atmosphere, and certainly will not penetrate the rock that will be overhead when we reach The Source."

"So we leave the rover outside, and a team of engineers to monitor communications," Fleet said and gestured with his hands vaguely. "It will work. It must."

"That is when things tend to not work," Mertensia said as she fished through the salad to pick her favorite vegetable, squash.

"With that attitude, nothing will work," Fleet waxed philosophically. The other three snorted.

"We will make it off of this planet one way or another," Kilo supplied.

Aqi absentmindedly left the conversation and her mind wandered to Rhea. The Warchief was finally starting to look less peaked and claimed that she felt stronger. Strong enough to drive a rover. Aqi let out a titter of a laugh.

"What?" Fleet asked suspiciously.

"Thinking to myself," Aqi said with a smile. The look in Fleet's eyes suggested he knew damn well what Aqi had been thinking about. Let him, once they had been rescued or were forever stranded at The Source, the time of the Commanding Family would be over. It would be Aqi and Rhea's time.

The vehicle jolted to a halt and snapped Aqi from her pleasant reverie. Immediately the sound of squabbling and chaos erupted.

"Stay in here," one of the palace guardsmen said as he opened the passenger side door and stepped into the sand.

Fleet, Kilo, and Mertensia tried to see through the windshield and craned their necks without getting out of their seats.

"As if," Aqi said as she flowed from the vehicle. Despite crawling over the two shackled servants, she was quite graceful.

It didn't take her long to see what the matter was. One of the rovers towing a trailer full of water sank into the sand, resulting in it tipping and spilling its precious contents. The water drained through the greedy sand in seconds, while what was left on the surface evaporated in just as little time. The guards had managed to save some of the water by righting the containers but only a few gallons remained in each. Around the wrecked rover stood a crowd of commoners, yelling and shaking fists at the men who had just wasted their precious resources.

Terra Mortem

Aqi made out the number '16-21-18-5' and she sighed. It was the uncontaminated barrels that had been lost. The number was a code, not a very cryptic one, and likewise the drums fouled with hydrazine were marked '4-9-18-20-25'. If only those had been lost instead. The guards were trying to de-escalate the scenario, with little success. Their attempts to calm the crowd only infuriated it. Aqi parted those seeing red and stepped between the soldiers and the plebs.

"We can't get the water back. It has been taken by the sand, like so many things in our lives. Our only choice now is to hasten to The Source, where we will have enough water to last the rest of our lives. But if we hesitate now or fight amongst ourselves, we will never make it." She surveyed the crowd as she spoke. Initially, she had to shout to be heard, but as she continued the din lessened until all she saw was nodding heads. "Help right the rover, and we will be on our way once more."

She drifted back towards her rover, not looking over her shoulder when she heard the groan of metal and the hiss of sand. As heavy as the vehicles were, many hands made for light work. Inversely, they also ruined soup. But the only soup she could think of currently was the three Family Members who hadn't stepped from the safety of their militaristic palanquin. She stepped back into the rover. "Crisis averted."

Ethan Proud

Chapter Thirty-Three

Rhea sat in the passenger seat, while Gana drove. A strange dynamic shift, but after the first two hours it was clear that Rhea lacked the stamina. The bags beneath her eyes had an oily sheen and her skin was yellow. Just a little exertion had her looking like a corpse. In the back, Lago, Utria and four other soldiers rode in relative silence.

"What do the other chieftains think of this?" Gana asked after several minutes stretched nigh an hour.

"If I had asked, then perhaps I would know. But since the other chieftains answer to me, I did not," Rhea answered darkly.

Gana chuckled. His counterpart smirked slightly.

"So are you two, like, t-together?" Lago asked, his gaze shifting from one to the other. His good eye settled on Gana's mutilated ear and he pensively touched his now blind eye.

Rhea and Gana laughed and bit their tongues to ignore the stutter.

"Not a chance," Gana said easily, and Rhea managed to stop laughing.

"Harsh," Lago said as he watched for Rhea's reaction.

"He doesn't have the right hardware for the job," Rhea chuckled. It took Lago a moment to catch on, but when he did, he simply said "Oh".

"Anyhow, back to the subject at hand. The chieftains will follow whatever orders I give them. And for now, this sojourn is our peoples only hope," Rhea stated.

"And if it wasn't?" Gana pried.

"Then we never would have left." Rhea had resumed all seriousness after the banter.

"Do Jorgen, Dmetri, and Jana know that you talk like this?" Gana laughed. Being a member of the scouts, he felt comfortable joking with his superior about the heads of the other branches.

"If you were privy to our meetings, then you too would know who runs the *Shrike*. Ran, I guess," Rhea corrected.

"I think everyone knows who thinks they run it though," Gana said, before both he and Rhea said, "Fleet."

"The old windbag will realize soon enough. Now that the structure of The Wreckage has crumbled and the system that has stood in place for a millennium will no longer work, real leaders will have to step up to ensure our survival."

"Are you talking about another rebellion?" Lago asked incredulously.

"No, I'm talking about the natural order taking over. We are about to go to war with a species we know nothing about. Not everyone has the strength to lead in war," Rhea explained, and Gana nodded.

Around them, droves of shuffling commoners walked. Dust and grit kicked into the air behind them leaving a wake that reached all the way back to their abandoned ship. It had been the only existence they had ever known, and now they would have to fight for the chance to live long enough to escape the dead planet.

"And you think you're the one to do it?" One of the other soldiers joined the conversation.

"Nobody ever accomplishes anything alone," Gana snapped, illustrating his point perfectly.

"I think we will be surprised when we discover who speaks for the Shrikers when the Second Earthling ship arrives," Utria said.

Rhea twisted and pointed at the woman with her right index finger. "That is the attitude that is going to keep us alive."

Another rover pulled up along their right. Jana, the Captain of the Police, honked brazenly on the horn twice before speeding by to the front of the column.

"And that's the attitude that is going to get us killed," Gana mused.

"She is a glorified bully," Utria sniffed. "All she does is catch petty criminals."

"Excuse me?" Gana said, twisting around to look at Utria.

The woman looked terrified. "Did I say something wrong?"

Rhea scoffed at her boldness. She clearly didn't see the familial relationship between her second and the Police Chieftain. Both had strong noses and jawlines. Nor did Utria note the careful consideration of the spelling of the names Gana and Jana. Gana turned so he was facing forward again, but didn't grace Utria with an answer.

"They're s-siblings, you idiot," Lago whispered, and Utria blanched.

"Your apology is unnecessary," Gana said with a smug look.

The rover erupted in laughter, though it would be the last time any Shriker had a reason to laugh in a long time. With the loss of most of their clean water, there were very few reasons for mirth at the current moment. Rhea's throat was dry and felt parched no matter how much of the liquid she consumed. Now that her only option was to continue to poison her already weakened body, her chances for survival were slim unless they managed to take The Source quickly. There had never been a true war waged by the Exos though, and the Council of Warchiefs had never put their theories into practice. Laying siege to a species of cave-dwellers on their own turf was surely a recipe for a disaster.

Rhea pulled a small bag of molla caps and dipped a finger into the blackened spores. Generously, she passed them around the car and held out a gob on her fingertip so Gana didn't have to take his hands off the wheel. Their collective spirits rose, though it was only short-lived. The fight of their lives was coming whether they were ready or not.

Chapter Thirty-Four

They had to be getting closer to the surface, Taiga speculated. She couldn't voice her concerns aloud, as the sound of wing beats and suction cups were heavy in the air. The gonis were close. The three Exos were hidden away in a field of stalactites and stalagmites. Taiga couldn't remember the last time she breathed easily. Or had heard her companions exhale. She could, however, hear her pulse surge through her veins laced with adrenaline. Her palms sweated, and her clothes stuck to her body. She saw a trace of light as a goni floated nearer their hiding place.

On all fours she began to creep away. Lepiro noticed first and was right on her heels. Literally, for twice he accidentally grabbed her Achilles tendon instead of a rock. Jarrod shuffled along behind them. He had never needed to be quiet or work his muscles quite like the nomads had, and as such he was feeling the strain now. He felt gritty dirt covering his hands and neck, under his nails and in every crevice. He was beginning to wonder if they would survive their flight from the Greyling City. Or whether it had been worth it. They hadn't been certain they would be the next sacrifices, or when the next sacrifice would be…but now they were certain the gonis would devour them as soon as they caught them. At least they had the illusion of safety with the Greylings.

Terra Mortem

The squelch of goni suckers scuttled across the cavern ceiling above them, heralding yet another hunter closing in. *Qech, qech, qech. Qech, qech, qech.* Lepiro turned his eyes slowly skyward and saw the creature sinuously carve a path around rock formations without paying them heed. Suddenly it dropped from the ceiling, the wind whistling past its wings masking the sharp inhales of the Exos. They were not the intended prey however, and the beast collided with an airborne goni and ripped it from flight. The two creatures struggled on the ground, snapping at each other's soft bodies, tearing away crescent shaped pieces of flesh. More gonis flocked to the cannibalism, leaving the Exos with a route for escape. They wasted no time leaping to their feet and sprinting to the tunnel that they were sure led to their salvation.

They turned the corner and heard the flapping of demon wings in their wakes. Escaping the gonis seemed impossible now, but then a sliver of light appeared.

X

After the sojourn across the desert, tensions were high. No one could explain the pain in their bellies other than blaming it on hunger, but they had plenty of food. None but the Commanding Family and the soldiers knew they were all being methodically poisoned.

"That's it," Rhea said and pointed to a scar in the surface of AE625.

"The fissure?" Lago asked uncertainly as Gana slammed on the brakes.

The Commanding Family's rover pulled forward closer to the entrance to Hades.

Mertensia was the first to leap from the vehicle. She spread her arms wide like a biblical prophet and exclaimed, "This is our salvation!" Her eyes, hair, and grin were wild.

From the depths of the earth, a high pitched keening from many mouths erupted as three figures burst from the fissure, tripping over themselves and the sand.

Within the rover, Yuto and Dierde recognized the two hunters and Jarrod immediately. Rio's absence was not missed by either of them, and their expressions darkened. Behind the Exos, gonis ranging from six feet to fifteen feet long flew from the mouth of the cave. Four of them landed on Mertensia, each gripping a limb betwixt their jaws. With hardly an effort, their ropey necks flexed and the woman was shorn into quarters. As her head and left arm flailed through the air, the onlookers could see that her jubilant expression had not left her face.

The soldiers leapt from their vehicles and began peppering the air with bullets as the monstrous goni plucked civilian after civilian up in their jaws. It was over as soon as it had begun. Twenty or so gonis littered the ground, heaving their last breaths.

Aqi, Fleet, and Kilo all exchanged a concerned glance before stepping from the rover. Perhaps Mertensia's dismemberment was an omen regarding their fates as well. The Source would be more challenging to take than previously expected. But now they had plenty of food for several days. The commoners began skinning the gonis and quartering them. Jorgen, the Chief of the Palace Guard, stood between the Commanding Family and the new Hydras. Taiga, Lepiro, and Jarrod stood uneasily. None more so than Jarrod. He was sure their retribution would be swift.

"You must be from Hydra Seven," Aqi said graciously. "And welcome back, Jarrod."

She smiled warmly, but Jarrod still did not trust her.

"Jorgen, take these two to the rover and reacquaint them with their friends. See to it that they get water and food first," Fleet said, and Jorgen nodded and led them away.

The other Warchief, Dmetri, was shouting orders to his infantrymen. They were setting up a camp. Food and resources in the middle, while barricades were erected at the mouth of the cave. The barriers were pitiful, upturned carts mainly, but also anything else that could be repurposed for protection. The empty water drums went into the completion of the wall as well.

"We need to send a recon mission to determine the lay of the land," Kilo suggested.

Rhea, Gana, Lago, and Utria ghosted up as if summoned.

"Not you, Rhea," Aqi ordered. "You need to rest up. The rest of you will go team up with Jana and six of her police."

Rhea glowered but did not protest. The anger emanating from her chilled the very air around them, though. The three scouts made themselves scarce as they began their preparations.

"We need to interrogate the Hydras before we let any of our people go underground," Kilo offered sagaciously.

The remaining Family Members turned back to look at their rover as a loud clang echoed from within it.

X

Jarrod's head was slammed into a quarter panel before he was roughly shoved inside the rover with his hands cuffed behind his back. Lepiro and Taiga went much more gently, surprised when they recognized the two Exos already occupying it. Their hearts sank when they realized they would have to break the news of Rio's death.

"Where is he?" Dierde seethed.

No one answered right away.

Finally Taiga began, "He was sacrificed-"

"You son of a bitch!" Yuto said and lunged at Jarrod, though he didn't make it very far.

Dierde, however, was much more flexible and resourceful. Her heel flashed out and caught Jarrod in the jaw squarely. The sound of tooth chipping on tooth sounded several times as she kicked twice more. Blood dribbled from his jaw as he made to argue his innocence.

He never got a single word out. Dierde's thighs wrapped around his head like pythons and with two sharp twists of her hips, his neck cracked. She gracefully moved her weight underneath her and sat back in her seat as if nothing had happened. Jarrod's lifeless eyes stared right at her. Her chest heaved with either grief or rage but she did not cry. She steeled her jaw and looked over at Yuto in disgust.

"I'm sorry," Yuto answered as tears glimmered in his eyes.

"Me too."

Then the door clicked as Fleet pulled it open. Jarrod's corpse rolled from the vehicle onto the sand. Looking over his shoulder, Fleet addressed his fellow commanders. "You can't say he didn't have it coming."

"We all have it coming," Aqi said with a sigh and ran her hand over her close-cropped hair. "Call Jorgen and have him uncuff them."

Kilo barked an order over his shoulder and moments later the four Hydras were free. In a sense. The Commanding Family stepped into the rover and shut the door behind them for privacy. Whatever information the Hydras had, they would decide how to disseminate it.

"We need to know what you know about The Source," Fleet said. It sounded friendly, but his eyes were not.

"We don't know much," Taiga offered. "The creatures below the surface seem civilized and initially helped us."

Fleet's eyebrows arched.

"But they offered one of ours as a sacrifice to a massive goni in a lake," Lepiro jumped in sourly. "Along with many of their own. It was barbaric."

"The meaning of barbarisms shifts between cultures," Kilo said reflectively.

"I suppose you would say we are barbarians," Yuto growled sharply.

"Indubitably," Fleet said flatly. "But we are not asking *you* questions at the moment. What can our soldiers expect to encounter below the surface?"

"Violence," Taiga said simply.

"Perhaps some landmarks that would help?" Kilo asked politely.

"They'll have to cross fields of molla and a lake," Taiga said and shrugged. "It's dark, we couldn't see much. If it weren't for Icharus, we would have been blind."

"Our scouts will have flashlights," Aqi said and opened the door to exit the vehicle. She offered a bowl of molla spores to the Exos. "I understand you have a certain affinity for this. And please, mingle with the Shrikers and introduce yourselves. I think you will find we are not so different."

Dierde accepted the bowl first and dipped her fingers into the basin. She smeared the spores around her eye sockets, and dragged her fingers vertically across her lips, giving the impression of a skull.

"A flair for the dramatic," Fleet noted as he too exited the rover, followed by Kilo.

Once the Shrikers had left, Dierde passed the spores to Yuto. He too painted his face and passed the proverbial olive branch. Lepiro and Taiga did not immediately follow suit.

"We are the last of our people. We might as well be already dead. Why not let them know they are facing ghosts?" Yuto snarled and the other two Hydras assented.

"Do you want to know how Rio passed?" Taiga asked softly.

"He is dead. That is enough." Dierde sniffed. Then she stepped through the open door and into the blazing heat.

The whispers began immediately. Most of the Shrikers hadn't seen a Hydra until recently. Their only impression of them was that of vicious nomads who had destroyed their homes. Now four of the demons stepped from the Commanding Family's transport with terrifying face masks. Their eyes were dark and shifted constantly as if assessing threats. These were truly beings to be afraid of. Children shuffled behind their mothers, while the women stared in horror as the strangers made their way to the water station. Even the men scattered, with good reason. Even the weakest of Hydras had faced more perils than the Shriker Warchiefs. And here, four stood in the midst of an uprooted Shriker city.

Chapter Thirty-Five

The flashlight beams led the way for the Shriker recon mission. Ahead of them, the sound of chattering and footfalls alerted them to another presence. Many presences. Then came the whirling claws, red eyes, and gnashing teeth. A spray of bullets dropped the first charge when a glowing figure glided into view and tackled one of the police. The gonis mouth closed around the man's face and shattered his skull. After centuries of eating gonis, the gonis were eating them back. The triumphant creature let loose a shriek which was answered over and over and over. The recon team of ten was surely not enough to face the onslaught.

Lago squeezed the trigger again as more Greylings rounded the corner. Three dropped, then four more came, then six more, then, too many to count. None of them bore any weapon, but they were just as deadly. They avoided the light and Lago had to constantly scan for approaching enemies. His flashlight would land on one and like static it would dance out of the light as another entered the beam. He missed more times than he connected. The policeman next to him collapsed on the ground underneath a flurry of teeth and claws. He peppered the assailants with rounds, but the man beneath the Greylings was dead. Gana and Utria stood next to him, their faces almost serene despite the chaos around them. The only way to survive in battle was to remain calm. Utria stopped a charging Greyling with her foot and forced it onto its back before placing a bullet between its eyes.

A quick scan by Gana revealed that his sister was nowhere to be seen. The sea of Greylings was receding, and Gana could only deduce that his sister and her men were their new focus. He barreled after the Greylings as they dipped into an accessory shaft. A moment later he ducked as a spray of gunfire dropped the creatures. Jana was the last of the police still on her feet, though it looked like at least two were still alive. Lago and Utria appeared behind Gana, and the sound of chaos stopped as abruptly as it had begun.

"Take up a defensive position at the mouth of this tunnel," Gana ordered and the other two scouts obeyed. Gana looked Jana over. Her hair was swept across her face, most of it drenched in blood. None of it was hers, though. Her dying men gasped where they lay. But none of them moved more than a spasm. Most of them were eviscerated or were missing parts of their throats. Jana wasted no time and eased their pain.

Her brother stood in shock. Mercy killing wasn't a practice often employed at the Wreckage. They had doctors and barely encountered any real danger.

"If I meet a similar fate, show me the same kindness," Jana said roughly. She was the elder of the two, neither of them were squeamish and both had a natural bloodlust without being warmongers. But Gana had lived his whole life looking up to her, and she had inherited the best traits from their parents—now he saw her in a different light. Her love wasn't the nurturing type. It was tough, but it was there.

"Do we go deeper or retreat?" Gana asked.

"Deeper, we have a job to do," Jana answered as she collected the gear she could carry from her dead comrades. "We at least need to locate the first lake."

A warbling cry echoed overhead. More gonis were in the area.

"And kill as many of those things as possible."

"We have company!" Lago shouted and the cavern lit up with the crack of gunpowder and firing pins.

The siblings rushed the corridor's outlet and saw a myriad of neon lights rushing their way. Some of the gonis crawled along the walls, while others dove through the air. Their bullet riddled, mangled bodies squished against the rocky floor. Yet more still came.

Three of the creatures landed directly in front of the Exos. Their wings were folded up neatly, as if they were ready to negotiate. They let loose wails worthy of banshees. The gonis were no match for the bullets and died before they had finished their hellish calls.

Then a sound rattled the very foundation of the planet. The cry clearly belonged to a goni, but one the size of a dune. The slaughter of its progeny had enraged it.

"What was that?" Utria panted as the remaining gonis scattered.

"It's the goni the Commanding Family warned us about," Gana said and shone his beam deeper down the cavern. "This way."

"This is crazy," Utria said in disbelief, but she didn't hesitate before plunging deeper into the dark.

"This is survival," Lago said direly.

"Shut up. And dim your lights. We want to see it before it sees us," Jana ordered.

A moment later, they were in nothing but darkness. Their eyes adjusted and they could detect the roughest of outlines, or perhaps they imagined it. Or their brains fabricated it from the gentle echoes they produced. Either way, after fifteen minutes of blind creeping, Utria walked into a soft fleshy form that was at least the height of a man. With a shout of alarm and a few well-placed shots, the molla cap tumbled from its stalk.

"It would appear that we are headed in the right direction," Jana said aloud, no point in whispering now. Their location had been announced to all. A moment later they heard a sound completely unfamiliar to them. Had Taiga or Lepiro been with them, they could have told them it was that of an immense body sliding into the water. It was the sound of death personified.

With their lights on low beam, the Shrikers advanced. Picking their way between the massive 'shrooms, they were on high alert for hidden dangers. Of course, nothing revealed itself. The Greylings were counting on their deity to take care of these new intruders. The sapling sized molla eventually gave way to smaller clumps, growing amid a garden of pebbles and broken shale. The Shrikers were mere feet from witnessing their first body of water.

The lights began to bounce off the reflective surface and illuminated the entire cavern just as Lago's toe broke the surface. He jumped back at the cold sensation and felt excitement bubble up his chest. No matter the peril they were in, Exos were always delighted by the precious commodity of water. Not only was the lake lit by the cavern, but it was also emitting its own red light. The goni lifted its head from the water and let loose a screech as it swam towards its next prey. None of the Shrikers had the fortitude to stand before it and turned on their heels and fled before it had even reached the shore.

The goni behind them didn't pursue them into the molla farm, it was probably struggling to drag its mass onto the rocks, which bode well for the recon team. However, the Greylings who had been hiding now revealed themselves. They leapt from behind the molla stalks and tackled the fleeting Exos. Jana felt claws slide deep into her abs as she blasted her assailant off her. She felt warm blood pool in the shallow of her hips and ribs as it also came bubbling up her throat. She leveled her barrel at another of the aliens and it too met its end swiftly. She could feel her organs press against her threadbare skin and squeeze past her diaphragm. Gana dealt with his attackers just as deftly as his sister and rushed to her side as she slipped back to the ground.

"No, no, no…" he said as he pressed his fingers against her stomach, forcing her intestines back inside her. "You're going to be fine… you're going to be fine."

Jana smiled, her teeth red. "You have to get the others out. Remember what I told you."

"We're all getting out of here. I can't do that," he said as pandemonium reigned around them.

Jana smiled again. "You have to. This is bigger than any individual. Our people need to reach the Second Earth." She feebly reached for his pistol in its holster but couldn't pull it out.

Tears ran down Gana's cheeks as he withdrew the weapon and pressed it to her chest. "I love you," he whimpered as he felt the kickback.

Jana had a smile on her face as she sailed into the afterlife, if there was such a thing.

Gana stood and shouted at his fellow scouts. Lago and Utria abandoned the vicious melee and followed him as he led them back to the surface. The Greylings did not relent in their pursuit, even the occasional gun blast did not stop them. They were determined to repel the invaders from their home. However, as a sliver of light appeared the creatures faltered. The night was their territory, but they were unwilling to face their foes in the light.

The scouts emerged, ragged and bloodied. The expressions on the faces of their fellow soldiers and the commoners were of pure shock.

Rhea was at their side in an instant. "What happened?" she exclaimed. She was relieved that her own men had emerged, though she still felt the loss of the military men and women who had not made it.

"We did our best," Gana said miserably.

Rhea blinked back her own tears and embraced him. "You did good. I am so sorry about Jana." Rhea felt Gana let out a sob into her shoulder. She squeezed him tighter as his body was wracked with grief. He let out a muffled cry and Rhea placed her hand on the back of his head.

"We will get off this planet," she assured him, although she knew it did little good.

The Commanding Family approached the soot-streaked, blood-smeared scouts.

"Take a rest. You deserve it," Fleet said. His mouth was sticky with fear. Of the ten soldiers sent into the earth, only three returned. And it appeared as though they had been through hell. "Dmetri!"

The Chief of the Infantry came trotting over.

"Take forty men with you down there and establish a foothold," Fleet commanded without communicating with his fellow leaders.

"Yessir." Dmetri nodded and barked out an order. He mobilized his men quickly and disappeared into the fissure. The clamor of battle echoed for many hours, with each passing minute the dissonance seemed further and further away until it stopped altogether.

X

Dmetri reached the surface some time later and was met by expectant stares. His face was haggard and his eyes hollow.

"We've taken the lake."

The cheers were deafening.

Chapter Thirty-Six

"This water isn't for you," the man said heatedly.

Taiga smiled through her skull mask. "Chances are, my massacred people found it for you." She dipped the cup into the cool surface. Her fingertips rejoiced at the feeling.

"It's rationed." The speaker was a guard and male, but Taiga was not intimidated. The guard, however, was, especially when three other Hydras seemed to appear out of nowhere.

"I think we will take some too," Yuto said and dipped a flask into the barrel. Bubbles streamed from the mouth as the air was forced out by the water.

"Don't make me put you in cuffs," the guard said without much conviction.

"We've been drinking piss for years so you can drink clean water. We are collecting what's due." Dierde spat into the water and the Hydras left the guard in peace. Or relative peace, as many of the commoners saw the display and were attempting to reenact the shake-down to get extra water. They weren't as successful. Comparing the Hydras to Shrikers was like wolves to purse poodles. One was dangerous by nature, while the other could only act it.

Lepiro watched in disgust as the Shrikers ate the gonis that had been slaughtered hours earlier. Icharus sat on his shoulder, concern evident in his little eyes.

"And they called us barbaric," he laughed. "The gonis are the only reason our kind even survived here. This is how they show their thanks."

"Should we at least try to assimilate? Looking like we do, we will never be accepted," Taiga commented.

"I'd rather die than be one of them," Dierde said haughtily and Yuto agreed.

"You misunderstand me. We are targets," Taiga growled.

Everywhere they went, eyes followed. It wasn't just the commoners who were watching either. Fleet approached them with a purpose.

"Look out," Lepiro hissed as the man neared earshot.

"I trust your stay has been hospitable."

None of the Hydras could tell if the statement was meant to be ironic. None of them answered, either.

Fleet continued undeterred. "If it is not asking too much, we would like the four of you to be on the next mission to The Source."

"It sounds like you want to get rid of us," Yuto smirked. "Maybe if you give us guns we can be persuaded."

"Do you know how to use them?" Fleet asked beneath a furrowed brow.

"We'd need training, you moron," Dierde said in disgust.

"Speaking as someone who has seen those horrors, I would prefer to decline," Lepiro said. He was determined not to be the next sacrifice to the god in the lake.

"I personally would like to kill some of those creatures," Yuto said.

Taiga knew he wanted vengeance for Rio, and felt a pang of jealousy.

"This was recovered on the last mission," Fleet said and tossed a flat palm sized rock on the ground. Inscribed on its surface was a single number. "Hydra Nine. You're more similar to them than you are to us. Come with me, I'll have Jorgen equip you."

Fleet turned and left the four staring at the symbol on the ground.

X

Four empty barrels, each bearing the marking 16-21-18-5, were set up as targets. Rocks were set in the bottom so they wouldn't blow over each time one of the Hydras hit their mark. They shared looks of approval when the sound of metal tearing plastic was heard, and chuckled when an attempted shot was only met by a burst of sand.

"I like the war paint." Jorgen nodded. "Squeeze the trigger. Don't pull it. Exhale."

"It's not war paint. It's for those we've lost. Both to the Greylings, and to you," Dierde snarled. A moment later a bullet ripped through the drum.

Down the line, Taiga and Yuto stood in cold silence. The reunion between husband and wife had been lacking.

"Are you going to say anything?" Taiga asked and fired another burst from her rifle. She wasn't pleading or begging. She was simply angry that her husband had shown no concern for her safety.

"We haven't loved each other in a long time. There's no point in continuing the ruse," Yuto said rudely.

"I never loved you. Other than Rio we were the youngest in Hydra Seven," Taiga answered. "You were the only choice left."

Yuto stiffened at the mention of his deceased friend.

"Would you like a hug?" Yuto asked without looking at his wife.

"Not from you." Taiga laughed smugly.

Yuto let the gun go slack in his hands and looked over at Lepiro and back at Taiga.

"Are you serious?!" he asked incredulously but without anger. "When did you have time to do that?"

"There's not much to do underground," Taiga said simply and Yuto laughed.

"I have missed you," he admitted.

"I've missed you too. But not like that," Taiga said and took aim again.

"I guess the four of us are all we have left."

"Indeed."

Jorgen interrupted whatever was going to be said next. "I think you are ready. Or as ready as you are going to be. Lago! Escort these soldiers to the base camp at the lake."

"On it," Lago said and smirked at Dierde. "L-long time no see."

She only curled her lip in response.

Lago didn't seem perturbed. "We will get outfitted with lights and canteens before we go down. Follow me."

"You were on the first team that went down there, right?" Yuto asked. The Shriker stiffened, but didn't answer. "So you know what it's like seeing your friends killed? Imagine if it had been done by your own kind. Like our colony."

"Am I supposed to pity you?" Lago sneered.

"No, but your friends will after they see you die," Yuto continued casually.

Lago whirled around. "Is that a threat?"

"Only if you have friends." Yuto shouldered past him, and Lago could do nothing but stand there dumbfounded.

"So those lights and water?" Taiga asked as she too stepped by him.

Lago growled but did not offer any more argument. He said little as he distributed flashlights and water to the Hydras.

Moments later, they were slipping into the fissure. The darkness engulfed them, but being hunters they were used to exploring every cavern and hidey-hole encountered. Lepiro and Taiga knew what awaited them and their pounding pulses were from the same nauseating fear that Lago felt. Yuto and Dierde felt a different kind of anxiety. Theirs was driven by a need for vengeance. Whether it was reserved for the Greylings or Shrikers, they weren't sure yet. Yuto stared at the flat gap between Lago's shoulders and thought of putting a bullet into his spine. He wasn't sure how long he stared at the man's back, thinking of pressing the barrel against it and pulling the trigger. It would be so easy. But then where would he go? Back to the surface? No, he still needed to avenge Rio. He would have to take part in the battle for The Source. Then turn on the Shrikers.

"Can you stop shining that th-thing on me?" Lago cast his gaze over his shoulder and his eyes locked onto Yuto's.

"My bad," Yuto said lamely but raised the flashlight so it shone directly in Lago's eyes. He let the beam fall a moment later.

Great. Lago thought. *I'm more likely to get jumped now by the Hydras then I am by the Greylings.*

Why hadn't the Commanding Family sent more men down with him? It was probably a show of faith to win over the Hydras. Stupid.

The clamor of war echoed from the cavern, like a roar building in the back of a throat.

"I hope you actually know how to use those," Lago said of the guns before sprinting in the direction of the sound. He nimbly avoided rocks and cracks that would have surely tripped him and probably cause him to discharge his rifle right into the bottom of his skull.

The Hydras behind him made no noise as they slunk between the pillars of rock formations, Lago's own careful footsteps suddenly sounding impossibly loud. Taiga ghosted by him, she remembered the way to the first lake clearly. She hadn't been under the same duress that Lago had been on his first journey beneath the surface and the landmarks were coming back to her.

The molla farms passed by her in a blur as she descended deeper into the grotto. She saw the dim glow of the scorpion moths and their spawn across the lake. What was in the forefront of the scene stopped her dead in her tracks.

Gonis screeched and dive-bombed the infantrymen beneath them, picking them up and dropping them in the lake or against the rocks, or devouring them as the creatures climbed back into the air. The flash of fired shots caused a strobe effect and it seemed like the fighting was a series of stills shown on a projector. Not a battle unfolding right before her eyes.

Her attention was snapped from the airborne aliens and focused instead on the lake shore. Emerging from the water were dozens of Greylings. She saw more dark shapes cutting through towards the shore, barely making a ripple in the surface.

Ethan Proud

Chapter Thirty-Seven

Lago saw what Taiga had and wasted no time before charging into the fray, his gun leveled for the Greylings that had just reached the shore. He roared a warning to his fellow Shrikers, but of course it was lost amid the din. After only a moment's hesitation, the Hydras followed him.

The Greylings moved quickly as soon as the element of surprise was lost and broke off into groups of five or six. One group headed for Lago and the Hydras, while the rest cut into the unsuspecting line of infantrymen still looking skyward.

Lepiro squeezed the trigger, felt the absence of recoil, and knew he needed to reload. Yuto and Taiga stepped in front of him to provide cover while he fumbled with his clip. Opposite them, Dierde stood impassively, spraying bullets at the oncoming wave of Greylings. Her eyes seemed blank and did not even emanate the hatred she felt deep in her gut.

A lucky Greyling made it past the strafe of death and raked its claws down Lago's side. He twisted his body and slammed the butt of the rifle into the creature's face, shattering the bones and leaving it writhing on the ground. He fired a shot to halt another approaching alien before finishing off the one on the ground. He felt naked without his fellow scouts. The Hydras would obviously defend their own before considering helping him. He looked behind him up the shoreline and saw that the infantry had split their attention between the gonis and the Greylings storming the beach.

"Fall back," he ordered to the Hydras. In unison their heads whipped towards him, ears cocked like dogs.

"FALL BACK," he repeated louder, and they backpedaled obediently, never taking their eyes off the threat.

A goni dropped from the sky above them, its jaws leading the way. Dierde pivoted and fired straight into its gullet and sidestepped the corpse as it pummeled the ground where she had just stood. She casually dodged its still writhing tail.

From behind the line of Shrikers, and from the tunnel leading back to the surface, came a flood of Greylings like rats from a storm drain. The Shriker force was now split between three fronts, the threat from the air, the beach, and the onslaught that just cut off their retreat. They had been hemmed in. A solid object hurtled through the air into the Greyling swarm on the shore. The grenade exploded on impact and sent chunks of gore splattering their comrades and the Exos closest. Dierde ducked, narrowly avoiding being struck by an eyeball and part of a nose.

The Exos formed a defensive ring and mowed down the incoming assailants. Soon the cavern was littered with the bodies of gonis and Greylings, though very few Shriker lives had been claimed. The Greylings receded back into the lake and the crevices they had come from just as mysteriously as they had appeared.

"Clear the tunnels, set up a defensive position," Dmetri ordered. His face was covered in blood that no doubt belonged to the soldiers who had died next to him. He smeared it away with the back of his hand and found Lago.

"Go back to the surface and find Drips. We need to start pumping this water immediately. Have Rhea send us reinforcements, too. We need to cross the lake and we can't hold both shores with our current numbers," he ordered.

Lago nodded and turned to the Hydras. "Come with me."

"No," Dmetri began. "We will need them, they know what to expect."

The scout's expression soured, but he didn't argue. Instead, he took off at a light jog for the surface.

He had little trouble following the path since he had already been down it twice. The shadows at the edge of his light beam and peripherals kept shifting as if they were enemies, hidden in the dark. Below the sound of his footsteps, he imagined he heard whispering voices calling his name, softly yet forcibly. He sped up his pace.

X

When he finally emerged, it took him a second to adjust to the searing light. His temporary blindness inspired a tactic he couldn't believe no one had already thought of, but he had a job to do first. He would run his plan by Rhea after he found the waterworks engineer.

He began navigating the camp, but the lay had changed since he last descended. Fleet found him before he managed to get his bearings.

"Why are you not with the rest of the squadron?" Fleet inquired, fear evident in his eyes.

"We are still holding the lake but need to cross, and need reinforcements to do so. Dmetri thinks it is safe to begin pumping water," Lago explained.

"And what do you think?" Fleet asked.

"W-what?" Lago silently cursed himself. He had managed to string several sentences together without stuttering, but couldn't say *what*. But then again, a member of the Commanding Family hadn't just asked him what he thought.

"About pumping the water. Is it safe? Do we have a solid defensible position?" Fleet explained.

Lago cast a sidelong glance at the water barrels. All of them bore the code 4-9-18-20-25. D-I-R-T-Y. An alpha-numeric code wasn't hard to crack. "It's safer than what we are drinking now."

"If we lose the equipment, we won't have another chance and we will have to stay in close proximity of the lake." Fleet did not appreciate the snarky comment.

"We won't lose it," Lago said and strode off in search of Rhea.

Fleet remained there, flabbergasted. He hadn't dismissed the scout, and had half a mind to call the man back. If Lago didn't obey the order, he would look even more foolish. He held his tongue. Then he went off in search of Johan.

When Lago found Rhea she was engrossed in a conversation with Aqi. Rhea looked grey. She was slowly deteriorating. Lago doubted she had much longer to live if she kept drinking the contaminated water. Her body had been exposed to such a high dose and was now slowly accumulating more. Even though the Exos had stronger kidneys and livers than Earthlings, Lago doubted they could survive this kind of chronic poisoning. Concern was evident in Aqi's eyes. It wasn't the emotion reserved for a subordinate though, it wasn't coming from a sense of responsibility. Lago recalled the conversation in the rover. Then it clicked in his brain.

"S-sorry to interrupt," he stammered.

"Lieutenant Lago," Rhea said, and though she stood straight, her voice and eyes betrayed her exhaustion.

"Dmetri requests more reinforcements. He means to cr-cross the lake."

"Then we should send the rest of our troops," Aqi said pensively.

"I agree," Rhea said. "We can't let our men get trapped on the other side if it doesn't go well."

"Is it just the one city?" Lago asked. The two women's expressions darkened.

"What?" they asked in unison.

"How do we know there aren't more cities or outposts under the surface?" Lago said calmly. The thought had just occurred to him.

"We don't," Rhea stated. "We must be ready for whatever comes."

"Ready the army," Aqi said to Rhea, who nodded.

Rhea opened her mouth to answer but Lago interjected. She glared at him patiently, mindful of his impediment.

"Do we have a light generator?" he asked.

Rhea chuckled. "Why would we need one before this? I think we can fabricate one easily enough, though. Now, go find Gana and have him mobilize the scouts."

Chapter Thirty-Eight

The citizens of the Wreckage watched as the mouth of the underworld swallowed up the last soldier in the Shrike Colonial Military. Kilo accompanied the soldiers, while Fleet and Aqi remained above ground.

Rhea stood at Aqi's side. "I should be going with them."

"You are in no state for combat. Once the main army has secured both sides of the lake and set up a camp from which we can spearhead our next attack, you may go," Aqi said calmly despite Rhea's mounting anger.

"With all due respect, that is not your decision." Rhea struggled to sound polite.

"If you did not agree with me, you would already be down there. You just need someone to confirm what you already know. You feel guilty, but you should not," Aqi said gently, and Rhea deflated.

"We both know my time is limited, anyway," Rhea said without conviction.

"That's not necessarily true. But it doesn't mean you need to rush into it," Aqi admonished her.

"I'd rather go out in battle than waste away here."

"There's still time for that. We might all face our deaths at the hands of the Greylings."

They both laughed lightly before falling into silence. Their eyes were focused on the sandy dunes that framed the fissure. Periodically, a noise would escape the depths. Whether it was the echo of a conversation or a whisper of the wind it was hard to tell. A noise more distinct than the others reached Aqi's ears. It was neither the wind, nor the idle conversations of the soldiers. The sound was indeed words, but not the likes of any that Aqi had ever heard.

A face peered at the Exos who stared back fearfully. The alien blinked twice before darting back beneath the sands.

"Will it come above ground?" Fleet asked midstride as he approached the two lovers. They held back the urge to roll their eyes.

"No. The sunlight hurts their eyes," Rhea replied. "We have a clear advantage, and we have nothing they want."

"Should we dislodge them from the cavern mouth?" Fleet pressed.

"We sent our entire army to hold the lake. Jorgen will have to send the palace guard," Aqi answered.

"You two don't seem concerned," Fleet observed.

"I have faith in our soldiers," Rhea answered.

A barrage of gunshots was heard and Kilo stepped into the light, flanked by two of his soldiers. Behind them Drips followed, counting on them for safety just as they counted on him for setting up their water. Three more engineers emerged, running three long hoses.

Kilo cut a straight path for Aqi and Fleet while the engineers rigged the hoses to the drums.

"We have control over the lake for the time being," he began. "We will begin pulling water to the surface. Three pump stations have been set up with guards positioned at each. We may not have enough power to draw the water to the surface, though. Bringing our people beneath ground to the lake shore is the best bet for clean water. If we rig up enough light generators we should be able to repel the Greylings."

"We don't have enough flashlights and bulbs. That is the current prototype, unless something has changed?" Aqi stated. Using the flashlight lenses and bulbs would produce enough light to deter the Greylings but it certainly would not be enough to guarantee safety.

Kilo nodded. "We are going to pull the headlights and taillights from the rovers as well as the batteries. We also pulled the UV lamps from the hydroponics and will pair those with the solar panels from the rovers to supply the batteries with continuous power."

"Will that even work?" Rhea asked as she scrunched her brow.

"I have no idea. Drips assured me that it has a fifty-fifty chance of frying the bulbs or simply not starting." Kilo laughed. "But we must do something."

"It only needs to last until we are rescued," Fleet said in agreement.

"Let's pray that the Second Earthlings come sooner than anticipated," Aqi said. "I will find volunteers to help Drips get the light generators ready. Someone find

Jorgen and have him prep our supply caravan to continue on foot."

"I will find Jorgen," Kilo said and started off at a brisk pace through the camp.

"If it hadn't been for the Hydras…" Fleet said to himself as he made no move to do anything.

Rhea curled her lip in disgust but said nothing as she began breaking down the tents nearest to her and directing the commoners to do the same.

X

Deep below the earth, at the second pump station, Gana stood watch with Utria and two other soldiers. An engineer adjusted several knobs on the pump as it began to whir. At first the pump made an awful sound, speeding up and slowing down suddenly, almost to the point it died before the engineer had it purring. The water began running uphill through the hose. The cool liquid gurgled as it was pulled from the lake. Even though the plan was to take the lake, the Commanding Family were a shrewd group and wanted to have clean water at the surface in case of failure.

"It's working," Utria said excitedly.

"Please don't say that," the engineer said. "I'd hate for you to jinx us."

The water in the hose halted and began to recede. The pump still ran, but it was only pulling air.

"Looks like you just did," Utria said and pursed her lips, thoughtfully. "Is there any way we can tell if the first pump failed?"

"It had to have. When it died, air got into the water column and we lost our pressure." The engineer scratched his chin.

"How do we know that it's the pump that is dead and not its guards?" Gana asked darkly.

"I'm willing to bet it's the guards," Utria answered.

The pitter patter of bare feet alerted the Shrikers to the advancing threat.

"How do we get so lucky?" Gana drawled dryly.

The first Greyling stepped into the light and a bullet tore through its chest and buried itself in the creature behind it. An object went flying through the air and Gana barely ducked in time.

"That was part of the pump's engine!" the engineer exclaimed, before a second piece struck him beside the head. Blood burst from his temple, and judging by the way his eyes rolled into his head and blood pooled past his lips, he was dead on impact. Not to mention, the shrapnel sticking from his skull.

"Looks like we won't be getting that water to the surface," Utria said between the reports of gunfire.

"Let's focus on saving ourselves before we try to save humanity," Gana said through gritted teeth. He swung the butt of his rifle into the teeth of a Greyling before it sank its claws into his neck.

The assault hardly lasted a minute, but the damage was done. One pump was clearly destroyed and they had lost an engineer.

"What's our next move?" Utria asked Gana.

He didn't answer immediately as he considered the possibilities. The first pump was ruined, no point in checking on its status. The men with it were more than likely dead. The third pump could be compromised as well. But with only two, the water wasn't going anywhere. He settled on the third option.

"We return to the lake. Either the Greylings have multiple routes to the surface, or they have broken through." Gana turned to the other two scouts. "Return to the surface and warn them."

"You think we can handle an army of Greylings on our own?" Utria laughed, but the wild look in her eyes told of her excitement for a challenge.

"We won't be rushing in. If all hell has broken loose we can steal away unseen. If we can help, we will." Gana trotted off in the darkness. He dimmed his light to where he could just see the ground. Utria followed suit. The other two soldiers didn't hesitate before darting back to the sands.

Terra Mortem

Chapter Thirty-Nine

It was still on the far side of the lake. The Hydras, Lago, Dmetri, and a contingent of infantry stood bathed in the light of the glowworms. It would be hard to pass through the tunnel undetected, but they had little choice. They had repelled a small band of Greylings, but no doubt more would come. Across the lake a small battle raged. The Shrikers had been pushed back from the pump, which the barehanded Greylings destroyed.

Dmetri scowled. "We may end up trapped if we continue. But whatever route those creatures took is down this tunnel. We need to find its entrance before we get cut off." He said it aloud, though it was his own thought process. He wasn't asking for second opinions.

"Icharus may be able to find it," Lepiro volunteered.

"Are you implying that it knows what you say?" Dmetri stared at the little morsel floating in the air next to its companion.

"Not hardly. But sometimes he can tell what I want," Lepiro said with a shrug.

"It's our best shot," Dmetri began. "Maybe we shouldn't have been eating them."

"You think?" Dierde said behind a curled lip. She was relieved that Dierde and Aileen were somewhere in the desert, probably gorging on molla, instead of being gorged on themselves.

Dmetri didn't grace her with an answer. Lepiro whispered a few words to Icharus, and the goni left his shoulder and drifted down the tunnel, its light dwarfed by the insectoid creatures crawling on the walls.

The squadron crept forward like thieves avoiding creaky floorboards. The footfalls of their neighbors naturally sounded louder than their own and many glares and scowls were exchanged.

Over the sounds of the soldiers moving, the shimmering of desiccated chitin polymers bound into hardened shells came dancing up the tunnel. The scorpion-moths in the air landed on the men and began to flex their wings, tiny hairs on the surface creating a chirp of friction in answer to the cloaked figure approaching the grotto.

Drums and mollawind instruments added to the haunting dissonance. Taiga and Lepiro blanched as chills crept up their spines.

The first forerunners of the ceremony came into view, their arms outstretched as their feet wove their sinuous bodies around the mineral deposits on the cavern floor. Their faces were turned upward, and they paid the Shriker soldiers no heed, not even when the first rifle blast tore into their molla stained bodies. The ecstasy of the presence of their god propelled them forward. It took three more bullets to drop them. More and more of them came.

"What's going on?" Dmetri shouted and grabbed Taiga by the shoulder.

Wide-eyed, she answered, but it was drowned out by a scream that engulfed the entire tunnel.

She repeated herself as an uneasy still overtook the grotto.

"They have summoned it," she said ominously.

"What did they summon?" Dmetri demanded, but the Greylings answered his question.

GONI, GONI, GONI.

"We should have eaten more of them," Dmetri murmured as the tunnel was overwhelmed with a red light. "Retreat to the boats!"

The clamoring of booted feet was deafening now that the need for stealth had evaporated. The men splashed through the water as they pushed the dugouts from the shore and leapt inside. The massive goni was right on their heels. Dmetri and the Hydras pushed the last boat into the water just as it reared back and plucked Dmetri from the water. It tossed him into the air, caught him, and swallowed him whole. His screams could be heard until he was halfway down its gullet.

The Hydras managed to get out of its reach by the time it turned its attention back to them. They navigated between the boats full of Shrikers and avoided being the next meal. The goni's huge mass slipped into the water where its agility increased tenfold and the disturbance it caused created ten foot waves that capsized the boats. The occupants desperately grabbed the still buoyant crafts but didn't dare take the time to right them. Instead, they kicked as furiously as they could, trying to cross the lake to escape the goni while not drowning at the same time. Their ammo and guns weighed them down and some were pulled to the bottom before they got a purchase on the slick watercraft.

With an insatiable hunger, the god opened its enormous maw and water and men were pulled into the Charybdis-whirlpool. On the opposite shore, Kilo watched in horror as his warriors drowned or were devoured. They had successfully repelled the Greylings, or perhaps the creatures had retreated knowing that this fiend was coming to defend their homes for them. The symbiotic relationship between the goni and the Greylings was a powerful one.

X

Above the chaos, Gana and Utria surveyed the scene. The outlook was bleak, the goni would surely kill everyone in the lake and reach the close shore. But if the Shrikers retreated here, they would die of thirst before they reclaimed the lake.

"Is that Lago?" Utria pointed, and Gana followed the line between her index finger and the scout amid the roiling waters. The bright green spot of Lago's hair was an obvious identifier, though bathed in the red light as he was, it only appeared lighter than the rest of his shock of black hair. He was out of the way of the monster's mouth, but he was still in danger of being crushed by its wing.

"Yes," was all Gana said. There was obviously no chance of them rescuing the man. "He will have to fend for himself."

"Should we return to the surface or join the fray?" Utria asked, as she too, weighed their odds.

"Neither, just yet. No need to bolster the dead with our own bodies," Gana said tactfully.

"Prudent." Utria nodded and sank lower to the ground. To her amazement, the Shrikers on the shore broke rank and fled. Some brave souls remained, Kilo among them.

She tracked the deserters as they made for the surface. Their escape was cut off abruptly as they ran right into the convoy led by Aqi and Rhea. Utria didn't need to hear the words that escaped from Rhea's lips to feel her fury. Fleet emerged from whatever position of safety he had chosen to add his two cents.

Gana and Utria couldn't hear what transpired between the absconders and the Shriker Leaders, but they knew it would be best if they were found at the lake with Kilo rather than hidden amongst the crags. Wordlessly, they stole down to the shore.

The scouts easily blended into the army while the defectors and the commoners arrived. Kilo and Jorgen broke away from the army to meet Rhea, Aqi, and Fleet. It was a bleak moment for the members of the Commanding Family and the Council of Warchiefs.

The power was already shifting with the loss of Mertensia, Jana, and Dmetri.

"The Greylings have all fled. But we have that monster to contend with…and none of our men can get a good shot at it," Kilo reported.

"Why can't anyone get a shot off? It's huge," Fleet said sardonically.

"Our men are in the way," Rhea observed. It was true, the goni was ninety percent submerged, any conceivable target blocked by the Shrikers frantically trying to swim away.

"So we just watch our men get eaten?" Jorgen said and winced as more screams pierced the air.

Rhea didn't answer, but stared at him flatly. Her gaze wasn't focused on him, however, and the gears were whirring behind her irises.

"We need to get the light generator up and running on the shore," Rhea said before coughing up a bleb of phlegm and blood.

"What are you planning?" Aqi demanded, her tone not lost on the others. Not that they had been very discreet since the fall of the Wreckage.

"I'm going to kill their god."

Chapter Forty

Amid the thrashing water, Lago did plenty of thrashing himself. The goni's head was dangerously close to him, and though it hadn't noticed him it nearly crushed him several times. Other than its massive red glowing frame, Lago could barely see anything else in the cavern. Between trying to breathe and only spluttering out water, his lungs were screaming. When he felt something solid bump into him he didn't hesitate before latching on. The shape began to struggle and Lago realized it was one of his fellow soldiers. Regardless, he finally had purchase of oxygen and his survival was dependent on the man beneath him drowning. As luck would have it, an overturned boat floated by and Lago released the poor sodden warrior and lurched for the craft. Lago had barely heaved himself onto the keel of the boat with a sigh of exhaustion when from the opposite shore, the clang of a lever being pulled was the only warning before a blinding light engulfed the cavern.

X

"You can't do this," Aqi argued, but Rhea hardly looked at her. Soldiers were dying and she had a duty to protect them.

"Let her do it," Fleet said, and Aqi's hand snapped into the air in an order for silence.

"Someone has to do something," Rhea said as she shouldered her rifle. She pulled her goggles over her face so she could see in the brightly illuminated cave, then bent over in a fit of coughs while Kilo, Fleet, Aqi, and Jorgen looked at her with concern.

Rhea turned to stalk down to the shore when Aqi grabbed her by the shoulder and spun her around. Rhea expected her to protest further, but instead felt her lips pressed against her own. Aqi's strong, lean arms wrapped around Rhea's waist and pulled her close for a moment, before she pulled away and pushed Rhea towards her fate.

With a smile on her face, Rhea reached the shoreline. With her index and thumb pressed against her tongue, she let loose a piercing whistle. Despite being blinded, the gigantic goni began charging across the water, its blind eyes roving in all directions at no accord of what the other was doing. As it sped through the water, all in its path were crushed beneath its furious mass.

Calmly, Rhea flicked the safety off and rested her trigger finger right outside the guard. The beast wasn't as close as she wanted it to be yet. She could feel her pulse pounding wildly in her throat, but her hands were steady and her mind still. What did she have to worry about? If she failed, she met her inevitable death. Ellie the Hydra was surely taking her vengeance via the hydrazine. Rhea found the thought oddly amusing. If she succeeded here, she saved the human race and the army could hasten to destroy the Greyling City.

The creature crossed the span of the lake in only a few seconds, though it had seemed like an eternity to Rhea. The beast stopped fifteen feet from her and reared its horrible head. Heat pits lined its mouth, each one easily the size of a human head. With this infrared sight, the goni had found the infidel that dared to stand before its might. With a deafening shriek, it cursed her existence before its maw sped towards her. With a gentle squeeze of the trigger, Rhea sent the bullet spinning towards the Greyling god. It tore through the soft palate, entered its cranial cavity, and failed to exit on the other side of the skull. Instead, it ricocheted an impossible number of times, scrambling the goni's brain. The creature's body suddenly went limp and its neck slapped the gravel next to Rhea a moment before its head crashed into the rocks with an empty thud. The Scout Warchief put another bullet in its brain for good measure. Suddenly, she felt exceedingly weak. Her limbs throbbed, her lungs were struggling to pull in enough air. Her kidneys ached, and she felt the burning of acid in her throat.

Woozily, she sat down on the goni's dead head and felt the thundering applause of the Shrike Colonial Military as well as that of the citizens.

Slowly, the Shrikers stranded amongst the waves began to drag themselves from the water. Their clothes weighed pounds more than they had when dry and their bodies felt waterlogged, if that was possible. They shielded their eyes until they adjusted to the artificial sunlight filling the underworld.

Rhea swooned and before she fell over, Aqi swept her up in her arms like a child too tired to walk in from the car. Rhea smiled up at her, before she heard the padding noises of bare feet.

None of the Shrikers dared to utter even a breath as an innumerable host of Greylings filtered from every shadow imaginable. Now with the light generator, they could see the honeycombed pattern riddling the cave walls. Hundreds of the creatures came crawling from the rocky precipices, their numbers rivaling the Shrikers.

The Shrike Colonial Military took a deep breath in unison as they steadied themselves for the coming bloodshed. A still overtook the arena and neither side moved for several long moments. A single Greyling broke ranks. He wore a crackling cloak of chitinuous shells and his body was aglow with orange ichor offset by dark streaks of molla spores. The other Greylings stayed back, cowering from the light. Clearly this individual was their leader or representative of sorts.

Cautiously, he approached the corpse of the slaughtered god, but his eyes were focused on the woman who had come to the rescue of the soldier who killed the lake monster. Clearly, this woman wielded some power among her people. Aqi didn't balk at his approach, though no other Shriker had the courage to move. Aqi met the creature's gaze, even when he was less than a foot away from her face. Much to her surprise, he shed his cloak, draped it around her shoulders, and fell prostrate at her feet. At once, the entire population of Greylings lay down and accepted her into their pantheon. Aqi was now the Greyling Queen.

The creature at her feet turned his eyes upward, and Aqi saw in his eyes what he wanted. With a grim smile, she supplied her name.

The grotto became overwhelmed with the rhythmic chanting.

AQI. AQI. AQI.

Whether it was light or dark on the surface, it was the dawn of a new era on AE625.

Ethan Proud

Chapter Forty-One

Weeks later, Aqi and Rhea lounged in their new home. Rhea was beginning to recover now that she had a clean supply of water from the lake. The Greylings had housed them in one of the nine towers built around the shore. The only goni that had been seen in weeks had been Icharus. The Greylings doted upon him with daily gifts of molla, though it was nothing compared to the treatment Aqi and Rhea received. They were both adorned with jewels mined from the deep, though most of the rocks sparkled an opaque blackness that only deepened the dark around them. Their bodies were painted with the orange hemolymph. They were also fed a delicious meal that was chewier than the goni flesh had been and very rich in flavor and texture. It was undoubtedly flesh, though whether it belonged to Greyling sacrifices or sand dingoes hunted on the surface, it was impossible to tell due to the language barrier. Fleet had been sulking since the couple's rise to power, though Kilo stopped by frequently and informed them on the progress of the Second Earth rescue mission. It was a mere week away. Salvation was at hand.

"How do you think we will be received on the Second Earth?" Aqi asked.

"Like prodigal sons," Rhea answered. "They'll slaughter the fattened calf and all will be happy."

Aqi could tell she wasn't serious.

"Is that how the Hydras were welcomed by us?" She mulled the thought over. No doubt they would be seen as uncouth pariahs, no matter the state of affairs on the Second Earth.

"You need to stop feeling guilty for the sins of the past Commanding Families. Besides, I believe the ruse was partially due to the Hydras who believed the spring was tainted by hydrazine," Rhea said. It wasn't meant to be comforting. It was an order.

"That doesn't mean it was right to continue with the illusion. It caused us a lot of problems and I won't blame the dead for the mistakes of the living," Aqi argued lightly.

"Since when have you become a martyr?" Rhea laughed and traced Aqi's jawline.

"Hindsight is twenty-twenty," Aqi said and bent down to kiss Rhea.

X

Across the camp, a discussion of a different kind was being held by the Hydras. They sat cross legged on the floor, passing around a few caps of molla. Taiga and Lepiro had allowed the skull paint to wash off, but Yuto and Dierde still donned the macabre masks.

Lepiro held up a cap of molla into the air and Icharus alighted on his arm and began feasting greedily.

The other three stared enviously at the last living goni-human symbiosis.

"I think we should seek our revenge, before we are rescued and the chance is lost to us forever," Dierde said, her eyes just as wild as the night she, Yuto, and Rio made the pact to leave. She had the strange sensation of déjà vu.

"The rescue is in a week or less," Taiga argued. "Why jeopardize our chance at getting off this planet?"

"And how do you propose we get revenge?" Lepiro asked dryly. Clearly neither he nor Taiga would be joining in the crusade.

"Assassinating the Commanding Family," Dierde said flatly.

Taiga and Lepiro turned to stare at her, before looking at Yuto. He wasn't shocked by this, clearly the two had deliberated it beforehand.

"That won't go over as easily as you think it will," Lepiro warned.

"Ye of little faith," Yuto hissed. "You are clearly opposed to the very thought of it. A model Hydra if there ever was one."

"Excuse me?" Lepiro growled and tensed, but made no further move.

"Always pleased to serve the Original Settlement," Yuto continued with a sneer. He would have said more but Dierde held up a hand for peace.

"That's why we are asking for your assistance. It will be difficult with just the two of us. But the four of us could easily do it."

"We will need to think about it," Taiga answered, while Lepiro's body language suggested he would do very little thinking. And if Yuto knew Taiga she had already made up her mind.

"Either you are in or you are out. It's simple," Dierde said sweetly. "We aren't asking you to kill them, just help us."

"I said we would need time to think about it," Taiga ground out.

"In. Out." Dierde gestured with her hands to illustrate her point.

"Out. But we won't stand in your way," Lepiro said, deciding right then and there.

"So be it. If you try to stop us, then you are our enemy," Dierde said as she and Yuto rose and made to exit the dwelling.

"If we are questioned, we won't lie for you. And we won't sacrifice our safety for you." Taiga stood and faced her husband and the woman who was going down a dangerous path with him.

"Then we part as enemies," Yuto said, his voice empty but his eyes showing the betrayal he felt. He sidestepped her and exited the hut.

Stepping out into the dark reminded him of a lifetime ago, when he would rise before the sun and hunt for water and molla. Yet it could have only been a month or two since Hydra Seven had been destroyed. He felt the loss of Aileen deeply at that moment, not that he hadn't been feeling it. He doubted she could survive on the Second Earth. For that matter, perhaps none of the Exos on AE625 would be adapted to whatever molecular differences the air held.

His feet made no noise and neither did Dierde's as they stole between the buildings. They admired the rock gardens, molla ristras, and other ornamentation. They had never had the luxury of personalizing their collapsible tents, nor did they spend much time in one area. Anything more than the essentials was a waste of pack space and too heavy to consider bringing.

Other Shrikers were milling about in the streets, or sitting on stone benches, though they were always segregated by workers and soldiers. Very little interaction occurred between the Greylings and Shrikers, though the occasional interspecies gathering could be seen when one bold individual joined a group of the other species. So far the language barrier hadn't been breached. It probably wouldn't ever. Soon the Shrikers would leave the Greylings without a god— leaving nothing behind but a wrecked civilization. There would be no concern for another species beyond their own, but then again, hadn't that always been the way? There was a reason they had to attempt to colonize other planets, fleeing their homeland for another world to destroy lightyears away.

Terra Mortem

The two hunters continued stalking through the city. The prey they sought now would be much easier than the elusive water they had spent their lives searching for. Sure enough, their first victim crossed their path with a courteous nod of his head. Kilo was headed to the surface, surely to communicate with the Second Earth ship sent to rescue them. In tow was Lago. Dierde and Yuto smirked devilishly. They vividly remembered being thrown to the ground and bound. This had just sweetened the deal. Dierde fantasized taking Lago's other eye before killing him.

The Hydras lagged behind casually before trailing the Shrikers towards the surface. Once they reached the lake, they stopped and patiently waited for the boat to cross to the other side. They listened to the idle conversation, or at least the parts they could hear. It wasn't very exciting. Finally, the grate of gravel on keel let them know their prey had reached the other side. They still waited, rather than letting the sound of paddles ruin the element of surprise. The Shrikers had taken the guns back from the Hydras, and could easily defeat a noisome assailant before the threat had even gotten within striking distance.

When they were certain their quarries were out of earshot, they slipped into one of the boats and began the painstaking process of crossing the lake without making a sound. The Hydras took a great deal longer than Kilo and Lago, but at long last they gently touched land and began their pursuit to the surface.

Ethan Proud

Chapter Forty-Two

Gana and Utria sat post at the edge of the City Lake. What exactly they were supposed to be guarding, neither knew. In the weeks between Rhea achieving her Godslayer status and Aqi ascending as the new god, Gana had found time to mourn for his sister. Now he needed to make it to the Second Earth so her death wasn't in vain. The grief was still too near for him to focus on such thoughts, but it was always in the back of his mind. Utria picked up a rock and skipped it across the surface.

After its last bounce, it sank gently beneath the waves, and another *plop* echoed eerily back to them.

"Do you think the gonis are extinct now?" Utria asked Gana.

"We haven't even explored a worthwhile section of this planet. I'm sure there are more, and there are things we haven't even begun to imagine here," Gana answered, his eyes fixed on the vast expanse of water. It was mesmerizing. He would have loved to swim in it all day and never leave, much like the Greyling's deity.

"I'm kind of sad we will be leaving this place forever," Utria said and Gana fought back the urge to scoff. "It's been our home for nearly a millennium, maybe it's nothing compared to what's waiting for us…but we never really appreciated it."

Ethan Proud

"You are right, but there is more to living than simply existing. We haven't even left a mark on this planet, other than the crater. Once we leave, the sands will erase any mark of our passing. No one will remember the Shrikers," Gana answered, and blinked away the dark thoughts before they rushed to the forefront of his brain.

"Well, we are out of time to do anything meaningful now," Utria said and skipped another stone. This one was round and sank with a loud splash.

"You don't think what we've done is meaningful?" Gana asked, watching as Utria searched for a flat stone.

"Meaningful to us. But as you put it, nothing that will stand the test of time." Utria turned a rock over in her hands, examining it for imperfections. This one was a pale grey, speckled with blue. She put it in her pocket and began searching for another stone to cast.

"Maybe nothing stands the test of time. Just look at Earth," Gana mused. He felt a rock gently strike his ribs hardly a second later.

"Don't act like you used to live there." Utria laughed, an obnoxious but contagious sound.

"Let's go check out the city," Gana suggested. "What's going to happen if we aren't standing guard? We are living amongst our enemy as friends."

"If we get disciplined, it's your fault," Utria said and started towards the glowing lights of the city.

"I thought you liked that kind of stuff," Gana said and ducked before the next rock hit him in the face.

They weaved their way between the streets, seeing cages of the glowing moths, Greyling children playing in mock yards, and adults milling about between the groups of Exos. Assimilation was tricky, but the aliens were attempting to communicate with the Shrikers. One approached Gana and Utria. The soldiers had to resist the urge to reach for their weapons.

The Greyling before them babbled happily and reached out and patted them both on the heads. Once again, the urge to reach for a weapon was nearly overwhelming. Instead, they both smiled forcibly, and the creature grimaced awkwardly. Utria remembered the stone in her pocket and handed it to the Greyling. It took it, held it aloft as if to catch the light, and admired it with a cooing noise. The Greyling placed it gently in a satchel at its hip, the only clothing the savage humanoid wore. The Greyling didn't spend much more time on the interaction, but meandered past them, presumably to its house.

"Do you think it has a family?" Utria asked, watching it go.

Gana glanced at the children running about. "It either has a family or a litter."

"Must you be a cynic?" Utria said and lightly backhanded him in the stomach.

"Oof."

"Maybe we should go back to the lake..." Utria trailed off.

Gana met her eyes. "Can't think of any better place to go?"

X

At the surface, the sand buffeted the rover and the satellite receiver dish and antenna attached to it. It was almost impossible to decipher the static coming across the other end of it. The sandstorm rolling in appeared as an impenetrable wall of beige barreling towards them.

"I think we should park the rover below ground," Lago said as he turned to face Kilo. He was met by a blank stare. Blood bubbled past Kilo's lips and spilled over his chin. His hands were clutched over his middle, but Lago could see the bloodstained point protruding from his stomach.

Dierde pushed the dead man from her blade, one of the collapsible spears she had carried every day as a hunter. The Shrikers hadn't considered the primitive projectile a weapon. Yuto was only a few paces to her left. Their eyes glowed furiously from their blacked out sockets. Even through the skull façade, Lago recognized them.

"I should have killed you. The war paint is cute though." He reached for the pistol at his hip, but Yuto lunged and wrapped him in a bear-hug tackle and ripped him to the ground. Lago slammed his forehead into the Hydra's face and felt the skin break under one of Yuto's teeth. With a crack, the front tooth slipped from its hold in the jaw. Yuto reeled, and Lago twisted violently, a foot connecting with Yuto's chin. The Shriker leapt to his feet, barely missing being impaled by the spear. Quick as a viper, he reached out and gripped the haft just below the blade. He yanked as hard as he could and Dierde stumbled forward as she lost her grip. He whipped the butt of the weapon across her back, but she didn't cry out. Rather, she swung a fist right into Lago's groin. Lago swore, and retaliated with his own right-hook into her nose. It broke with a satisfying crack and a gush of blood. Both the teeth painted on her face and those in her mouth now ran red. Dierde was a wild woman, and a broken nose wasn't going to stop her. She snatched the green streak of Lago's hair and with all her force pulled his face down to meet the knee she rammed upward.

Sputtering blood and a tooth or two, Lago spun back.

"You Hydras really are the dumbest creatures this planet could curse us with." His dark eyes sent daggers at his two adversaries. He reached for the gun at his hip, ready to blow both of their brains out after kneecapping them. But instead, his hand settled into his empty holster.

"As you were saying, we really are dumb," Yuto said and leveled the gun at Lago's head. He watched as the hatred morphed into fear in the moment it took for him to pull the trigger. There wasn't much left of Lago's face after the recoil.

Yuto turned to Dierde and heaved a sigh of relief, they both looked like shit. Only two more Family members left. Then they heard the slow clapping behind them, just at the mouth of the fissure.

"Bravo. Bravo." It was Fleet.

Yuto trained the gun on him. "I don't know why you're so pleased. You're next."

Fleet was undeterred. The broad smile on his face was unnerving. "I think you'll want to know what I have to say."

"Doubt it. Blast him," Dierde said and wiped her sleeve across her nose.

"Last words. Make 'em good," Yuto said dryly.

"Rhea led the massacre of your village," Fleet said coolly. He sounded too aloof to be trusted.

"But you ordered it," Yuto countered.

"No, we ordered that she bring Jarrod back," Fleet began. "She did not have orders to destroy any colony that had interacted with him."

"I fail to see how this is going to convince us not to kill you as well," Dierde growled and gestured for Yuto to finish the job at hand.

"I told Jorgen that I was going to check in on the Hydras. Make sure you felt at home. Nobody knows you followed Kilo and Lago, but you will be suspects if I, too, go missing today. If I return alive, however, I can offer you an alibi for the two corpses there," Fleet said.

Yuto let the gun fall to his hip. "He's right," he said.

Dierde nodded reluctantly. "So we kill Rhea, what do you get?" she demanded.

"Aqi," Fleet said with a devious gleam in his eye.

"Good luck with that." Yuto laughed. "We will take care of Rhea, but the second part of your scheme is all you."

"How pathetic!" Dierde said under her breath, but judging by how Fleet's face darkened, he had heard it.

Ethan Proud

Chapter Forty-Three

Bare toes wiggling in the water, Aqi and Rhea sat on the shore of the lake letting the gentle waves lap up their calves. The grey wells beneath Rhea's eyes hadn't dissipated, but the unnatural jaundice sheen had. She was beginning to feel healthier now that she was drinking natural spring water. Her body was staving off the toxins that clung to her blood cells and circulated through her body like oxygen. Four Greylings flanked the pair. Whether they were basking in the glory, or fancied themselves as retainers, it was hard to tell. Aqi guessed it was the latter, since at least four of the aliens always attended them or stood guard outside their new abode. Though the Exos had their toes in the water, the Greylings stood stiffly a few feet back. Their red eyes bounced from one side of the cavern to the next, sometimes making eye contact with their brethren as if to communicate something unsaid.

The sound of footsteps alerted them to Fleet's bothersome presence. Apparently he was done sulking.

"Good morning or evening," he said pleasantly and sat down next to them. "I trust you are adjusting well?"

"This is a minor adjustment compared to what is to come," Aqi said simply.

"You mean our sojourn to our new home." Fleet stated the obvious. He glanced up at the Greylings and their wary stares. "They worship your beauty."

Rhea rolled her eyes, but Aqi was more tactful. "They worship me because of my relationship with the Godslayer. It is power, not beauty."

"Either way, will you take them with us?"

"What?!" Aqi and Rhea exclaimed incredulously.

"They are your people now. Will you abandon them?" Fleet pressed.

"And as such, it is my decision and my decision alone. This is their home. They will stay. We won't be missed," Aqi said through gritted teeth.

"I wouldn't count on that," Fleet said before he rose and left.

Rhea's eyes followed his shrinking figure. "He's planning something."

"He always is. Scheming will do him little good now though," Aqi said and paid no more heed to Fleet.

"Let's go. We've been here for long enough. I'm hungry." Rhea's stomach warbled as if to voice its agreement. Together they left the shore.

X

Yuto and Dierde stayed in the alleyways and the darkest of shadows. Their mouths were hot with the metallic anxiety of promised vengeance. They watched the tallest house built against the lake shore for hours on end. Their eyes strained in the darkness, focused on the six Greylings standing post. They wouldn't get past six Greylings and kill both the lovers unawares. It was a waiting game now, only the most opportune moment would suffice.

If crickets had ever voyaged out to AE625, no doubt their chirps would now pierce the stillness. Yuto and Dierde watched the house unflinchingly, like hounds. Their faces were smeared with molla and blood, only intensifying their skull-like apparitions. And like ghosts, they now haunted the Greyling City.

Suddenly the door opened and Aqi strode out, wearing a patchwork poncho and tall boots. Her golden embossed eyes glinted in the light. Even from a distance, the darkness of her irises was alluring. As she broke from the building with the grace of a puma, the Greylings turned to follow her. All six of them.

"Apparently she has faith in this Rhea," Dierde purred, and she too stalked off like a cat.

Weaving between huts, stalagmites, and potential victims, they eventually stood before the towering structure. They took inventory of their surroundings before creeping to the front door and pushing it open slowly. It silently swung on its hinges, a seeming impossibility for a slab of solid stone. When the gap was wide enough for a single person to slip through, Dierde darted in.

Yuto slowly sealed the door behind him. Surprisingly, the room was well lit. From the outside it had appeared the inside was pitch black. Martian Flares in glass cases, probably brought by the Commanding Family, were placed periodically, bathing the room in their strange light. A stairwell wrapped around the room and a ninety degree turn took it up to the second level. The only multi-level building the Shrikers had ever been in had been the Shrike. This was oddly reminiscent. They recalled Fleet's words, *Hydra Nine. You're more similar to them than you are to us.* Though they both thought it, they didn't discuss its ramifications. It had little bearing on their lives. They weren't concerned with where they came from anymore. They were concerned with where they were going.

They breached the second level. Still no Rhea, but a crude mockery of a table was set in the middle of the table. A pile of molla caps that rivaled a dune in height sat in the middle of it. Around it, nine chairs were placed symbolically. Clearly, it was a meeting room of sorts. A trough of water sat in one corner. Inevitably, Dierde and Yuto locked their eyes on the caps on the table. Out of the corners of their eyes they made contact and floated towards the table. They painstakingly pulled a cap each from the pile and scraped a fingernail across the gills. It seemed so loud. Not nearly as loud as what was to come next though. They tapped their fingers together as if cheering a toast and held them aloft to their nostrils. Slowly, they inhaled, a precise gesture, but in their need for silence, it sounded like a gale of wind tearing through the building. They heard Rhea cough from some floors above them, and froze.

For a moment, their eyes glazed over as serotonin and dopamine were released from their brains by the bucketful, but in the same amount of time the edge returned. Their eyes glowed greedily. Vengeance was at hand.

Up the next flight of stairs, and still no sign of their prey. This room was completely empty. Devoid of even decorations. However, three large bloodstains darkened the stone in the center of the floor. Dierde and Yuto didn't waste much more time debating the cryptic purpose of the room. For all they knew, Rio had spent his last days here. With heavy hearts they treaded silently up the final flight.

The penthouse was littered with more of the Martian Flare lamps, and chairs no doubt taken from the Commanding Family's quarters. Large bags of stitched molla filled with sand were placed on the floor and were evidently very comfortable, judging by the way Rhea was curled up in one of them. She looked so childlike, resting in the fetal position, her fierce Mohawk limp across her face instead of spiked into the air. The hair on the side of her head was beginning to grow back, though it was barely past being categorized as stubble.

Dierde seethed with rage and coiled up within herself, ready to strike. In the blink of an eye, however, Rhea was across the room without uttering a sound. Her eyes were not dulled and bleary with sleep but on high alert.

"Very poetic," Rhea snarled.

Dierde and Yuto smiled at each other, the face paint grin split to reveal actual teeth.

"At least this one didn't call us dumb," Yuto said and shrugged humorously.

"I'm not your first mark?" Rhea asked, the muscles in her legs bunched like she was ready to spring at any moment.

"You weren't even a target until we found out the role you played in the massacre of our colony," Dierde said.

She and Yuto broke apart to begin closing in on Rhea in a pincer movement, leaving the door tantalizingly clear. That last sentence was enticing enough that Rhea relaxed for just one second.

"Fleet no doubt told you." It wasn't a question.

"Yes, after he watched us slaughter Kilo and that demon with the green hair," Dierde supplied, shuddering when she remembered Lago pinning her against the desert sand.

"You should have tried to kill a few more before coming here. I'd hate to cut your spree short," Rhea said confidently, her hand slithering towards the knife in her boot.

Dierde tsked as a retort, and Yuto sprang.

Rhea flattened herself against the wall and grabbed Yuto by the shoulder, extended her leg and meant to toss him to the floor. But the Hydra were wild animals, vicious by nature and not like the guard dogs of the

Wreckage. He nimbly twisted on the ball of his foot and struck Rhea in the face with his elbow. Her skull cracked against the wall, but she was just as feisty. She snatched his arm with both hands and sank her teeth into the tender flesh of his underarm. With a yelp he leapt back and tripped over one of the sandbags on the floor, landing solidly on his back.

Out of her peripherals Rhea detected Dierde's advance. She turned and faced the woman squarely while drawing the knife from her boot.

Dierde saw the motion long before it had the chance to turn deadly for her. She stopped short, pulled her knee to her chest, and extended her booted foot with full force right into Rhea's chest.

The Scout Warchief joined Yuto on the ground, gasping for breath.

"My lover is dead because of you," Dierde hissed as she paced closer to the prone figure on the ground. "Now Aqi will feel the same pain that I have felt. Before you die, I want you to know that whatever pain she feels from losing you…it's your fault."

Not having recovered enough to gain her feet again, Rhea swung her foot at Dierde in an attempt to trip her. Deftly, the Hydra skipped over the leg and planted her next step right onto Rhea's stomach. She put her whole weight onto the woman and heard the gentle hiss of air slowly leaving her diaphragm. The knife on the floor caught Dierde's eye and she stooped to pick it up before looking back at her victim. Rhea's eyes were fluttering.

She was still too weak to offer up much of a fight, and now without oxygen the little strength she had was seeping out. Not even her desire not to break Aqi's heart gave her enough fortitude to fight back. Blackness crept into the edge of her vision and the last thing she saw was Dierde bringing the gleaming knife down towards her chest.

With the blade buried to the hilt in Rhea, Dierde stood up and wiped a hand across the back of her forehead, leaving a streak of blood. Yuto managed to press himself up on his elbows and coughed up a long tendril of drool. He heaved himself to his feet and swayed woozily.

"Are you serious?" Dierde asked and laughed lightly. "A concussion."

"I'll be fine." Yuto shook his head fervently as if it would clear his mind and ran a hand through his hair in exasperation. "We need to leave before Aqi and her retainers come back."

"I agree."

They clattered down the stairs together, the noise mainly Yuto's fault as he had trouble keeping his footing and Dierde had to assist him. They eased out from behind the door and into the streets and didn't bother meeting Fleet's expectant stare from the shadows. In fact, they said little to the man. He was a worm and didn't warrant their respect.

X

Ethan Proud

It wasn't long before Aqi returned to her new dwelling after a great sense of unease overcame her. She called out to Rhea as soon as she crossed the threshold, but of course no one answered. She dashed up the stairs with enough speed to rival an Olympic athlete and with the urgency of a fire engine. When she discovered what was waiting for her, she dropped to her knees. Had her hair been long enough to yank out, she would have, but instead she raked her claws across her scalp and face and let loose an anguished scream that was heard by all. Her cries continued for many hours and didn't lessen in intensity as she rocked the corpse of the one woman she had ever loved. Her throat was raw and tasted of blood, but she didn't stop. No amount of pain could rival what had just been taken from her.

Chapter Forty-Four

Tears dried, Aqi carried Rhea to the lake shore. None of the Shrikers had been able to get close to the woman, her Greyling guards made sure she had her space. Aqi reverently set Rhea's now cold body in the bottom of a boat, filled with jewel-like insects and molla caps. The Greylings poured the spores into her mouth, presumably they would inoculate within the cavity and digest her slowly over many months. A few handfuls of sand from the surface were sprinkled over her body before the watercraft was pushed into the center of the lake. Whether or not the lake goni Rhea had met in battle had usually eaten the corpses of the dead, her body would remain unmolested until the natural process of decay rendered her detritus.

Aqi knew that the murderer or murderers were somewhere in the audience. The entire known sentient population of AE625 was gathered along the lake shore. However, the Greylings prevented any of the Shrikers getting a good view of the Shakespearian love story's final act. Aqi clenched her jaw when she heard the murmurs begin to spread. She knew that Rhea would encourage her to get everyone off the planet. But until justice was brought down upon the conspirators, no one would be leaving the Greyling City.

With one final tear stained goodbye, Aqi pushed the boat out onto the water and watched as it listed slowly towards the center. She turned and marched back to the home she had shared with Rhea. It had been the first bed they ever openly shared and they had expected a lifetime of happiness now the old ways of the Wreckage had dissolved. That dream died in the same breath as the traditions had. Perhaps they had been too hasty. Had they waited until they were on the Second Earth, they would have been safe.

Aqi saw the Hydras clustered amongst the Shrikers. They stuck out like sore thumbs, especially the two wearing the death masks. Fitting, Aqi thought, all the Exos should have adorned themselves as such. It was only because of Rhea that they had won the Greyling War. Another thought raced through her mind. *What if they had been told Rhea led the massacre of Seven?*

Aqi's face snapped back towards the misfits, but only two remained. Yuto and Dierde had disappeared somewhere in the crowd. Her suspicion deepened. She knew where to start the witch hunt now. But who had told them?

Fleet. Of course.

Aqi's stride lengthened as if a weight had lifted from her shoulders. She still bore immeasurable grief, but now she had a purpose and an outlet for said grief. Before she started her hunt for the traitors, she needed to rest. Her heart was tired, and revenge was a task for the morning.

Taking the stairs one at a time, Aqi ascended to where Rhea had breathed her last. She collapsed on the floor and began to cry softly until she fell asleep. She was aware of two Greylings standing guard by her door. She cared not what they said or thought. She couldn't know that the only disdain they felt was for whoever had caused their new deity pain. Obviously, it had been one of her own. The sacrifice had seen no purpose and was barbaric in their alien eyes. They continued to stare at the goddess on the floor and were touched by her humanity.

X

When Aqi woke next, she knew not whether it was day or night, a common theme underground. She saw the Martian Flares around her had begun to wilt. Their petals were soft and limp, and brown necrosis speckled the margins and the sepals. She lifted the glass terrarium case around it, and gingerly lifted it until it was level with her face. Its anthers drooped and its stamen had collapsed on itself. The flares all around the room were similarly failing, their bioluminescent quality in various stages of degradation. What caused their sudden demise was a mystery, though Aqi surmised that their fungal symbiont had perished due to malnutrition. The plants had been fed by molla hyphae and stunted the production of the fruiting body, but produced a molla spore inside the seed capsule when pollinated. It was a beautiful process, one that mirrored that of the humans and gonis' symbiosis.

The clack of a booted heel on stone nearly made Aqi drop the Martian Flare on the ground. Instead, she tucked it back inside its terrarium and silently said a prayer for its recovery. She turned to face her intruder. None of the Exos were welcome in her quarters and none of the Greylings wore boots. For all she knew, it could be the assassins coming to finish their work.

Tension left her shoulders when she saw Fleet in the doorway. He stood their sheepishly, but still had purpose. If that was possible. He hadn't had much of a purpose since they left the Wreckage.

"What do you want?" Aqi grated her teeth together.

"To simply talk," Fleet said and splayed his hands in a gesture of neutrality.

"And what would we have to discuss?" Aqi said, no more polite than she had been when he first entered.

"Our people need to be led. We have lost Mertensia and Kilo. It is up to us to take the Shrikers home. We need to stick together during this time." His words were laced with cunning. As hard as he tried, he could never sound truly genuine.

"They had leaders, you just weren't one of them."

Fleet balked at this, but kept his façade. "I have always shown *our people* how to survive. If it had not been for the four of us, they would have died long ago."

"We simply followed the rules laid out by those before us. We were hardly radical or revolutionary.

With the systems that were in place, any fool could have survived." Aqi snorted humorously at Fleet's delusions.

"Aqi," he started sternly, "I am only trying to do what is best. Why won't you lead at my side? Like we used to." He smiled, and his eyes gleamed with desperation.

"I haven't been interested in being at your side in over two years," Aqi countered. "You had Mertensia and Kilo. You did not need a fourth."

"Our ancestors always had a quartet of leaders." Fleet's eyes darkened and tears welled at their edges.

"Little good it did them. Rhea and I were content to simply belong to each other. We weren't seeking to rule as Queens. I don't see why you were so threatened," Aqi said and sneered at Fleet's weakness.

"Why do you hold our traditions in such contempt? Until you met Rhea, everything was perfect in your book."

"Were you so jealous that you had to have the Hydras kill her?" Aqi said and seemed to grow two inches taller as wrath welled within her.

"I can't believe you would be bold enough to insinuate something of that nature." Fleet recoiled, his lip curled in disgust.

"I didn't *insinuate* anything. And you didn't deny it either." Aqi took a dangerous step closer to her ex-lover.

"Only the guilty deny anything. You should know me better than to think me so callous," Fleet said, faking a hurt expression.

"I know you all too well. You are scum. And you are the reason why Rhea is dead." Aqi spat on Fleet's face.

He flinched but didn't retaliate. Instead, he seemed to sag as if his resolve had been crushed. "I loved you, Aqi. Not Kilo, not Mertensia. Well, not in the same way." Tears streamed down his face.

"You are pathetic. You think murdering the woman I loved would make me fawn over you?" Aqi asked incredulously. The coals in her chest had been fanned by his admission and were now columns of red hot anger.

Drawn by the sound of arguing, the tower was full of Greylings. They crept up the stairwell and peered in at the two Exos. Silently, they slunk into the room, crouched and ready to spring at the slightest inclination from their queen.

Fleet took no notice of them. Instead, he continued to beg Aqi for forgiveness and her love. He groveled on the ground, on his knees he clawed at her pant leg, but she remained unmoved.

"Tell me you love me," Aqi said, her face as cold as the stone they stood on.

"I love you Aqi. I've already told you this, I love you more than life itself. I would die if I couldn't have you." He made quite the convincing plea, but Aqi's harsh features only hardened.

Terra Mortem

She scanned the room and surveyed the Greylings that had crowded in. There had to be at least twelve of them pressed against the wall, and she spotted just as many beyond the threshold of the room.

"Then die you must," Aqi said and Fleet looked up at her, initially terrified. Then angry. He opened his mouth to shout but Aqi held up a hand to stop him. She turned to the Greylings. "Kill him."

Like a pride of lions, they closed in wordlessly. They dismembered him with their bare hands.

Aqi settled into a high-backed stone chair. She patted the armrest. She could get used to a throne like this. But one overlooking the lake. She counted the days in her head, while her minions watched her, blood dripping from their hands and mouths.

The Second Earth ship would be landing in four days. But nobody would be alive to meet it. If Rhea couldn't travel with her to paradise then nobody would. The barbaric Shrikers didn't deserve to be saved. Aqi had passed her judgment and the twelfth seal had been opened. Her wrath would be fit for the First Testament.

"Kill them all."

The Greylings bowed their heads in understanding and stole from the room. The screams started before the last one had filtered from Aqi's tower.

Chapter Forty-Five

Gana stood in shock as the Greylings poured from the tower like oil and began tearing into the Shrikers with abandon. He lifted his rifle and fired three blasts and three of the aliens dropped. He wondered how Aqi fared, had they torn her apart first now that the Godslayer had been murdered?

Next to him, Utria leveled the barrel of her own gun, before seeing the futility. "We need to regroup and take a defensible position. We will be slaughtered unless we take cover."

Her companion nodded and together they took off at a light jog towards the last place they had seen Jorgen. The chaos around them deepened as more of the Greylings turned violent. They barely took three steps without pulling the trigger at least once. With each assailant killed, another two took their place. And with each Greyling killed, three Shrikers fell.

A blinding light pierced the darkness and the two scouts shielded their eyes with gloved hands. A hail of bullets surrounded them, and then the cave went silent. The light dimmed, to reveal Jorgen and a contingent of soldiers protecting Johan who was manning the generator.

"Gana, Utria. Good that you've made it. We need to round up all the survivors we can. If we get out of these tunnels, we can survive until the ship lands." Jorgen peered around the buildings. The Greylings had fallen back, but their glowing eyes could still be seen peering from behind the huts. Their hatred was tangible.

"We need water to survive four days on the sands," Utria cautioned. "We will need to take it before we flee."

"And that's precisely what we will do. We will set up a barricade at the edge of the tunnel to the surface, and send a squad to the lake," Jorgen said in accordance with Utria.

"Which lake?" Johan asked, as he fiddled with the generator. Its power was surging, but it had not yet gone out.

"The one closest to the surface. The City Lake, we poison with these." Jorgen smiled as he held up four canisters of hydrazine. They had been taken from the rovers. The visual claxon of yellow and black promised disastrous results.

"Serves these creatures right," Gana said and spat on the ground. "Has anyone seen Kilo or Lago?"

"We found them dead on the surface. It's not only Greylings we need to fear," Jorgen said direly.

"The Hydras?" Utria hissed through her teeth.

"Not all of them," Lepiro said as he and Taiga pushed past the crowd of soldiers.

Jorgen's face tensed grimly. "If you see the ones with the face paint, kill on sight."

"Not these, though?" Utria asked, her distaste for the nomads evident before she even opened her mouth. Her brows were knit together so tightly they nearly touched.

"No." Jorgen was firm. "These two warned us of their kindred's treachery. They will be rewarded for their loyalty."

"What if this is part of their plan?" Utria asked, but Gana put a hand on her shoulder.

"The Greylings are our enemy now. We need to focus on the immediate threat."

A silence fell over the group, and the clamor of hunting Greylings reached their ears.

"Not all of us are safe right now though," Jorgen said and waved the group into motion.

They began to sweep through the streets. At the edge of the light, fleeing shadowy figures were in no short supply. The soldiers tried to block out the sounds of the aliens closing in behind them, but it was futile. How many of the beings were there? It seemed as though there were infinitely more Greylings than Shrikers. The surface and escape seemed further away with every passing minute.

Rounding a corner, they bore witness to a graphic murder. The light of the generator fell upon a group of six Greylings ravaging the corpses of four adult civilians, while children huddled in terror behind earthenware pots. Either the aliens hadn't seen them yet, or they were simply toying with the young humans. Either way, it was sickening.

Terra Mortem

Teeth and claws were little match for the power of technology and all six of the beasts were rendered piles of flesh by many more bullets than necessary. Jorgen stepped forward and ushered the children to move, their little bodies shaking with fear or shock, their eyes wide and glassy. Jorgen scooped the littlest of them up and cradled him against his chest while he brandished his rifle in his free hand.

Several hours more of combing the streets yielded no more survivors. There had to be more though, seven hundred and sixty-four Shrikers had sojourned to The Source. Only forty-seven were in Jorgen's unit, including the three children.

"We need to fall back to the tunnels, we can't lose anyone we have right now. We need a volunteer to take the hydrazine to the lake though," Jorgen ordered.

Nobody immediately volunteered. They had all witnessed Rhea's deterioration after being exposed to the stuff.

Finally, one brave soul stepped forward.

"I'll do it," Utria offered.

"I'll go with her," Gana said quickly.

"No. We can only spare one soldier. She will be less likely to be discovered if she is alone." Jorgen's tone left little room for argument.

Gana tried, regardless. "You can't be serious. She will need help."

"I told you, no," Jorgen reiterated before turning to Utria. "Thank you, we will wait for you." He motioned for Drips to bring the hydrazine to her. Utria took it and slipped the containers into her pack and reshouldered it.

"See you on the surface."

She didn't wait for anyone to say goodbye. Instead, she darted into the nearest alley and cut a path towards the lake. The hydrazine containers made an imperceptible clinking within her pack.

The strange dialect of the AE625 natives reached her ears and she froze for only a moment before dipping behind some urns portraying the same craftsmanship as the ones the children had taken cover in. She turned her ear and attempted to eavesdrop on the aliens. Some of the words were a mockery of her own language, but others were completely indecipherable. The creatures passed, and Utria let out a long breath. When she inhaled again, a strange odor escaped the pottery and reached her nostrils. After hearing the Hydra's description of the rituals, she refused to look inside the urns. Instead, she crept back into the alleyway.

After making sure the coast was clear, she crossed the main street. The cacophony of battle told her that the danger was not immediate, but it was close. She moved a little quicker, she didn't want to get caught on the wrong side of the Greyling Army and be unable to reach the barricade. Knowing Jorgen and his zeal for efficiency, it wouldn't be long until it was up.

Utria saw the sliver of reflection on the lake surface. The little bit of light from the scorpion-moths was all it needed to shimmer like glass. The gravel crunched under her boots as she crossed the shore. Aqi's tower loomed some sixty feet to her left. She paid it no heed; for all she knew Aqi had been slaughtered within its confines.

Slinging her pack off her shoulder, Utria stooped to pull the first canister free. She froze when she heard footsteps coming from behind her.

She whirled around and drew her pistol, but let it fall when she saw Aqi. "We thought you were dead!" Utria blew out a sigh of relief and holstered the weapon.

Aqi made no move, nor did she make any comment. A single line of fiery ichor had been drawn from one earlobe to the other, crossing her cheekbones and meeting on the bridge of her nose. Another line of orange blazed from her lower lip, past the hollow of her throat, and stopped at her breastbone. The only effects she wore that were Shriker in origin were tall boots and the poncho she often wore on the surface to shield her from the blistering sand. She wore several stone rings on her fingers, and a crown made of living molla. The hyphae intertwined, the usually microscopic roots transformed into a thick braid. Feeding the saprotrophs were the wings and shells of the impish insects.

Aqi lifted her hand cryptically, and before Utria could ask, Greylings rose from the water and yanked her backwards. Holding her limbs against her sides they shoved her thrashing body to the bottom of the lake. In a flurry of bubbles, all her breath left her. Her lungs burned, despite the cool liquid flooding them. Her panic rose in her throat and she felt as if she would puke, but the water filling her chest was relentless. Blackness took her and she ceased struggling.

The Greylings pulled Utria's body from the lake several minutes later, to be certain she was dead. Her wide lifeless eyes stared at Aqi, though they saw nothing. The Queen of the Greylings turned and led her disciples towards the cavern mouth.

X

Behind the barricade, Gana paced. The Greylings had fallen back, but his mind was not on his own survival. His thoughts were consumed by Utria. If she had fallen, he would have lost everyone, Jana, Rhea, and Lago. He willed her to still be alive. He was similarly preoccupied when he spotted the striking figure cutting through the darkness.

Aqi was alive. In her eyes were brimstone and fire.

Chapter Forty-Six

The paddles barely broke the surface of the water. The two assassins had made their getaway as soon as the scourge of the Shrikers began. They wasted no time or morals deciding whether or not to wait for their fellow Hydras. They had made it clear that they were on their own. From across the still waters, the constant report of gunfire shook the rocks. Silt and small flakes of stone rained from the cavern ceiling.

Dierde and Yuto didn't say anything, their faces were smeared with sweat, molla, and blood, their breath hot in their mouths. They only had a few days before the Second Earthling ship landed and spirited them away from this damnable planet. Whether or not they were its sole Exo occupants was up to the Shrikers battling the Greylings. Dierde and Yuto hadn't been cruel enough to destroy the other boats, though the thought had crossed their minds. Had they discussed it, they probably would have done it. But both were too afraid of the other's judgment to say anything.

They both lurched slightly when they hit the shore, despite seeing it as it loomed nearer. Stepping from the boat, their feet splashed lightly in the water and their soles became wet within their boots. It would be the last reprieve before setting out across the desert again. Stooping over the water, they filled their Hydra backpacks and were temporarily jolted back to their previous lives. How many times had they hauled meager volumes of the life-giving fluid back to their camp? How many times had they trudged across the sand for days on end, parched and on the verge of death?

All their efforts had been in vain, two shining utopias with constant supplies of water had existed. Yet they had been doomed to wander. It was fitting justice that the Shrikers would have to wander as they had. Unless they defeated the Greylings of course, but the aliens had the home-turf advantage. The odds seemed pitted against the Exos.

"No going back now." Yuto broke the silence as he closed his pack with a drawstring before clipping a strap to keep the top compartment in place.

"It's what they deserve," Dierde answered coldly. She shared a grim smile with Yuto. Justice didn't always feel right, but it didn't make it wrong.

They wasted no time getting to the surface. The wind was howling as was the norm, and sand bit at their flesh. They pulled their scarves over their faces and settled their goggles on their eyes. They stared at the rover sitting unmolested between two dunes for many long moments before shrugging and slogging towards it. Yuto pulled the door open roughly and slid into the driver seat while Dierde crawled into the rear driver side seat and peered over his shoulder. Slamming the doors, they locked the gritty debris out.

"Think you can operate it?" Dierde's voice was muffled behind her balaclava.

Yuto pulled his bandana beneath his chin. "We'll see."

Over the past several days, or had it been weeks, he had seen plenty of rovers being driven. It couldn't be that hard. He experimentally pushed all of the pedals on the floor. Nothing. He twisting the wheel a few times. Nothing. Pushed a button on the dashboard. Nothing. Another button. Nothing. Moved the gear shift. Nothing. Put the gear shift back. Nothing. Twisted something behind the steering wheel. Suddenly it roared to life. And died a moment later. He twisted the key again, and this time pushed a pedal against the floor. The engine purred, but the rover did not move.

"Give up?" Dierde asking, ribbing him gently.

"Can't say I didn't try," Yuto said and pushed the door open, stepping back into the vicious winds. "Walking is what we were made for, after all."

Dierde laughed sardonically. Setting out across the desolate planet they felt naked without their gonis. The only solace was that this time, they weren't wandering, they had a map that would lead them straight to the landing site. Hopefully, along the way they would run into Aileen and Dierde, but they both knew they would have to turn the creatures loose before boarding. The chances that the gelatinous aliens would survive the atmosphere of a foreign planet were slim. It broke both their hearts, but the chance to say a proper goodbye would be worth it.

The nostalgia of the sands wasn't lost on them as they referred to the map one last time before setting a course.

Chapter Forty-Seven

"Aqi!" Jorgen shouted and motioned with his whole arm for her to cross the barrier.

"Stop," Gana said. "She isn't here to join us."

"What do you mean?" Jorgen hissed angrily.

"She's with them." Gana pointed to the Greylings clamoring behind their goddess. She was given a wide berth, but it was obvious that they were waiting on her.

"Don't be ridiculous," Jorgen said and hopped over the barricade and rushed towards Aqi.

She didn't break stride or acknowledge him, even when the Greylings pounced on him and dragged him from her path. She didn't even look his way as his screams intensified.

"Make it quick. I rather liked him," Aqi said hollowly, her lips hardly moving. Abruptly, the screams stopped.

From behind the barricade, Gana winced as Jorgen's head was separated from his shoulders. Aqi entered the ring of light, and the Greylings skirted the edge of it, like wolves plotting their next move on a lone elk.

Aqi pulled a pistol from beneath her poncho and leveled it at the figure next to the generator. The bullet shattered the air and lodged itself in the middle of Drip's forehead. Her next shot was aimed directly at the generator. With a loud pop, the lights went out and the Greylings closed in. They leapt over the barrier and beset themselves on the Shrikers. Aqi watched calmly as her people were slaughtered.

X

"We need to get out of here," Lepiro whispered as he tugged at Taiga.

"Take the boats?" she asked as she turned and outpaced him. "What about Yuto and Dierde?"

"What about them?" Lepiro asked.

"They either took the boats as soon as they killed Rhea, or I was born yesterday," Taiga replied as they left the carnage behind.

Lepiro peered over his shoulder before answering. "They couldn't have taken all the boats," he assured her.

"Either they sank them, or they will kill us before we reach the rendezvous point," Taiga answered.

"You can't be serious. He's your husband," Lepiro balked.

"They made it clear we are enemies," Taiga said solemnly. "I wouldn't be sure of anything."

"You are much too dire," Lepiro said, while Icharus' fleeting shape guiding them into the tunnels.

Taiga's retort was cut off when three Greylings did the same to their escape. Lepiro pulled the gun from his hip but was too late. Two of the aliens had already reached him and pinned him to the ground. He felt claws dig into his stomach as warmth spread out across his abdomen. He coughed up blood in lieu of a scream. The last thing he heard was Icharus' panicked shrieks above him.

Taiga eviscerated the first Greyling in one quick move before turning to dispatch the two that had taken Lepiro down. She killed another with a quick stab of her blade as it turned to face her, but the third was too quick and dodged the next killing blow and tackled her. With a well-placed knee, she sent it skittering across the floor in the fetal position. Another well placed cut, another dead Greyling.

She rushed to Lepiro's side, but he was already dead. The heat was receding from his skin as the cold cave air leeched it. Icharus sat screeing on his chest and Taiga tried her best to pull the creature from its dead master. The goni wouldn't leave. She tried to coax it with kind words, to no avail. With tears staining her cheek, she turned tail and fled.

X

The Greylings had broken through the barricade, but the Shrikers stood their ground. There were too many of the Greylings to stage an organized retreat. Defeating the Greylings here and making a break for the surface was the only option they had.

Gana felt oddly calm, despite the danger he was in. It was a last ditch effort to survive, but a stillness had overcome him. Only two outcomes existed in this scenario and he simply had to do his best. Most of the Shrikers would die below ground, but maybe a few would make it out alive. Gana counted each shot he fired, and when the trigger stuck after the last bullet, he discarded the magazine and loaded another. It appeared that they were beginning to stem the tide when a heavy figure dropped from the sky. Then another. Gana turned his eyes upwards and saw many more of the creatures emerging from a honeycomb of ancillary tunnels. The Greyling population seemed to have no end.

From the tunnel behind them, another host of the beings appeared. The Shrikers had been hemmed in. All hope for the human race was lost. The stillness that had settled over Gana evaporated. He kicked the creature closest to him in the chest before placing a bullet where his foot had been moments before. Gunfire erupted and the sound of bullets striking rock came from every direction. Gana felt a force hit him in the stomach, then a sudden heat. It wasn't necessarily painful, but he knew the damage had been done. He looked at the gunshot wound in his stomach and cursed. He had been felled by friendly fire. He sank to his knees and curled into a ball on the ground. Then he felt the pain.

It didn't last long before he bled out on the cold stone floor.

X

Terra Mortem

Taiga reached the edge of the lake before she was finally overtaken. The swarm of Greylings caught her just as she reached the boat. She slashed in broad wide arcs, each time her blade finding many Greylings but still they came. She was ripped to the ground, thrashing and screaming all the while. She managed to break free and her knife found another Greyling. Blood spurted from its wound, and the ground became slick and warm. She felt her forearm snap as an assailant bore its whole weight upon her. She screamed in pain, but was cut off as teeth found her throat. With a final gurgle, the last of the Exos below ground died.

Chapter Forty-Eight

Aqi strode purposefully among the destruction. None of her old people had made it out alive. Her new disciples had been victorious. She crossed the barricade and felt a small stirring of guilt when she saw Gana, struck down by a stray bullet. He and Rhea had always been close. She swallowed her feelings and moved on. There was no point in pitying the dead. In the tunnel leading to the first lake, she found Lepiro's cold body. Icharus still sitting on his chest. The goni let out a low mournful call when he saw Aqi. She stooped down and stroked his head gently. His sad eyes regarded her for a moment before turning back to look at Lepiro.

She knew she couldn't leave the creature in the cavern. She scooped him up and cradled him against her chest.

"Do you have a name?" Of course, he did not answer. She stared at his red glowing cartilage and chose a new name for him. "Vulpes."

Vulpes crooned at his new name for a moment, and allowed Aqi to carry him away from Lepiro's side and back to the Greyling City. In the coming days, he would begin to grow to a size that no Hydra goni had ever reached.

X

Terra Mortem

There came a great roaring as the ship made its landing. A flurry of sand was propelled in all directions and blasted the two figures celebrating the arrival of the Second Earthlings. Dierde and Yuto's faces were no longer reminiscent of skulls but instead resembled dirty miners, emerging from the depths. They were caked in soot and grime, streaks of blood evident.

A party of six humans exited the craft, their disappointment obvious. They had been expecting hundreds, if not thousands of Exos to rescue. A woman, outfitted in a bright orange suit, puffy boots, and vest with many clips and pouches, stepped forward.

"Are there more of you?" she asked, looking around the desolate planet in bewilderment. The *Shrike* could be seen in the distance, but no movement came from the walls that surrounded it.

"We are the only survivors," Yuto said grimly. His eyes were as hollow as his words.

"What happened?" the commanding woman inquired further.

"We encountered the natives. We were slaughtered," Dierde provided.

"I am so sorry to hear that," the woman said. "But we are glad that we arrived in time to rescue you. Come aboard, we will waste no more time here. My name is Tamora Brider."

"My name is Yuto, and she is Dierde," Yuto provided as they walked up the ramp into the ship.

"No last names?" Tamora asked, and when she saw the looks on Yuto and Dierde's faces she quickly changed her tune. "No matter, we can discuss that when you get settled in. We have a long trip and a lot to tell each other."

Epilogue

Drums pounding in her ears, Aqi sat in her throne positioned at the edge of the lake shore. Her hands rested on two skulls, while her back and head were supported by numerous ribcages. Molla grew from every gap and the result was quite comfortable. The eerie hum of mollawind instruments heralded the arrival of the beast in the water. Vulpes sped towards the shore as the Greyling children offered him bowls of molla and strips of meat. Aqi didn't question where the meat came from, but she had a hunch.

Vulpes emerged from the water and gorged himself on the offerings. In only a few short months, he had grown enough to rival a horse in size and was getting hungrier by the day.

Aqi watched as he slid back into the water and summoned her attendants to her. They lifted her into the air, still in her throne, and carried her back into the heart of her city. The bitterness in her heart had yet to erode, but she was hopeful that someday she would be at peace.

X

With a hiss, the airlock opened after the ship landed in a docking bay at the capital of the Gaia Colonies. The city was called Terra Omnia and was a shining jewel of technology. Each building was resplendent in white, with roof top gardens and solar panels. No cars moved through the streets, and no sand was anywhere in sight. The Hydras had never seen anything so green and lush. The air itself was so full of scents. It smelled sweet, fresh, and bountiful all at once. Like giddy children, Dierde and Yuto exchanged face-splitting smiles and stepped onto the soft earth. There was only the gentlest of breezes that lightly tugged at their hair and clothes. It was a welcome change from the howling gales of AE625.

As they looked around in utter excitement, Tamora couldn't help but smile. The sky opened up and pregnant drops of water fell slowly and softly, mingling with the smell of fresh earth. The Hydras looked up in astonishment.

"Welcome home."

Terra Mortem

Ethan Proud

ABOUT THE AUTHOR: Ethan Proud was raised in Pinedale, Wyoming and that is where he fell in love with reading, writing, and the outdoors. He published his first series the *Rebellion Trilogy* with his older brother, Lincoln. Ethan is an avid adventurer, whether it is on the page or in nature and when he is not writing or reading he can be found backpacking, rock climbing, or snowboarding.

Keep up with him at:
http://proudbrotherswriting.com

Made in the USA
Columbia, SC
06 April 2019